BLACK'S BEACH PARALLAX

A vibrant tale of government secrets and layered realities

SCOTT SPADE

Prologue

Package addressed to my grandson, Michael D. O'Malley, Associate Professor of Cognitive Neuroscience, University of California at Santa Cruz. Not to be opened until after the demise of Jack O'Malley.

June 12, 2038
Dear Michael,

I'm sure you remember our family vacation in Australia several years ago when you were twenty-two. You had just been accepted to the prestigious graduate program at UC Irvine in the exciting field of cognitive neuroscience. I alerted you then that this package would come to you shortly after I died. You seemed intrigued but probably assigned my mysterious forecast to the "crazy old coot" category. Before you jump to conclusions, please allow your scientific mind to evaluate my story fairly.

Your recent groundbreaking research on the effects of a new class of drugs on human behavior is sure to attract government attention. The CIA or some other agency may offer you financial support to carry out more directed drug studies. I cannot advise you on how to respond; options must be weighed carefully. The enclosed narrative aims to help your decision making by filling in essential parts of the historical void left by our mass media.

In his famous novel *Nineteen Eighty-Four*, George Orwell wrote, "He who controls the past controls the future. He who controls the present controls the past." Over my long life, I have often observed our business, political, and military leaders covering up stupid and reckless actions. In our system of tight corporate media control, he who controls the present does indeed exercise substantial control over the perceived past, at least for those unwilling to dig for truths under the surface.

The enclosed manuscript relates my experiences during the period of 1962–1982; several questions are addressed. Who started the shadowy company Integrated Parallax Systems? How did it gain access to government secrets, many not known even to the president? Who was the mysterious character known as the Colonel, and what really happened to him? Do secret government programs employ mind-altering drugs? How many media pundits are paid under the table to do their bidding? And what actually happened to Gene Stanford?

Gene and I spent many hours running on the beach while discussing explosive events unknown to the public. Some might think Gene guilty of treason, but in my view, his actions represented a profound patriotism. As I write this letter, I see his image clearly in my mind's eye, that of a handsome, brilliant scientist but most of all an exceptional human being. I also remember the shocking emergence of an entirely different Gene, one who seemed crazy and perhaps even dangerous.

Let me apologize for including personal stories that some might consider sordid, but all these experiences, including the improprieties, are part and parcel of my whole self. Who knows? Maybe they will be of some use in your own personal life. In any case, attempts to censor my history were disconcerting. So in the end I included all memories—the good, the bad, and the turbulent. If my language sometimes seems inconsistent with grandpa talk, remember that the dialog originates from a man in his 20s or 30s.

If you are shocked by some of the wild behaviors depicted, please consider the exceptional tenor of the times. The 1960s embraced a revolution in social norms about clothing, music, drugs, dress, and especially sex. The dishonesty of our government in the conduct of an unnecessary, unpopular, and barbaric war encouraged counterculture experiments. Not surprisingly, some experimental outcomes were good and some were not so good.

This package may add information useful to your consciousness research, at the very least by facilitating potential interactions with government agencies. I end, however, with a warning: keep this package and its contents secret, at least until you obtain tenure at your university. To do otherwise might be a career-limiting move.

I end by telling you how proud I am of the exceptional man you have become. Have a great life!

With love,
Grandpa

Jack O'Malley
Rancho Santa Fe, California

N

Encinitas

 Rancho

Solana Beach

Los Peñasquitos

Del Mar

Black's Beach

 Parallax

La Jolla

Crystal Pier

Astro

 Bicycle Bill's

The Body Shop

Downtown San Diego

Brown's

Bob's

Chapter 1

My watch read 7:58 a.m. as I jumped from my car in the Astro Dynamics parking lot. I was sixty yards away from one of the large walk-in gates. The twelve-foot fence topped with barbed wire surrounded Astro's enormous complex. It could have been easily mistaken for a medium security prison set down next to the San Diego Freeway.

The year was 1964, and I had been Astro's employee for two years—my first real job after graduating from UCLA.

Security guards were making moves to close the gate—damn, I'd better haul ass.

Several middle-aged men with crew cuts and dressed in coats and ties were running toward the gate through the huge parking lot. I was still in shape from my days on the track team, so I easily passed several of the overweight guys with sweat running down their desperate faces. I entered the gate with more than a minute to spare.

"Nice going, kid, but next time you'd better come a little earlier," quipped one of the older armed guards as he checked my security badge.

As I left the gate area, I turned around in response to some sort of commotion. One of the runners had collapsed just inside the gate and was being attended to by guards. I heard one say, "We'd better call an ambulance just to be on the safe side."

At the time Astro had nearly forty thousand employees, but this would not last long. Joe, one of the engineers in our group, had visited the Astro corporate headquarters in New York and wandered by mistake into the wrong office. He glanced at an open report visible on a large executive desk. The report said that Astro planned to reduce its work force to about fifteen thousand within one year.

"Guess what I saw in New York?" Joe excitedly told our engineering group when he got back to work.

"Come on, Joe," replied our boss, Earl. "You obviously misread the report. Your interpretation is just too crazy to be taken seriously."

We all agreed with Earl. After all, we were hotshot engineers doing essential defense and aerospace work under fat government contracts; our benevolent Uncle Sam would take good care of us.

In just a few months, there was a huge difference in our workplace environment. Each Astro department head was ordered to lay off his quota—on average more than fifty percent. Department heads were told to use their own firing criteria, but the company was helpful. One such action was to institute a check-in procedure at the main gate after the other gates closed. All those entering after eight in the morning were required to sign in on randomly selected days. The sign-in list was then sent directly to department heads. Get your ass added to this shit list and your chances of being fired went way up—hence the desperation shown by runners through the parking lot.

The random gate check resulted in a curious spectacle between eight and ten o'clock. Some late employees rolled the proverbial dice and bravely walked through the main gate. Others could be seen lurking behind parked cars like peeping Toms, waiting to see if the first group was stopped to sign in. If the gate check was in place, the latter group would leave and enjoy a leisurely breakfast at a restaurant called Astro Eats, located just down the street. After ten or so, they could stroll through the gate without having to sign in. Astro Eats enjoyed fantastic business during this period, as did the nearby topless go-go pizza joint where we held final Friday lunches for our unfortunate laid-off buddies.

Fortunately, the pizzas were not topless—only the girls serving them.

When I arrived, fresh out of UCLA in 1962, Astro Dynamics was essentially a medium-size city. It teemed with activity: humming production lines and changing organizational charts as a result of a flood of new employees. Outside of work, a wide range of clubs was available: sailing club, adventurers club, ski club, sports car club, and more. Missile Park, adjacent to the complex, sported an actual retired Atlas missile as

its symbol, a huge metal erection easily visible from afar. The park became the center of many activities, with tennis courts, picnic areas, softball fields, a clubhouse, and even a miniature train.

Astro Dynamics manufactured the Atlas missile, the first stage of a system originally designed to launch nuclear weapons but later used to put spy satellites in orbit. Vandenberg Air Force Base, located on the coast of California north of Santa Barbara, was the launching point.

I was invited to the San Diego complex for a visit in the spring of 1962 while still a senior at UCLA. The visit went well; I was offered a job and asked to report after graduation in June.

But first I made a visit to my mother and two older siblings in Cocoa Beach, Florida.

My dad, Connor O'Malley, had married an Irish girl when he was only twenty-one. She turned out to have a pathological Irish temper, once even attacking Dad with a knife. This union must have been conceived in that famous resort town known as Hell, where all non- Christians are supposed to end up. Divorce, however, was prohibited by the Irish constitution. After much soul-searching, Connor left his wife and immigrated to the United States, taking whatever low-level jobs he could find for the first several years.

My dad ended all connection with the Catholic Church, effectively a self-excommunication, and fell in love with a pretty, dark-haired Jewish girl named Rachel, who became my mother. Our hybrid family functioned well with little religious dogma to muddle our thinking. Organized religions were rarely discussed. Kids' questions about God, Jesus, the devil, the Holy Ghost, or whatever were typically answered by our parents with noncommittal statements like "Nobody really knows," "Be careful of people who claim to know things they cannot possibly know," "Find your own truths," or simply "Live and let live."

Our family faced a major crisis when my dad was laid off at age fifty-one from a midlevel administrative job with the Pan-American company located near Cape Canaveral. The resulting financial stress took a heavy toll. My mom took a minimal job loading bags at the checkout counter of a local grocery store. My brother, Daniel; my sister, Esther; and I all worked throughout our high school years.

In the summers I worked on construction jobs, hauling concrete blocks, mixing mud, and completing any other work that the more senior workers wanted no part of. For six days each week, I got up at six in the morning and rode my bicycle forty-five minutes to the job site. We usually finished work by half past five, and on good days I was home, tired and dirty, by half past six. While daytimes in Florida summers were hot and humid, the nights posed the biggest challenge. With no air conditioning, I woke up every summer morning in a pool of sticky sweat.

This tough but ultimately valuable experience caused me to focus on one goal: somehow I had to get my overworked ass into college. The bachelor's degree became my imagined ticket to a better life. Our formally middle-class family had become a poor family overnight. The toll was especially hard on my dad, who became deeply depressed and developed additional health problems. He had lost his insurance when he was laid off, so he had no money for proper medical care. Connor O'Malley died of a heart attack at age fifty-five.

When I accepted the job at Astro, I had only a vague idea of the kind of job I would be doing; the work was classified as *Secret*. On my first day, I hopped out of bed early, dressed quickly, and jumped excitedly into my first car. I sported a new 1962 blue Chevrolet Impala, purchased on credit for $2,800 a few days earlier at a dealership just across the freeway from Astro. No money down—just used my job-offer letter as collateral.

I arrived at Astro full of vim and vigor and entered the outer office of Earl Gold, head of the Guidance Analysis engineering group and my immediate boss. A tall, good-looking blonde in her late thirties greeted me with a warm smile. "Hi, Jack. I'm Nancy. Welcome to our little engineering community. Earl is expecting you; go right in." Nancy, who I would later come to know quite well, was dressed conservatively in a loose blue blouse and long white skirt that successfully camouflaged whatever body might lurk underneath. Was she blond all the way down? I couldn't say; this group knew how to keep their secrets. Nancy projected a big sister or perhaps even motherly image toward our group of young engineers. At the time I also put her in my big sister category, and no strong prurient interests popped up. But such innocence would not endure.

My boss, Earl, tall and thin with horn-rimmed glasses, a relatively old man at thirty-four, welcomed me warmly and spent the next two hours with introductions to the twenty or so members of his engineering group, most of whom were under thirty. Much of their banter with me concerned sports, mainly my track background and speculations about how my so-called legendary speed, as they generously called it, might be useful to the engineering group's flag football, basketball, and softball teams.

Jim, a short, stocky fellow whom I later discovered to be super smart and the group's informal intellectual leader, patted me on the shoulder and said, "We have here in our midst a genuine stud in Kovac," pointing to a tall, dark-haired fellow across the room. "He played quarterback at Michigan; I've seen him toss a football seventy yards. On top of that, we have two friends in the next building who were offensive linemen on top-ranked high school teams. They're at bit out of shape but can still guarantee Kovac plenty of time to throw. Our main limitation is simply stated; we have no speedy wide receiver. That's why we insisted that Earl hire you." He grinned widely. While this last pronouncement was delivered as a joke, I later wondered if it might contain just a grain of truth.

The pleasant social environment continued; it was all good, but I was getting bored. I kept wondering when I was going to get some real work. After all, I was getting paid $9,000 per year, a sum so excessive in my mind that I actually wondered how I could possibly ever spend it all. This naive monetary outlook was partly the product of my minimal experience with the so-called fair sex, hopefully a temporary condition.

Whenever I asked Earl what he wanted me to work on, he would go to his bookshelf, hand me a thick notebook, and say, "Here, Jack. Read this report and tell me at the end of the week what you think of it."

I noticed that only about half of our group seemed to be busy. The excessively relaxed environment was puzzling. Only a few years earlier, in 1957, the Soviet Union had placed the first satellite in orbit around the Earth. Sputnik, meaning "elementary satellite" in Russian, was a metal sphere about two feet in diameter equipped with four antennae broadcasting radio pulses back to Earth.

The Eisenhower administration's first response was low-key and almost dismissive. However, they had underestimated the reaction of the American public, which was shocked by the Sputnik launch and televised failures of American launch attempts at about the same time. A national sense of fear was inflamed by poorly informed politicians and professional cold warriors portraying the United States as woefully behind the Soviet Union in the space and arms races.

Not only did the launch of Sputnik spur America to action—it also led directly to the creation of new government agencies like NASA and

DARPA, the Defense Advanced Research Projects Agency. Sputnik also contributed directly to advancement in science and technology when Eisenhower enacted a bill called the National Defense Education Act. This encouraged students to study math and science in college; tuition fees would be paid by the government. Would my UCLA degree have been possible without such government help? I'll never know. A new emphasis on science and technology swept the land, and the phrase *shortage of engineers* became a media buzzword.

At the time of my early Astro employment, this media buzz raised basic questions. If there was such a shortage of engineers, why did I, as well as half the others in our group, have so little to do? It was only much later that I found an answer that made any sense: defense contractors operated under government cost-plus contracts—essentially meaning they received a profit equal to a fixed percentage of their costs. In short, the more they spent, the more they made. The more engineers Astro hired, the better for the stockholders—good old crony capitalism in action.

These kinds of cushy arrangements were sharply curtailed several years after President Kennedy appointed Robert Strange McNamara secretary of defense. McNamara instituted a much-publicized cost-reduction program. This dramatic policy change resulted in the massive layoffs at Astro after 1963.

In November of 1963, I clearly remember walking back to my desk from the coffee machine. A fellow Astro employee with fear written all over his face shouted to me, "The president's been shot." I couldn't decide if this was just a bad joke until I got back to my office and found everyone huddled around a radio. Sure enough President John Kennedy had been assassinated in Dallas. Vice President Lyndon Baines Johnson was sworn in shortly thereafter on the flight taking the president's body back to Washington.

The irony of McNamara's middle name, "Strange," later became prominent with his major role in the escalation of the Vietnam War under Johnson. By the late 1960s, Vietnam had come to dominate the daily

lives of many Americans, both war supporters and opponents. Some soldiers volunteered; most were drafted. Few had any real idea of why we were at war with this remote third world country with no prospect of threatening the United States. "Hey, hey, LBJ, how many kids have you killed today?" later became a familiar antiwar cry in response to the massive US bombing campaign.

When I came to Astro in 1962, I had never even heard of Vietnam. Who could have known that in just a few years, this country would dominate our nightly news?

Chapter 2

Before McNamara's intervention, Astro Dynamics operated in a care-free environment of unlimited taxpayer generosity. Given the luxury of having extra worker bees in place, we had plenty of time on our hands for personal side projects. We were trained in computer language and had free and unlimited use of the IBM mainframe at Astro.

A typical missile simulation run cost $3,000, or roughly $23,000 in 2015 dollars, about equal to the price of my new Chevy Impala. Make a programming mistake? No problem; just run the simulation over again. Want to enroll in a college course? Astro will pay the tuition. Come to the plant at night to study the course, and Astro will pay you time and a half for overtime.

Allan, an older guy down the hall from us, got interested in the casino game of blackjack. "Older" to us meant anyone over thirty. Allan ran hundreds of simulations in order to develop optimal blackjack strategy based mainly on counting the number of face cards played, thereby providing advance information about cards in the deck remaining to be dealt. He wrote a popular book, *The Casino Gambler's Guide*, showing that card counting could yield substantial profits, provided players could avoid being cheated by casinos or prevented from playing altogether.

Allan's book was published three years after Edward Thorp's famous *Beat the Dealer*, but Allan's card-counting strategy was easier to master. Thorp later directed his talents to Wall Street, where he became a highly successful hedge fund manager. The fact that Allan's computer simulations may have cost the US taxpayers several hundred thousand dollars never became an issue as we seemed to have infinite money in this pre-McNamara defense environment.

Steve, perhaps the second-smartest member of our group, possessed a near-photographic memory, ideal for card counting in blackjack. Over several months he made regular weekend trips to Vegas, typically returning with profits three to five times larger than his traveling expenses. My own card-counting abilities were not as advanced as Steve's, but I was still able to profit over several Vegas weekends, despite all the distractions of free drinks and scantily clad women with dollar signs in their eyes rubbing their boobs against my horny neck.

Alas, dreams of an exotic gambling career were crushed when Vegas barred Steve from play. "We decline your action" was all they had to say. Clearly, I could expect similar treatment if I began to extract serious money from these greedy bastards. No Nevada court or politician would even think of challenging their casinos' right to exclude whomever they wished. Only suckers were welcome—thank you very much.

Some of my own extracurricular activities were sports related. I labeled one of my side projects CAOS (computer analysis of scores), a program rating college football teams; to my knowledge no one had yet developed this sort of system. Each game produced a link in my simulated network and was labeled by the point difference of the game's score. I mailed my ratings to fifty or so sportswriters to judge their interest in adopting my services. Their defensive responses came as a surprise; many said essentially, "No computer can ever replace *me*."

I did, however, receive a very positive reply from Anson Mount, the sports editor of *Playboy*. Unfortunately, new fantasies of a career with explicitly erotic fringe benefits were dashed when *Playboy*'s editors rejected the idea based on technical deadline issues. Only years later did football computer ratings become commonplace in daily newspapers. Maybe the first successful programmer's uncle was a sports editor.

Anson Mount was also *Playboy*'s religion editor. Yes, they really had one. Hugh Hefner often invited religious leaders to lunch at his Chicago mansion. I'm not sure how many accepted such invitations or if any participated in the proverbial bunny hops. All I can say for sure is that Jack O'Malley remained purely bunny-free.

During high school and most of my college years, the quality of my relationships with girls ranged from zero (if the measure of success was actual sex) to mediocre (if "mediocre" meant having friendly interactions with a little smooching and fondling). For one thing, I worked part-time jobs while completing my schoolwork during all of these years, so I was always busy. But this was just a convenient excuse. If truth be told, I was terrified of girls and especially of being rejected.

Just calling a girl for a date involved major trauma. I would nervously approach the phone like it was a savage beast or the edge of a thousand-foot cliff. Then I would back off and try to gather enough courage to try again, repeating the process multiple times. The Cowardly Lion from *The Wizard of Oz* could have won the Medal of Honor in my pitiful dating world.

I knew that this fear was irrational. Maybe my dad's influence, otherwise helpful and loving, was partly to blame. He tended toward the conservative side on sexual issues, possibly never fully shaking his strict Catholic upbringing. He preached superhuman respect for women, surely a good thing, but even my mother thought he sometimes went overboard. "Conner," she told him. "Surely, I want Jack to respect women, but let's get real. Women are not saints; they're flawed human beings just like men. Your experience with your first wife should have taught you that." My dad would reply with something like "Oh, darling, that can't be right, because *you*, in fact, *are* a saint" or some similar Irish blarney.

I actually had another role model of sorts to help me overcome my girl fears: my high school buddy Sam, for whom female rejection was no more serious than stubbing his toe. One sunny day when we were seventeen, we were walking along an upscale shopping street when we spied a gorgeous, well-dressed blonde of perhaps twenty-four. Sam decided that *we* should pick her up. I said, "No way," but to my horror, Sam proceeded toward her until I wrapped him in a bear hug and wrestled him down to the sidewalk.

The object of our attention turned around, immediately assessed the situation, looked at us with deep disdain, and spit out just three words: "Forget it, boys." If I had possessed a tail, it would have been located squarely between my legs. I went home in low spirits, But Sam just laughed the whole thing off, repeating the story several times at school the next day, even suggesting that he might have had her except for my interference. Oh, to be such an optimist!

I finally lost my virginity at a drive-in movie in my junior year at UCLA after my date, a plump dark-haired girl named Roxy, got just a little drunk from the bottle of Southern Comfort that I had stashed in the trunk of a borrowed car. Roxy was twenty-three, two years older than me, and far more experienced in the ins and outs of lovemaking. We parked in the darkest corner of the drive-in that we could find. Fortunately several of the closest light bulbs were burned out—probably sabotaged earlier by horny students.

In the backseat, I expertly brushed off a stale hamburger bun onto the floor. Aha, I thought, first obstacle successfully overcome! I then gently pushed Roxy down on her back and removed her shoes. I unbuckled her jeans and carefully pulled them down over her ample ass and legs—all the way off. She said in a soft voice, "Oh…don't…oh…oh," but to my mind, three moans more than canceled out one small "don't." Engineering training encouraged such quantitative judgments; my professors would have been proud.

Her panties came down next; in my haste I left them hanging around one leg. I was so excited by my first good look at her beautiful patch of silky black pubic hair that I could hardly breathe. Coming before I even had a chance to enter her was a looming danger. I opened her legs, shoved my face forward, and tried to lick her in a manner that I had once read about in a trashy novel, something like *Pink Panties and Short Dresses*. I had, however, only an approximate mental map of her clitoris area. How was I supposed to know just where to find it? My book didn't have pictures. I proceeded slowly at first and then faster and faster.

Apparently, I was close enough to pay dirt based on her enthusiastic response. At her first orgasmic-sounding scream, I entered her soaking wet vagina in a single motion and came immediately. "Oh, wow!" she said later as she pulled up her panties. "That was fantastic! But next time let's make it last longer."

I looked down at my long-suffering friend, who actually did appear close to being ready for the "next time," and thought, OK, Johnson, we finally did it.

The next morning I visited the UC medical library and found a crude line drawing of the female genital area with labels and arrows—better late than never.

Roxy and I dated for six more months, finding places for urgent sex that were much superior to the backseat of a car—my dorm room, the Santa Monica Beach, and even once in the bathroom of a late-night train. Sex, however, was about all we had in common; interests in intellectual pursuits of any kind were not part of Roxy's psyche. Our passion just kind of died slowly.

Shortly after we mutually agreed to end things between us, she found a new boyfriend whom she later married. I was even invited to the wedding but respectfully declined; it just didn't feel right. At that time, I couldn't imagine being at ease with the groom after all the good stuff I had done with his new bride. Later I would overcome such trivial hang-ups.

I was less successful in my search for a replacement squeeze than Roxy. The actor and singer Burl Ives once did a song called "Call Me Mister In-Between." His lyrics included the line "I'm too old for girls, and I'm too young for women," a sentiment to which I could closely relate.

One morning in the summer of 1964, my brain was immersed in a technical problem as I worked in my tiny cubical at Astro Dynamics. Several of the engineers from the 1962 group were long gone; some left voluntarily, more had been fired. The atmosphere of unlimited resources and free time for outside projects had flipped 180 degrees. My concentration was broken by a silent brush of soft hair on my neck and a light touch on my arm.

Nancy spoke softly, her face snuggled close to my ear. "Earl wants to meet with you; come to his office." I managed to stutter, "OK...mm... thanks, Nancy." I wondered how to react to Nancy's provocative behavior toward me. We had known each other for two years, and this level of friendly touching was new and unexpected. Not that I didn't like it, mind you; it was just that I couldn't interpret it. Was this the way she behaved with other male friends, or was she sending me a subtle message? I hadn't the slightest idea, but I felt too stiff and uncomfortable for the meeting. I opted for a bathroom break to clear my heads.

When I arrived at Earl's office five minutes later, Jim and Steve were already present. These two were our group's heavy hitters, so I assumed that Earl's issue was serious, although the reason for my presence was not clear. Earl was all business, producing none of his usual friendly banter.

"Guys, we have problems. Our new computer dial settings for the next Vandenberg launch are off by twenty to sixty percent from the last settings. If Vandenberg uses these numbers, we have no idea where the missile might go."

"Shit," Jim exclaimed. "For all we know, the fucker could hit the White House."

"OK, we have both a short-term and a long-term issue here," said Earl. "First, we must send plausible dial settings to Vandenberg by next Monday. Second, on a longer time scale, we've got to find out what's wrong with our methods; it's obviously something very fundamental."

Atlas missiles launched from Vandenberg were controlled with computer and radar systems. Every second, the computer received six pieces of information from the missile—three spatial values, the x, y, and z coordinates, and three components of velocity. The computer then calculated a new trajectory, and appropriate commands were sent back to the rocket engine. A second-stage rocket later placed a spy satellite, hopefully in the right orbit, to take the desired pictures—let's say to get a good shot of Nikita Khrushchev cooking hot dogs in his backyard in Moscow.

An air force officer with zero understanding of the sophisticated computer programs underlying this process was sitting in front of the Vandenberg computer. His job was simply to turn three little knobs on the computer, the three dial settings supplied before each launch by our engineering group, Guidance Analysis. These three settings typically changed by only small amounts before each launch based on error corrections estimated with our missile simulations in San Diego.

Earl continued the discussion in his office. "I have a suggested solution to our immediate problem. Our last three dial settings show a weak trend, changing by about one-half percent in consistent directions. I'm thinking we just send Vandenberg extrapolated settings based on these trends."

Jim laughed. "In other words, we fudge the settings."

Earl looked peeved. "*Fudge* is not a good word here, Jim; I prefer *extrapolated*. But, in any case, let's agree that this little discussion not leave this room. With all the talk of layoffs, I'm sure you can appreciate how important it is to avoid even the appearance of impropriety."

We all nodded our heads wisely; nobody advanced counterarguments.

"Normally, I would assign our second problem, the apparent inaccuracy of our mathematical methods, to Jim or Steve. But you two guys are already heavily committed on critical short-term projects for the next week or two. That's why you're here, Jack. Jim suggested that you organize the effort and maybe make some progress toward a solution over the next two weeks or so. Then, Jim and Steve can get on board, and the three of you can finish the job and get us out of this mess."

"Sure, I'll start right away," I said with more confidence than I felt.

Chapter 3

I immediately got hard at work on Earl's assignment to get the computer dial setting problem worked out. To make a long story short, the kid from Cocoa Beach got real lucky. It turned out that when I got past all the verbal fluff and the unrelated math and computer code, the source of the problem was simple. Within one week, I had found the error. By the end of the second week, I had formulated several possible solutions. I was on cloud nine—maybe even ten.

"Son of a bitch," said Jim with a smile. "You haven't looked this good since last year when you made that one-handed catch in the end zone of Kovac's pass."

I could not have known it at the time, but this particular engineering glitch and my lucky solution were to set in motion events that transformed my life in a new and unimaginable way.

Several days after I had presented my results to Earl, he called me to his office. "Jack, it turns out that your findings have implications that extend well outside our small engineering group. This other stuff is classified *Top Secret*, and you have only *Secret* clearance, so I can't tell you much. But I just finished talking to Dr. Stanford of the Astro Dynamics Basic Physics Group, and he wants you to present your analysis to a select group of military and scientific personnel next Friday."

"Who's he?" I asked.

"Jesus, Jack, Dr. Stanford just happens to be a famous physicist, probably the most high-powered brain at Astro, and he enjoys excellent relationships with the military to boot. I can't believe you've never heard of him."

Just then, Nancy stuck her head in the office. "Dr. Stanford is on line one." Earl picked up the phone and uttered a series of short replies. "Yes, yes, OK, he'll come at two o'clock today."

Earl looked at me like he had just received orders from the Pope. "He wants to talk to you privately at two this afternoon, before the military gets involved."

I wandered into a disorganized suite of offices with blackboards containing complicated math in an obscure building near the back of the Astro complex. No secretary or receptionist was in sight. I spotted a tall, handsome athletic-looking fellow with dark hair, maybe thirty years old, wearing a casual white pullover shirt.

"Excuse me. I'm looking for Dr. Stanford."

"Well, look no further, Jack," he replied. "And by the way, my name is Gene."

I was speechless, having expected to meet some old guy with white hair and a formal demeanor.

"Gene" smiled; he saw the origin of my confusion right off. After all, he was accustomed to this kind of reaction, but he avoided comment. "I asked you here so we could go over your analysis before we meet with the big brass on Friday. These generals can sometimes be a pain in the ass, so I want to be sure you and I are on the same page. It's not wise to piss them off."

We then went over technical details for several hours. Gene stayed low-key the whole time, keeping me mostly at ease, but I was well aware that he was testing me, albeit in a friendly manner.

"See," I said, pointing to three simple algebraic equations in my notebook. "When Vandenberg moved to the new launch series, our basic equations used to compute the three computer dial settings became ill-conditioned. Instead of three equations and three unknowns, now we effectively have only two independent equations, so our so-called so-lutions are nonsense. But, between Jim, Earl, and me, we were able to derive a third independent equation."

When we finished, he said, "I'm surprised this turned out to be so simple; science is not always like that.

"I just had a thought. I've been asked to do some work for the Advanced Planning Group on a future Venus probe. I'm busy on other projects, so I need a smart guy like you to help me out on a temporary basis. What do you know about orbital mechanics?"

My head was spinning. "Well, other than that they follow directly from Newton's laws, not a whole lot. I did have to learn some of the basics in connection with my current work in Earl's group, but I'm no-where near an expert."

Gene smiled. "It's not all that hard. If I point you to the right books, you can pick up all you need in a few weeks, no sweat. So what do you say?"

I suppressed my excitement. "It sounds really interesting, but I'd have to check with Earl; he might not be too happy about losing another one of his guys with all the layoffs and all."

Gene waved his hand dismissively. "This is just temporary—maybe three months tops. You let me take care of Earl; I'll find a way to make up for his loss. Do you want the job or not?"

I accepted without further hesitation. How could I say no to the Pope?

A few days later, Earl called me to his office. He wasn't entirely happy with my move to work with Gene but understood my position. "I'm OK with this as long as it's limited to three months. Dr. Stanford did get the brass to give me some overtime hours to make up for your loss."

I spent the next two weeks studying the two books on orbital me-chanics that Gene loaned me. Every few days he would call me to his of-fice to check on my progress and suggest small problems for me to work on. He knew just how to challenge me without burying me with so much arcane technical detail that I became discouraged.

The advanced planning for the Venus probe was part of the Pioneer program, a series of unmanned space missions designed to explore the planets of the solar system. The Venus orbiter mission was not expected to take place for five to ten years, so my work was very early in the game.

After six weeks I was finally beginning to generate useful results with my computer runs.

Gene called me to his office, and I presented a rough outline of my findings on orbital error analyses. In short, suppose the first-stage launch rocket introduces such and such an error in position and velocity. What does that mean for errors in the spacecraft's trajectory on its way to Venus, and how much correction will be necessary?

"OK, good, Jack." Gene handed me a handwritten yellow pad full of technical material. "It's time for you to start working on a formal report for the Pioneer people. You are off to a good start, but much more is needed. I have listed the new calculations required in your report. Let's plan on meeting for an hour every other day to check your progress. I definitely want to have you back with Earl within the three-month time frame."

A lot of hard work, I thought, but that was what I was being paid for.

Then Gene hit me with a surprise. "By the way, I try to get in a good run three or four times a week. Why don't you join me tomorrow? We'll take a long lunch break and drive to Black's Beach. I know you're somewhat of a running legend at Astro, but I can still do five to ten miles at a pretty good pace, so maybe I can keep up."

Gene and I soon became regular running partners, and this continued after my return to Earl's group.

Over the next months, I learned that Gene's father, George Stanford, had retired early from the military and started his own company when he was forty-two. George had impressive contacts; one was a longtime friendship with Dwight Eisenhower. Within four years the company was doing more than a hundred million dollars per year in sales, partly due to George's contacts but also because he proved to be an astute businessman.

Their family had no obvious connection to Leland Stanford, the famous tycoon, industrialist, robber baron, and founder of Stanford University. Probably some sort of relationship with a distant cousin was involved, but I never heard anybody speak of it.

One might say that Gene grew up with the proverbial silver spoon, but his chosen path was highly unusual for a rich kid. He obtained his PhD in physics and astronomy from UC Berkeley with research on quasars, the quasi-stellar radio sources. The prefix *quasi* indicates point sources like stars rather than sources spread out like galaxies. However, the energy output of a single quasar might be as much as a thousand times the energy of a typical galaxy containing billions of stars. Strange objects, indeed. The nature of quasars was controversial until the 1980s when they were identified as compact regions in the center of galaxies surrounding super massive black holes.

Rich kids were rare in my science and engineering classes. Why work your ass off when you can get a cushy job in Daddy's company? But Gene was an enigma, a walking paradox; he consistently moved in directions counter to stereotypes. He could have had a faculty position in some prestigious physics department and worked on whatever scientific project interested him. With his family's wealth to back him, the best of all professional worlds was his for the asking. Only later did I come to a better understanding of Gene's real motivations.

Gene was raised in a socially conservative environment but had a rare ability to interact effectively with just about anyone, be they academic, business, or military. His family consisted of patriots in the traditional sense; God and country came first. While he greatly respected these attitudes, he was quick to appreciate other viewpoints. Shortly after obtaining his PhD, Gene married his longtime girlfriend, Marie, a smart, petite, brown-haired girl and another child of wealthy business parents.

Two months after returning to Earl's group, I received a rude shock. Kovac pulled a chair into my cubical and stretched out his impressive frame. "Well, buddy, it looks like I won't be playing for Guidance Analysis this fall; you'll need to find a new quarterback. Astro just gave me the ax."

I didn't know what to say. Kovac—everyone called him by his last name—had been a good friend for two years. He was largely responsible for the success of our football team.

The year before, in the fall of 1963, we went undefeated in our six-team company division, consisting of engineers and technicians, part-time jocks now past their prime. We were quite full of ourselves until we faced the winner of the other Astro division, a team from the mail room that we had never seen play. It turned out that the mail room was loaded with former top high school and college players; two of their guys may have been even faster than me. We were slaughtered 42-6. Our only score came late in the second half when their safety fell down and I was able to grab a long pass from Kovac.

Although flag football has no tackling, it does allow serious blocking, and boy, could these mail room guys block. Pretty much everyone on our team was seriously banged up. I had bruises from head to toe and a severe limp and had to skip my beach runs for three weeks. Poor Jim, who was in way over his head at this sporting level, was knocked out of the game in the first half. He was forced to wear a neck brace for six weeks. Even our super jock Kovac broke his finger. It seems that no matter how good you think you are at something, there is always someone somewhere who is much better.

We said good-bye to Kovac at our Friday lunch, as we did with every laid-off colleague from our group. The nearby topless go-go pizza joint provided the usual venue. We ate pizza and drank copious quantities of cheap beer while girls danced the go-go and twirled the tassels on their breasts. Our jokes were confined to black humor. In our somber moods, nobody gave a rat's ass about bare tits, tassels or not. We hated to see Kovac go but were even more concerned about our own futures. Many more Friday lunches were in the works. "Hey, bartender, make sure to keep the beer and breasts ready for duty every Friday."

I was not accustomed to so much alcohol, especially in the daytime. My college experience consisted mainly of tough engineering classes, part-time jobs, and training for the track team. I never joined a fraternity and had very little bar time under my belt. Thus, Friday afternoons after our go-go lunches presented me with a real challenge. I was always fighting to stay awake when we returned to Astro. Sleeping at my desk was a bad idea; it could move me up on the layoff list pretty fast. My first solution was to sleep on the john, resulting in major leg cramping and, at best, fitful sleep.

Jim, however, had a better idea. "Look," he said, "with all the layoffs, we have plenty of free cubicles. We also have a huge pile of boxes containing old reports waiting to be shredded. Because many reports are marked *Confidential*, it will take forever for these reports to be processed, especially with Astro's loss of manpower. We can build a little castle out of boxes placed in the entrance to a cubical with a tunnel to a private space that can accommodate one or two sleepers on the floor."

We waited until everyone cleared out at the end of the day and constructed Club Snooze in less than an hour. This frivolous project proved to have a profound influence on my life, but who would have thunk it at the time?

Chapter 4

For me, the most disturbing layoff targeted our oldest engineer. Henry was forty-two with a wife and three kids; he had worked for the same company in Saint Louis for fifteen years. He accepted a higher-paying job with Astro Dynamics and moved his family across the country to San Diego. After just six months on the job, he was out the door with two weeks' notice. At our final Friday go-go and good-bye lunch, Henry's heroic attempts at putting on a brave face were painfully transparent.

As we gobbled pizza and washed it down with pitchers of cheap beer, I flashed on alternating images of the downtrodden Willy Loman from *Death of a Salesman* and my own father, laid off at fifty-one and dead at fifty-five. Also going through my mind were Thoreau's words, "Most men lead lives of quiet desperation and go to the grave with the song still in them." These depressing thoughts put me in a foul mood. I got especially shit-faced that day but still managed to stagger back to Astro by two o'clock.

In my alcohol-induced stupor, I badly needed the luxury accommodations of Club Snooze. When no one was looking, I crawled through our box tunnel into the dark womb-like spot on the carpeted floor; I was fast asleep within a few minutes. My next awareness was of voices that I didn't recognize and the commotion of heavy objects being moved. Forget it. I went back to sleep.

The next thing I knew I was being wacked sharply on the back of my head and an angry voice saying, "You! Turn over so I can get your badge number." I looked up to see some big gray-haired guy in an air force uniform writing notes on his pad. The proverbial shit had hit the fucking fan.

When I came to work the following Monday, Club Snooze had been dismantled and the boxes hauled away. Other than a bit of whispered "damns" and eye rolling by Jim, nobody said much to me about the incident, although I suspect much was discussed out of my earshot.

When I saw Earl, he just turned an ashen face toward me and shook his head sadly, contributing to my deep sense of foreboding.

Several weeks went by with no apparent repercussions; the incident seemed to have blown over. After all, I encouraged myself, I had spent three months as Pope Gene's assistant. I was also the one who rescued Guidance Analysis from the abyss by discovering our erroneous missile calculations. Maybe I had even saved the White House; I was hot stuff.

But not long after my newfound optimism surfaced, Earl came to my cubical and asked me to follow him to his office. My anxiety level rose immediately because normally Earl would have just sent Nancy to fetch me. Then when I entered the outer office, Nancy carefully avoided eye contact. Isn't it interesting how much critical information can be gleaned from such minor social cues?

I was not surprised when Earl spoke. "This is the part of my job that I hate with a passion. I'm sorry Jack, but you're being let go; you have two weeks from today."

"Because I was caught sleeping on the job?" I said.

"You also had bad luck," Earl replied. "In most cases I could have saved you, but the security people got wind of this little incident and alerted General Trainer, who happened to be visiting this area. Trainer is based in the Pentagon and is known to be a real hard-ass. He personally wacked you on the head and took your badge number. It's a good thing the fanatic wasn't armed; he might have shot all of us.

"Of course, I am partly to blame for turning a blind eye to the nefarious activities of your Club Snooze members. Fortunately, I was able to limit the damage done to Guidance Analysis. To be honest, you are somewhat of a sacrificial lamb. I'm truly sorry."

How did the security people get involved? Did they think Club Snooze was hiding secrets? Did they think we were tunneling all the way to Moscow? I never found out, but in my last week at Astro, my emotional reaction to being fired turned 180 degrees. Dad used to tell me that when life offers you a lemon, make lemonade. Or maybe, gin and tonic, I thought. I focused on the facts. I was twenty-four and in excellent health with no one to support but myself. Without the limitations of my nine-to-five job, I could surf, play volleyball, run on the beach, or do most anything else whenever I felt like it. Hell, I could even sleep until noon in my exclusive version of Club Snooze.

Most of all, my prospects with women actually appeared to be looking up as I got a little older. I now had longer hair and sported a mustache; I seemed to be finally getting old enough for women—thank God. It was time to focus on personal development, so to speak. The world, or at least San Diego, would be my proverbial oyster. I would not become another Willy Loman or Connor O'Malley. All I needed was a minimal source of funding to cover expenses. Put that in your pipe and smoke it, General Trainer.

The next day, Gene called to express his regrets. "I'm really sorry, Jack. I tried to use my influence to protect you, but Trainer just wields too much weight around here. He has a lot to say about Astro's contracts with the Pentagon, and his financial bite can be even worse than his bark.

"On a positive note, you're a smart guy and will find another job. Unfortunately, California is now saturated with laid-off engineers, so you might be forced to move back east. You may even be forced to wear a coat and tie and cut your hair. I can make some inquires with other defense contractors if you want; my recommendation is probably worth something."

"No, thanks, Gene," I responded. "I'm staying in San Diego. I'll tell you my new plans when we next run together."

When the time came for my Friday good-bye lunch, I was enjoying one of my best days ever—even getting a minor kick out of the girl's twirling tassels that had come to be so associated with layoffs. Jim insisted that I join him and his wife for dinner the following Sunday.

Others offered similar invitations for get-togethers over the following weeks. What irony. Just a month earlier, my emotions had reached a low point when Henry was let go. Now here it was my turn to hit the streets, and I was as happy as the proverbial clam, excited about unknown future adventures. Jim and Earl could not understand my giddy demeanor.

Earl was truly mystified. "Are you really OK or just fooling us? What are you plans? You do understand that I fought like a son of a bitch to save you, don't you?"

"Hey, Earl, the truth is that I feel like a huge weight has been lifted from my shoulders. I just paid off my only debt, my car loan. I'll receive unemployment payments for twelve weeks, and I have some savings. I'm really looking forward to sleeping late. If I get desperate, I can always move in with you and your wife; I'm sure she wouldn't mind."

Jim laughed heartily, but Earl managed only a weak smile in response to my black humor; he was far better at hiring than he was at firing.

I was a little disappointed in Nancy's reaction to my firing; she had barely mentioned it in the two weeks prior to our Friday good-bye and was especially quiet during lunch. For a while, it seemed that she didn't really care that I was leaving. But as we all stood up to leave the bar, she walked past me, saying nothing but shoving a piece of paper in my hand. It read *call me*, with a phone number below.

On my drive home, the radio was playing one of my favorite tunes; it seemed like a good omen:

Oh please, say to me
You'll let me be your man
And please, say to me
You'll let me hold your hand

I wasted little time; that same Friday night, I called Nancy, and she answered after two rings. We talked for more than an hour, gossiping about Astro personnel as well as several aspects of my personal life. She probed lightly about my female relationships, but this was, of necessity, a brief interchange. Was this all big sister stuff, or was there more to it? Without much thought, I finally blurted out, "Can I take you out to dinner sometime?"

She replied quickly, "No, Jack. The unemployed have to watch their spending. Come to my apartment tomorrow at seven, and I'll fix us a nice dinner."

Nancy's modest one-bedroom apartment was located a few blocks from Crystal Pier in Pacific Beach, a suburb five miles north of downtown San Diego. I found her place by half past six but waited somewhat nervously until seven before knocking on the door. To my mind *dinner* was a code word, but did Nancy have the same interpretation?

As I stepped in the door, I reached over to give her a friendly hug, but her response was not "friendly" at all. She threw her arms around my neck and moved her body up against me. My friend Johnson popped up like a reliable jack-in-the-box. "Mmm," she said as she pressed harder, "you're either packing a gun or just really glad to see me."

Nancy was wearing a fitted black dress and was barefoot. I kneeled down and pulled her dress up over her waist, revealing matching black panties. I began rubbing her lightly between the legs. In contrast to my earlier sexual experiences, I detected no resistance whatsoever in this eager partner. If anything, she seemed to want to go faster. We kissed, and the alcohol on her breath was pervasive; apparently she had started drinking well before my arrival. I pulled down her panties while she helpfully held up her dress. No she was not blond all the way down—one of Astro's secrets was a secret no more.

We moved toward the closest chair, and she kicked the panties off her ankle. I lifted her right leg to the chair, unzipped my pants, ran my fingers through her full brown bush, and entered her slippery cave with much gusto. Success! Jack was inside the box. I started moving slowly, but she moaned, "Don't wait. Let yourself go. We have the whole night ahead of us for a more leisurely pace." I eagerly followed her wishes and finished in what felt like a small nuclear explosion.

The next fourteen hours were a blur. Nancy and I talked, kissed, petted, ate snacks, drank whiskey, slept short periods in her big bed, and made love multiple times. Her orgasms outnumbered mine by at least four to one. I learned more about sex that night than I had in my previous twenty-four years.

I became familiar with her body. She was tall and thin with large breasts, but most would not really call her beautiful in the strictest sense. At thirty-nine, she showed some signs of age; her breasts were just a little bit saggy, and she had a little extra fat around her middle. But I could not have cared less about these so-called imperfections. On this night she was my beauty queen.

Nancy drank like a fish. When I commented in passing on how she could drink me under the table, she turned serious. "Jack, you should know the truth. I am a full-blown alcoholic. I've quit drinking several times and tried AA but always end up backsliding. I trust you to not mention anything to anybody about our intimacy or my drinking, especially your friends at Astro. My job might be on the line."

"No problem. My lips are sealed." Later, I used the code name "Piper" for Nancy when discussing our relationship with my friends. I avoided any details about sex; they probably wouldn't have believed me anyway.

Over the next two months, Nancy and I continued our passionate encounters several times per week. Then one morning we were lying in her bed right after we finished making love. She came up with a real shocker right out of the blue. "Jack, I can't see you at all next week; please don't come close to my apartment and don't call. When the coast is clear, I'll call you."

At first I thought she was kidding, but when I realized she was dead serious, I insisted on an explanation. Finally, she just blurted it out. "My boyfriend will be in town all week."

What the hell! I guess I had kind of thought that I was the so-called *boyfriend*, not that we ever discussed limitations with other people.

Nancy told me the whole story. "When I was twenty-five, I fell in love with a married man in his forties, a well-known scientist. He now lives with his family in New York, but he visits the West Coast on a regular basis. When he comes to town, I drop everything to be with him. That's just the way it is."

I was nearly speechless; all I could say was "OK, call me when you can." I got dressed in record time and left without another word. I was angry and deeply wounded, much more than I would have admitted to anyone.

I was not in love with Nancy; I just liked her a lot and was deep into our energetic sexual exploits. In the next few hours, I ruminated over and over about this other boyfriend, who now had to be in his fifties. Quite a contrast to poor young Jack, now cruelly revealed as nothing but a second-stringer in love's game. No question about it: I was one jealous son of a bitch.

Unfortunately, I was not yet sufficiently mature or experienced to tell Nancy just how hurt I felt. For one thing, my pain seemed totally irrational; after all, we had never agreed to have an exclusive relationship. I feared that any attempt to express my stupid, jealous feelings would be interpreted as a demand to drop the first-string boyfriend. I knew that was never going to happen, nor did I really want it to. In truth I didn't fancy being tied to an exclusive girlfriend; I was just now getting my feet wet, so to speak.

After his first visit, Nancy and I never again really discussed the other guy. We typically ate dinners at her apartment, and I even acquired some limited cooking skills. We often visited her favorite bars where she was well known and liked. We also kept our eyes open for good movies. One evening we attended the black comedy *Dr. Strangelove*. The plot seemed outrageous at the time. Brigadier General Jack Ripper, played by actor Sterling Haden, decides on his own to deploy a nuclear attack against the Soviet Union. Attempts to recall the attack fail. When Soviet bases are hit, the feared doomsday machine is triggered. Only later would I come to appreciate that the fictitious General Ripper was not so fictitious after all.

Nancy and I continued our relationship for another year, and the first-stringer came to town several more times. I disappeared without protest during his brief invasions. I learned to accept it, albeit grudgingly, and began dating other women. I owed Nancy a lot. In some ways she was one of my most important mentors, and I would always feel affection for her. Our lives, however, were headed in different directions.

Chapter 5

Gene parked his car near the private road in the La Jolla Farms subdivision, walking distance to UCSD, which was located up on the bluffs four hundred feet higher than Black's Beach. We jogged slowly down the half-mile private road to warm up until we reached the white, sandy beach. Later Black's would become a famous nude beach, but during this period it remained mostly deserted. We picked up the pace and headed north, past Torrey Pines Golf Course on the bluff and the Del Mar racetrack where the coastal railroad track paralleled the beach.

Gene was a natural athlete, but with the exception of years of private karate training, he had avoided high school and college sports and focused on his studies, apparently due to parental pressures. I sensed that he regretted missing out; his initial attraction to our friendship had a lot to do with sports. He often asked about my former track adventures and even my modest football exploits. On my side of things, I was in awe of his knowledge of the world, not to mention his raw intelligence, all contained in a package free from arrogance. Later, as our friendship deepened, our running discussions took on a much more serious flavor.

"So, Jack, explain to me again just how you plan to support yourself," Gene said as we turned around and headed south. "Your experience with counting cards in Vegas shows that the casinos will never allow you to win consistently. Furthermore, it is my understanding that the Mafia controls much of Vegas. Rumor has it that the surrounding desert contains more than a few permanent occupants who have crossed the wrong people."

"You may be right, Gene. But I have no intention of playing poker or blackjack or anything else in Vegas. San Diego's card rooms are small mom-and-pop businesses, closely regulated by the city. It's a whole different ball game; the typical player in the smaller games is not especially skilled. I think I can consistently win enough to live on. I plan to give it six months and see what happens."

At first Gene was quite skeptical about my financial game plan, but he later changed his tune and even occasionally began to visit the card rooms himself.

One of my few recreational pursuits in college was poker with friends. In my senior year at UCLA, I had made a fascinating discovery of the seedy section of downtown San Diego. This intriguing area sported a variety of businesses aimed at sailors from the local naval air station, college students, businessmen, lawyers, and others, including several subspecies of old men, whether they be dirty or maybe just a little dusty. Attractions included bars, strip joints, the Pussycat Theater, and legal poker rooms.

The state of California banned "games of chance" but allowed "games of skill"; distinction between the two was left mostly to local governments.

For many years, San Diego hosted a dozen or so card rooms, which were closely regulated by the city. Each card room was limited to a maximum of five tables and a modest hourly rate set by the city. These small businesses were small potatoes and held no interest for organized crime. No cutting of the pot was allowed, in sharp contrast to the universal practice of greedy casinos. The stakes ranged from small-limit poker to relatively high-stakes no-limit, where you could bet all your chips in one go.

The only game allowed was California five-card draw in which the joker was wild only when used with aces, straights, and flushes. No lowball, no stud, and no Texas hold'em—nothing but five-card draw could be played legally. Even Go Fish was a no-go if played for money. Also, the card rooms were not allowed to advertise or accept checks; the poker business was all cash.

When the good people of San Diego passed by card rooms, most thought they were viewing innocent bridge games, having no idea that such sinful gambling was afoot in their neighborhoods.

Given my meager bankroll, I had little choice but to begin my poker career in small-stakes games, playing two-dollar-limit at Brown's Cardroom on Fourth Street. Later I graduated to no-limit games at various locations downtown, as well as at card rooms in other San Diego neighborhoods like Point Loma, Ocean Beach, and Pacific Beach right next to Crystal Pier.

In small-stakes games, the simple strategy of playing "tight" pretty much guaranteed breaking even or small profits; "tight" meant you just stayed out of marginal hands and avoided loose calls. A number of retired folk played nearly every day in the small-stakes games, often supplementing their social security checks by essentially taking small amounts of money from the loose players in the majority. At higher stakes, winning strategies were, of course, much more subtle.

The modest hourly charges facilitated environments in which perhaps the top one percent or so of players might earn a reasonable living "wage" at the tables. Early on, in 1965, after leaving Astro, I was averaging about $2 per hour after paying costs. In comparison, the federal minimum wage at the time was $1.25. My $2 "wage" was equivalent to about $15 per hour in 2015 dollars, and it was all in cash with no deductions for taxes, social security, or anything else. Sorry, Uncle Sam; eat your heart out. My income was small potatoes to be sure but enough to support an ascetic lifestyle. As time went on, both my game and my wage were to progress nicely.

My friends often assumed that my UCLA math training allowed me to beat the game by calculating odds, but this had little to do with how money was actually made. The label *poker* refers to several different games; the importance of knowing odds differs substantially between games. San Diego's law allowed only five-card draw, in which players are dealt five cards facedown, followed by the first betting round. Players remaining after the first round then draw up to four new cards in exchange for an equal number of discards. After the draw, each player normally has a new hand of five cards, and the second and last round of betting takes place.

Aside from modest fees, the essential features of five-card draw are simple. First, no cards are ever exposed, unlike in games like stud poker and Texas hold'em. Second, many games are no-limit, meaning that any player can bet any amount up to all his or her chips on the table. These features effectively eliminate most considerations of odds from game strategy since experienced players typically follow reasonable statistical strategies intuitively. Success depends almost exclusively on understanding the mental states and behavior of opponents, including an appreciation of how one's own self is perceived by other players. A good player must try to read the minds of opponents and see himself through their eyes. Each game is essentially a controlled experiment in folk psychology and unconscious action.

When I first started playing in college, I fundamentally misjudged the nature of the game by vastly underestimating its critical psychology component; one might characterize my play as "autistic" in this subculture. Mathematical training was probably a handicap; I knew the rules and odds, but I was abysmally ignorant of the game's essence. Fortunately, I became aware of my error several years before I was fired from Astro and poker became my regular job. Later, as an experienced player, I often observed the same autistic play by (otherwise) intelligent newcomers.

The critical distinction between human financial and social goals in various "games" is not always appreciated. This is nicely demonstrated when professional poker players appear on television and the host suggests a demonstration game played for pennies or matchsticks. To appreciate the silliness of this idea, imagine challenging a tennis professional to a "match" played without balls. You swing your racquet, and I'll swing mine; we'll just pretend we're hitting the ball.

In my San Diego games, a full table consisted of eight players arranged in a circle. Cards were dealt in turn by the players; no paid dealers were involved, keeping costs low. My seven opponents might consist of five acquaintances and two strangers but typically no friends. Although the players engaged in (mostly) civil conversation, these games differed greatly from the typical friendly home game.

Regular players were labeled with colorful names that mysteriously emerged from the subculture—names like Sailor Alan, Tomato John, Bicycle Bill, Fast Eddie, Chicken Art, Dick the Contractor, and Jack Box. Professionals were well-known and mostly welcome, accepted members of a subculture where status was partly defined by the ability to accumulate chips, a plausible mini model of the "greed is good" American society.

The atmosphere of these games is perhaps illustrated by an old joke about a player asked by a friend why he continued to play when he knew the game was crooked. The player answers, "Yes, I know, but it's the only game in town."

One incident that sticks in my mind concerns Pigeon Pat, a player on a losing streak who kept borrowing more and more money from other players. We were playing no-limit at Bob's Card room, an especially run-down joint in the downtown area. Under social pressure, I had loaned Pat fifty dollars but refused to extend more credit. When others did the same, he abruptly left the game, shouting, "Save my seat!"

Shortly after, Pat returned with a big wad of cash and resumed playing. About an hour later, the police came and arrested him. It turned out that he had walked around the block to the nearest bank, robbed it, and returned directly to the card room. I never saw Pat after that; my fifty bucks were history.

Good basic poker involves playing tight, that is, folding most hands so as to leave plenty of time to observe other players closely. My decisions to play a hand, call a raise, or fold were based on both conscious and unconscious processes. The most important decisions depended on complicated information sets. Objective data included my opponents' positions relative to the dealer, the sizes of their bets, the number of cards drawn, and the number of chips remaining in our stacks. Subjective data included (mostly) unconscious memories of past play, my best guess as to how opponents expected me to act, my opponents' mannerisms, and perhaps other visual, auditory, and possibly even olfactory information available only to my unconscious.

I typically made critical decisions in a second or two, based mostly on intuition apparently originating in my unconscious. Just as in sports play, it was often better to make choices without actually thinking about them. In my many hours of professional play, these choices were often wrong; they were just less wrong and wrong less often than most of my opponents' choices.

We are all faced with many analogous situations in our daily lives in which choices must be based on very limited information. We rely on some combination of logic and intuition, but the world's complexity often overwhelms logic, and intuition must play a dominant role in decision making. In the years ahead, I was to return to this thought on numerous occasions.

Chapter 6

In late 1966, Gene invited me to join him and his wife Marie for lunch at their home on the Mount Soledad bluffs high above the beach at La Jolla Shores. Their house was one story with his and her office wings extending on either side of a central kitchen and living room area. Both Gene and Marie enjoyed private workplaces; Gene even had a large telescope in his home office. They had no children, so two bedrooms and two offices were all that were needed. The home was upscale but not excessively so. On the other hand, the 180-degree panoramic view of the Pacific Ocean with hillside homes and a golf course in the foreground took my breath away.

Gene introduced me to Marie, a petite woman in her late 20s, natural looking with little or no makeup, and very attractive with long brown hair and small breasts. She wore a long slinky purple dress that spoke of big bucks. Gene was his usual gregarious self, but Marie seemed cool toward me at first. I guessed that she didn't quite understand why her brilliant husband was spending time with this unemployed kid, a poker player looking just a little like a hippie with long brown hair bleached blond by sun exposure. Of course, this "kid" was now twenty-six, just six years younger than Gene.

I soon realized that Marie was one smart cookie; she had a master's degree in some esoteric area of the biological sciences that was unfamiliar to me. She worked for a high tech start-up in La Jolla near the Torrey

Pines Golf Course. Once our more serious discussions of scientific issues and world affairs got going and Marie noticed that I held my own, she warmed considerably. But, unlike Gene, her formal demeanor never allowed me to forget her wealthy family background. Despite her engaging personality, she maintained just a hint of the sense of control and entitlement characteristic of the very rich.

After lunch, Gene gave me breaking news that he had previously revealed only to Marie. "I've given my notice to Astro Dynamics; I'll need about a month to finish ongoing work, but then I'm out of there. I've accepted a new position with a small company called Integrated Parallax Systems, or IPS for short, located in Sorrento Valley, the industrial park in north San Diego. My office will be close to Del Mar, pretty convenient for our beach running and lunches with Marie. The new job involves government contracts with an interesting combination of scientific and policy work."

"Policy work? Is IPS like the Rand Corporation?" I asked.

"Yes, it's a think tank," Marie answered.

Gene adopted his professorial demeanor. "IPS apparently shares some characteristics with the so-called think tanks like the Rand Corporation that aim to improve government decision making through research and analysis. The big difference is that IPS is very small; almost nobody has ever heard of it. Their office has no visible sign, their phones are unlisted, and publicity is strongly discouraged. IPS is a very private company."

"This is a little weird, Gene," I said. "How many employees work for IPS? What kind of science will you be doing? What government agencies are paying the bills? These general questions are not usually classified in my experience. If you classify bathroom locations, everyone will just piss on the floor."

Gene frowned. "I'm sorry, but everything you asked is secret. My job offer required a level of security that I had never even heard of, way above *Top Secret*. I will not be discussing my work with anyone, not even Marie, except to say that I'm extremely excited about the new challenges it offers. It will afford me an opportunity to really make a difference in this crazy world, especially to promote and protect America's future."

I was incredulous. "That's it? You can't even give us a hint? Just who is your boss, by the way? Would I recognize his name?"

Gene presented us with an evil smile. "That's it, period, end of story," he said. "If I told you anything, I'd have to kill you."

A few days later, Gene and I met on the sidewalk in front of the Crystal Pier Cardroom in Pacific Beach, located just half a block from the sand and surf. We were not planning to play poker that day; rather, we were dressed in our running gear. Gene wanted to see the card room up close. He was quite curious about my poker exploits and whether it was actually possible for me to make a living this way. I could see that a part of him really wanted to play, even though the money itself was, to him, negligible.

Poker is a game that attracts a broad cross section of the population. It's possible to find games in which millionaires, PhD scientists, rich lawyers, and skid row bums are all playing at the same tables. But how do the bums get money to play? This can be a mysterious process; maybe the "bums" are not always what they seem. But sometimes the answer is simple. Any so-called bum who also happens to be an excellent player can often find financial backers in certain poker environments where the cash flows freely.

My own poker career had advanced nicely in the two years since I'd gotten my ass canned by Astro Dynamics. I was now playing only no-limit poker, which required much more skill than the limit variety. Plenty of bluffing and check raising took place before and after the draw. It was no longer possible to win consistently by simply playing tight; one might say that I had almost learned to "grok" opponents. That is, I came to understand their poker behavior in some depth, strangers or not. A minor reputation as a good professional player was only the small part of my reward. By the end of 1966, I was averaging fifteen dollars per hour after costs in fifty-cent ante games, or about one hundred dollars per hour in 2015 money. Two nights in the card room easily covered my monthly rent plus several trips to restaurants and bars.

As we ran south along Pacific Beach, Gene quizzed me on my personal background. He was especially interested in my successes and failures in sports. "I recall you played flag football in the little Astro league. Did you play high school football?"

If the truth be told, I was rather proud of my accomplishments, so I was more than happy to relay my story to Gene. "After my dad was laid off, our family's dire financial state required my sister, brother, and me to work after school nearly every day. Participation in school sports was nearly impossible. But in my sophomore and junior years, I was able to obtain enough compromises in my schedule to make myself free for the football team. I was an average-size player at one hundred seventy pounds, but I was pretty fast and managed to make second-string halfback on the varsity team. Of course, at this level I played only sparingly in real games, but the track coach noticed my speed in practice. In the fall of my junior year, he mentioned that he was looking forward to seeing what I could do on the track in the spring. I told him that my work schedule would not allow me to do track or even my senior year of football.

"'Look, Jack,' he said, 'You can do most of your track training on your own schedule and still keep your job. While I hate to see you drop football, your potential on the track is greater. I'll write down a workout schedule, and you can start training when football ends.'

"For much of the next year, I ran my ass off—two or three days per week running the five miles to school early in the morning and then using the coach's borrowed key to the locker room for a quick shower before my first class. I ran home in the afternoon, showering again before showing up at my job with the grocery store by half past five. On other days I focused on shorter early-morning speed runs. By the time track season started in February, I was in top shape; however, my 100-yard dash time of 10.1 seconds was still no better than the times of a dozen or so runners statewide.

"At the beginning of my senior year, the coach called me to his office. 'Jack, with all your extra training, you should move to the 440;

it combines the speed of a sprinter with the endurance of a middle-distance runner—perfect for you.'

"Success. Near the end of my senior season, it seemed I might even be the fastest 440- yard high school runner in the state. Sorry, I mean the fastest white boy. I missed out on the 440 state championship run because the coach decided that by loading the relays, our team would score more points. His strategy didn't work. I ran well in the relays, but our team still placed only sixth in the class-A division. I was afraid I had lost my chance for a college track scholarship.

"Our coach saved me by calling one of his friends, a coach at UCLA. 'I got a guy here with a great work ethic; on a relay he ran the 440 in 49.2. That's not impressive by California standards, but I think he has good potential. Florida's times look pretty slow to Californians, but track is not a big sport here; we don't train like you do. While nobody talks about it, the colored kids have their own schools and track meets; their times, no matter how fast, remain under our radar.'

"As a result of the coach's efforts, UCLA offered me a partial scholarship and part-time job—just enough to allow me to scrape by for four years without going into debt, robbing banks, or selling my body to the beautiful babes lurking in my wet dreams.

"American track adopted the metric system; 400 meters equals 437 yards. My best time in the 400 meters at UCLA was 47.7, good enough to run relays, enjoy good times with teammates, and later catch footballs from Kovac, but it was still far from world-class. I would not be going to any Olympic Trials. The 1964 Summer Olympics were held in Tokyo; the four hundred meters was won by Mike Larrabee in 45.1."

After a period of silence, Gene said, "I'm curious about your attitude toward so-called colored people. Of course, this label is now considered offensive by many, so let's just call them blacks."

I thought for a while. "My mother is Jewish, and my father was Irish Catholic, groups that have experienced discrimination in the past. My parents would often make little comments to us indicating their opposition to all discrimination, especially that directed at black people, but they never made a big deal of it. After all, people like us who lived on the financial margins held little power to change the system. To our family, black people were essentially invisible. My only black contacts were a few maids working for the well-off parents of some of my friends. Blacks were barred from white schools, restaurants, movie theaters, sports events, and so forth. If any black guy ran a fast 440 while I was in high school, I would never have known about it. It was totally unfair, but that was the system throughout the south.

"The department stores and other large businesses allowing black people had separate bathrooms and water fountains marked *colored*. By the time I was thirteen or so, I knew there was something very wrong with this system, but most white people seemed to be either unaware or uncaring. Generally, the lily-white churches supported segregation as being 'God's will'; I'm not sure what they had to say about the occasional lynching. The issue remained safely under the rug until the civil rights movement got going in the early 1960s, well after I moved to UCLA."

Gene thought for awhile and then recounted a bit of history. "Benjamin Franklin protested vehemently when white vigilantes in Pennsylvania massacred Indian women and children in the 1760s. He cited such massacres to illustrate that no race had a monopoly on virtue, likening the vigilantes to 'Christian White Savages.' Franklin praised the Indian way of life, their customs of hospitality and their councils, which reached agreement by discussion and consensus. I sometimes wonder if we have really progressed so much in two hundred years."

Chapter 7

The anti–Vietnam War movement really got going with the war escalation. In South Vietnam in March of 1966, twenty thousand Buddhists marched in demonstrations against the policies of the military government supported by the United States. Tens of thousands of US antiwar demonstrators picketed the White House and rallied at the Washington Monument.

"The sixties" embraced the counterculture revolution in social norms about clothing, music, drugs, dress, and sex. Conservatives typically denounced this as irresponsible excess, flamboyance, and decay of social order.

The events that I attended became progressively more interesting, often consisting of various eclectic species of psychologists, antiwar activists, sexual-freedom advocates, drug users, astrologers, new agers, draft dodgers, college professors, doctors, lawyers, and Indian chiefs—you name it. Conversations could range from intelligent interchanges of ideas to new age gibberish and anything in-between.

At a party one evening in 1967, I was approached by an attractive hippie-looking girl of about twenty with blond pigtails and a long full dress made of some sort of flimsy see-through material, revealing the apparent absence of any undergarments, top or bottom.

She smiled knowingly as I made a quick scientific study of the situation. "Do you like my dress?" she asked.

"Si, Owi, Da," I answered, thereby overcoming potential language barriers and impressing her with my multilingual sophistication.

Our interchange at first seemed off to a great start, but attempts to find common ground were less successful. She was into crystals, astrology, and something that sounded to me like "anal mind reading." I could never figure that last one out. In an apparent attempt to bridge our communication gap, she asked, "By the way, what's your sign?"

I decided to be funny and answered, "Positive." At that she just looked at me for about five seconds, said, "Bye," and walked away. But at least I learned a lesson. After that, whenever asked for my sign by an attractive woman, I answered with appropriate gusto, "Aquarius!"

At first, I had feared that Gene's secret new job would put a damper on our friendship, but just the opposite occurred. Although Gene was clearly excited by his new work, he was also stifled by boring social contacts, which were, in any case, few and far between. The spooks and military types he worked with were apparently not much fun to play with after-hours. Another social problem for Gene was that his work contacts were mostly much older than his thirty-three years.

Marie seemed to have similar feelings about some of her own scientific colleagues and didn't like the few spooks she had met through Gene. I began to get regular invitations to their home. I even felt that Marie and I were on our way to becoming good friends.

"I have some news," I announced after one of our dinners. "I'm moving out of my apartment. I've rented a five-bedroom house on the bluffs in La Jolla, within walking distance to the UCSD campus and Scripps Pier. I'm taking the master bedroom with en suite bathroom, which are upstairs and offer a nice view. Two housemates are already on board, and the three of us will be doing interviews for the remaining two spots."

"Is this going to be a commune? How come you get the master bedroom?" Marie asked.

"Because I organized the whole thing and put down the deposit. Plus, I'm paying a little more. About four nights a week I don't get home from the poker and bar scene until after two in the morning; I need quiet before noon to get my beauty sleep. It's not really a commune. We have agreed to make dinner together twice each month. At those times we will work out any problems that develop in the household. Otherwise, we will do our own things."

Gene offered his input. "I guess my first question is why. Also, who are the current housemates?"

"While not a commune, we do envision a little friendly community of like-minded people. In fact, we know of several other groups trying similar living arrangements. Some, like the Rogers and Tori groups, are closely associated with the humanistic psychology movement. Perhaps relationships of some sort will grow between these initially separate groups. This seems like it could be fun; we'll see. But, on the practical side, I will be living in a beautiful house in a great location, all at an affordable rent. Ava and Bob are clinical social workers in their late thirties; they form a sort of part-time couple."

Marie raised an eyebrow. "What's a part-time couple?"

I patiently tried to explain the new social arrangements that were mostly foreign to Gene and Marie given their conservative upbringings. "It means they have an open relationship. Each one is the other's significant other, or maybe you prefer the label *main squeeze*. They have their own bedrooms and mostly sleep with whomever whenever they want. On the other hand, they respect each other's feelings. So, if Bob tells Ava that he feels real bad about her scheduled date with John Doe, Ava may decide to skip the fling with this particular John. Most of the time, they sleep with each other."

Gene shook his head. "That's crazy. Can you imagine the potential complications, the jealousies—the potential for destructive behavior?"

Marie's eyes lit up. "Wait just a minute! Jack, come clean. Just how in the world did you convince the owners of this expensive house to rent to a poker player with long hair and promiscuous roommates?"

I felt just a little sheepish. "My view is that our landlord should care only about getting his rent and knowing that his house is well cared for. So I felt justified in instituting a creative solution—based on my deep understanding of mathematical physics, of course. I convinced Bob and Ava to dress up and present themselves to our glorious capitalist pig landlord as Mr. and Mrs. Keyster, upstanding members of the medical community. Also, in residence will be Ava's younger brother, known as Jack, plus a few additional relatives."

Gene and Marie rolled their eyes and expressed more misgivings about these living arrangements. But all objections were presented in friendly good humor. I sensed that they were basically intrigued by at least some of the counterculture revolution, maybe even enjoying some secret fantasies of their own.

A week later, Gene showed up at the Crystal Pier Card room at seven in the evening. We agreed to go separately since playing as known friends could create issues with other players. Gene was hooked. He lost about two hundred but didn't care; the poker game as a sociology experiment fascinated him. After that, about once or twice a month, Gene escaped from the spook business to the card room.

But, surprisingly, Gene fell into the "autistic" category when playing poker. He didn't play often but couldn't resist the challenge, especially after hearing of my adventures while we ran on the beach. Gene had a favorite strategy in no-limit games: he would play tight most of the evening and later attempt a big bluff to steal a rich pot. It rarely worked; he got called almost all the time.

"How could that guy call me after I had been playing so tight all night?" he would complain to me.

"The basic problem," I replied, "is that you are unable to see yourself as others see you. Your empathy tank is empty. Better you stick with science."

Gene asked me for more detail, so I replied, "It took me quite a while to understand how closely a player's chips represent that player's feelings of self-worth. Understanding the depth of this emotional involvement is essential. In some games my chip stack represents fifty percent of my financial net worth, subject to loss in a single hand. Across the table from me might be a millionaire with a very small fraction of his wealth at risk, yet he typically seems every bit as attached to his little pieces of plastic as I am to mine.

"Your bluffing strategy doesn't work because you project such a strong, self-assured presence. Yes, the other players see that you play tight, but this observation is trumped by your demeanor. They actually expect you to challenge them; in essence they are thinking one step ahead of you. The irony is that while they are expecting big bluffs, you could probably get by easily with a series of small bluffs."

As time went on Gene and Marie became more and more curious about the new counterculture, including the unconventional parties I attended. As we were sipping a wine before dinner in an upscale lounge one evening, I said, "Why don't you join me next Saturday? There will be a so-called evening of exotic adventures at the home of a woman I know slightly named Betsy. I'm not sure what the fancy name means, but it's some kind of party with games and good conversation. She has a large solar pool that she heats to ninety degrees; no Jacuzzi is needed. I went in once before and enjoyed it."

To my surprise, Gene and Marie accepted my invitation. We showed up at a large house in the moderately upscale neighborhood of University City. Betsy greeted us at the door and asked for a donation of five dollars each to pay for wine, grass, pool heating, and towel laundry. She was a tall, well-preserved woman of about fifty dressed in a red sweat suit. We were introduced to several other guests covering a broad age range.

I recognized one guy of about forty from an earlier party, a physics professor at UCSD named Frank Halpern. We joined a discussion on Vietnam. "Much of the official stuff coming from the White House and military is bullshit," said Halpern.

Gene looked interested but kept quiet. He wasn't about to say anything that might reveal his profession. Not knowing much about the war's history, I asked Halpern a series of pointed questions ending with "Where can I get good background information?"

Halpern's friend Trudy answered, "You can start with a pamphlet called *How the United States Got Involved in Vietnam*, written by a journalist named Bob Scheer. Start there and follow the references. Give me your address, and I'll send you a copy."

Later I was to get to know Trudy much better and to call Halpern by his first name. The next year, 1968, Frank ran for US Congress as a candidate of the newly formed Peace and Freedom Party.

The early part of the evening consisted of a series of short games, some challenging and some quite silly but all serving to loosen us up. A few joints were passed around to supplement the cheap wine. Later Betsy announced that the last few games would take place in the pool. "Don't worry. I keep it plenty warm. And remember, I don't allow bathing suits, so throw off your capitalist shackles and strip down to your bare asses!"

I glanced at Gene, who seemed a bit taken aback. I expected them to quietly sneak out the door, but to my surprise, Marie piped up, "Come on, Gene, let's do it. I know you can't wait to see all these old broads naked. Besides, if we leave now, Jack may have to walk home."

We undressed. Gene stood out from the others as especially lean and muscular, but my attention was directed to Marie, who entered after most others were already in the warm water. I made my top-to-bottom bodily survey, along with a dozen or so other bathers, as she self-consciously stepped into the water: long brown hair, small turned-up nose, small round breasts with pink nipples, generous patch of brown pubic hair, and near-perfect freckled legs.

Later that night I tried to remember the exact quote from Exodus. As I recalled, it went something like "Thou shalt not covet...thy neighbor's wife, nor his ox, nor his ass."

Nor even his neighbor's wife's ass for that matter, I thought.

Several weeks later Gene and Marie invited me to join them at the Del Mar racetrack, where they advertise that *the turf meets the surf.* This famous spot hosts a longtime tradition dating back to 1937 when Bing Crosby greeted the first guests; in the following year, Seabiscuit won the main race by a nose.

It was a beautiful August morning. We entered the main gate and passed by corrals where the horses waited for their moments of glory. There were also plenty of amateur gamblers hanging around to get good looks at the horses before placing bets.

We entered the stands, and Gene called my attention to several men near the finish line. "That guy on the right is Clint Murchison, Texas oil billionaire and owner of the Dallas Cowboys. He also seems to be part owner of the Del Mar track but operates behind the scenes. Do you recognize the guy sitting next to Murchison?"

I looked closely. "Jesus Christ on crutches, it's good old J. Edgar himself," I said.

Gene nodded his head. "My father knows these people but is not especially friendly with them. Hoover loves to bet on the horses, so Murchison sets him up with a box seat at the finish line. When Hoover's horses fail to deliver, Murchison covers his losses.

"For years Hoover has enjoyed free vacations at the Hotel del Charro off Torrey Pines Road in La Jolla. Apparently, Murchison is part owner of the hotel through a secretive holding company. Other famous guests have included a large assortment of movie stars, mobsters, and gamblers as well as Joe McCarthy, Richard Nixon, and more. For many of these guests, food and lodging are pro bono. Hoover and Nixon are longtime friends, partly because of these visits."

"Is this capitalism in action?" I asked.

"More like crony capitalism," he replied. "Since the thirties Murchison has used gifts to high officials and their relatives to get what he wants. He often puts it this way: 'Money is like manure; if you spread it around, it does a lot of good.'"

As a kid I loved listening to the radio program *Gang Busters*, billed as "the only national program that brings you authentic police case histories." The program started with a barrage of loud sound effects—a shrill police whistle, a wailing police siren, machine guns firing, and tires squealing. The series dramatized FBI cases, aired with the approval of J. Edger. But I didn't recall any episodes involving payoffs to FBI directors or even scenes at racetracks for that matter.

Chapter 8

As time went on, I became closer friends with Gene, and he opened up a little about his work environment at IPS. There were, it seems, some things he could tell me without actually killing me. The IPS offices were located in an ugly nondescript warehouse in Sorrento Valley, a few miles southeast of Del Mar. Gene had no idea of the company's actual size and no knowledge of possible company locations outside the San Diego area. Even such basic information was secret.

Gene had met about ten other "associates" of IPS; the word *employee* was never used. They seemed to range in age between about forty-five and sixty-five, and all apparently traveled a lot, spending more than half their time away. Only first names were ever used. The big boss, called *the Colonel*, seemed to be amazingly well connected in Washington.

"I once overheard him on the phone refer to McNamara as *Bob*," Gene said.

Gene was somewhat hesitant in giving me his direct IPS number. After one of our beach runs, he added a stern warning: "Be careful of what you say on this line or even my home line for that matter. No personal stuff and certainly nothing about your quasi-socialist lifestyle. Let's agree that all substantive discussion is to be limited to the beach."

"Quasi-socialist? Come on. Poker playing is pure capitalism in action," I replied. "Don't tell me you're concerned about wiretapping; I thought that was illegal?"

"You don't get it, Jack. IPS works for government agencies that do pretty much whatever they want. Tapping my phone, your phone, or even the phones of congress, if they thought they had reason, would be nothing to them."

"You mean IPS is a CIA front?"

"No," he replied, "IPS might work for any or all of several agencies— the FBI, CIA, NSA, DARPA, or other spook caves whose very existence is top secret. For example, when the NSA, the National Security Agency, was created by President Truman in 1952, its existence was not known to the public; the intelligence community then often referred to the NSA as 'No Such Agency.'

"I'm really not supposed to be telling you much of anything about IPS; if anyone found out, I could be canned in a flash. So let's agree to limit any talk about sensitive subjects to beach runs. If either of us has something urgent to discuss, we can just interject a code word—let's say *paradox* or *paradoxical*—into our phone conversation."

Why was a code word necessary? Did Gene have some hidden agenda that he would only reveal later? Or, maybe he just needed a friend to talk to without worrying about the potential repercussions from IPS. As it turned out we would come to implement this code far more than I could have expected at the time.

I expanded my poker venues to include Bicycle Bill's Cardroom in Point Loma, a subdivision next to San Diego Bay. Bill took up poker while a UCSD philosophy student. Still only a few years out of school, he purchased the card room and connected with a girlfriend, Ruthie, an attractive blonde ten years his senior. The environment was just a little upscale—walking distance to boat slips on the bay. Bill's had four tables, one less than the maximum allowed by the city. Ruthie and I would often have drinks at the bar down the block when the card room closed at midnight in accordance with city law. Bars closed at two in the morning.

One night around ten, I was in almost full control of my table. I had implemented successful bluffing strategies and other aggressive plays. I was winning big to the point that I could sense players chomping at the bit for a chance to nail me to a cross big-time.

I raised a player known as Jersey Joe before the draw on two pair, kings up, normally a bad idea against a tight player but possibly effective against a loose player like Joe, who might well call with a poor hand. But from his demeanor when he called, I figured him for a middling to strong hand and was pretty sure he had me beat. Furthermore, bluffing was out of the question; I expected him to call whatever I bet.

I was ready to cut my losses, but then Lady Luck smiled on me. I drew one card and caught a king, giving me a big full house, not unbeatable but good nearly all the time. Joe checked, and I bet my entire stack—about $400.

Joe hesitated; I knew he really wanted to call, but maybe I had overdone it. Perhaps I should have bet only $200. The longer he hesitated, the more certain I was that he would eventually call.

But just then a wild bull of a man came bursting through the card room door. Obviously very drunk, he started swinging wild punches toward our table, causing all players to scatter except Joe and me.

The two of us went down on our knees on the floor, trying to dodge punches while at the same time holding our cards above the table. If our cards left the table, house rules demanded that the hand be ruled null and void. Fortunately for yours truly, the bull was finally corralled, and Joe made the call. I happily raked in and stacked my chips, feeling pretty smug but trying to avoid showing it.

Later, after buying Jersey Joe and several others drinks in the bar, I treated myself to a very late steak dinner in downtown La Jolla. That night, I slept like a baby bear in my new master bedroom.

A few weeks later, I received a call out of the blue from Judy, a family counselor whom I had met two or three times at various gatherings. She had visited our La Jolla house with a large group of friends interested in various kinds of community building. "Hi, Jack, remember me?" she said. "Next weekend I'd like to visit Sandstone, but they don't accept singles; I need a male partner."

"Thanks for thinking of me," I replied. "But just what is this Sandstone place? I've never heard of it."

Judy then provided a comprehensive description. "Sandstone Retreat is located in Tuna Canyon in the Santa Monica Mountains overlooking Malibu and the Pacific Ocean. It was started a few years ago by a former manager with Lockheed Aircraft; he later made serious money with his own company. This guy and his wife believe that monogamy is unsatisfactory and prevents people from having full lives. Their retreat is clothing optional, and open sexuality is encouraged. I hear it's also in a beautiful setting, although I've never been there."

Holy guacamole! How could I say no to this offer?

We drove up together in my still-functional Chevy, now five years old. Judy was an intelligent woman of twenty-five with brown hair and green eyes. She was good-looking with a nice figure—perhaps not in the beautiful category but plenty good enough for my uncritical tastes.

I did have several concerns that I didn't share with Judy. Just what expectations did she have about our weekend relationship? Sure, we were going as a couple to satisfy the rules, but did that mean we would be sleeping together?

Another general concern was one that I probably shared with most men when they first attended nudist camps. How would my friend Johnson behave when he detected a bunch of naked women? Would he be a good boy and stay down? Would he shrivel up like he was immersed in frozen yogurt? Or would he jump up, bark, and generally behave like a bad dog?

Sandstone consisted of multiple small buildings in back of the two-story main house, which overlooked an enormous round Jacuzzi just below and the Pacific Ocean in the distance. The main entrance led to the upper level, which consisted of a kitchen and a richly carpeted living room larger than many houses. The lower level was almost all open and furnished with beds everywhere and no separating walls. A side room, called the *ballroom*, was semiprivate and contained no furniture—only a heavily padded floor. Later, I was to get into big bad trouble in the ballroom.

We arrived late in the afternoon on a Friday. Many other guests arrived between six and seven. Hollywood was well represented; I recognized several minor character actors from familiar movies, although I couldn't remember their names. At least one major male star appeared, but he received only minimal extra attention; these people were not easily impressed. I became engaged with several interesting groups of scientists, authors of fiction, medical doctors, and others. The experience was intellectually stimulating and great fun but totally nonsexual in the early evening.

Unexpectedly, I ran into one of my old UCLA professors, actually named John Smith—no kidding. I had taken a basic humanities course with him in my sophomore year. He was there with his wife, Maggie, a small dark-haired woman, not unattractive but sort of mousy looking, if you know what I mean.

After hearing of my recent history, John quickly came to focus on a more immediate topic. The Smiths had one child, a girl of six, and had decided to go for a second. But first they would have one last fling at Sandstone—sort of like eating a big meal before starting a major diet. I opened my mouth to ask something that would have probably been stupid, but before I could say "cheese," Maggie grabbed my arm and escorted me to the ballroom. The experience that followed was OK but largely forgettable. I seriously doubt that they named the new kid after me.

At about ten at night, I removed my clothes and entered the enormous round Jacuzzi. Shortly after, it became filled with five more men and six women, not arranged as couples but randomly located around the huge circle. We became engaged in an interesting political discussion, but after a short period, three of the women somehow became perched on top of and facing male partners, moving up and down in a manner that left little to the imagination. All this time the conversation between the six unpaired bathers continued unabated.

Noisy orgasms began to break out on a regular basis, interrupting my train of thought; sort of like strong static on the radio. After each glorious blast, the participants reentered the ongoing discussion as if they had never left. It was really getting too surreal for me so I hopped out of the Jacuzzi, grabbed my clothes, and headed back to the main house. I was getting tired and decided to see what Judy was up to.

I found Judy in the large living room in a lively discussion with a middle aged man and two women; she seemed happy to see me. "I wondered what happened to you Jack. Let's get some wine from the kitchen." After some good conversation over the next hour, Judy and I became quite comfortable with each other; sleeping in the same bed seemed the most natural of all the options. We spent that night in one of the downstairs waterbeds and engaged in what I would describe as friendly and loving relations but quite tentative. Judy was no problem; she was great to be with. The bizarre environment and lack of privacy were the culprits, at least for the two of us who were quite unaccustomed to such extremes of public sexuality.

My related problem that night was lack of sleep. Multiple orgasms created an almost-continuous roar all night that would have put Niagara Falls to shame. It seemed like a contest; did Sandstone actually offer prizes for the loudest or most intense blast?

Feeling groggy from lack of sleep, the next morning I headed for one of the bathrooms for a much-needed crap. As per Sandstone policy, none of the bathrooms had doors. On an intellectual level, this made perfectly good sense; one bathroom could obviously service multiple customers at the same time. Nevertheless, I feared major constipation issues when a smiling, tall, attractive, nude woman, a minor movie celebrity, bounced in happily and brushed her teeth right next to me.

Still tired, I searched desperately for a quiet place to catch forty winks. I wandered into the empty ballroom and curled up on the padded floor in one corner. I was soon fast asleep but was then awakened by two women and two men, all naked and engaging in some version of "linear" sex right next to me. It was a creative version of a little-known non missionary position—for want of a better term, *back-front-back-front.* Or maybe it should be labeled *the quadruple doggy bunny hop.*

It almost seemed as if they were insisting that I join the chain—at which link, I'm not sure. Despite my scientific curiosity, I decided to try to ignore this doggy game even when they bumped into me. After all, I'd already had a week's worth of sex in one night, not to mention a good crap completely spoiled.

I was just getting back to sleep when the Sandstone manager shook me. "What are you doing?" he demanded. "Don't you know that we don't allow sleeping in the ballroom? I will have to ask you to pack up your stuff and leave. We just don't put up with this kind of behavior."

He had barely glanced at the naked foursome, who continued their enthusiastic bunny hopping as if no one else were there. Maybe they were really ghosts who were only visible to poker players.

Amazing. I had the dubious distinction of being fired twice for sleeping inappropriately, first at Club Snooze and now at Sandstone—in the latter case, essentially for failing to properly "dog" the bunnies in the ballroom. Shame on you Johnson; you failed the critical managerial test.

Chapter 9

In the four years since being canned by Astro, I had enjoyed a carefree life. My only financial obligation, other than supporting myself, was a seventy-five dollar check that I mailed to Mom in Florida every month. My brother, Daniel, and sister, Ester, had covered my share for the first year of my unemployment, but after that I was able to restart my regular contributions. With two-twenty-five from the three of us plus the six hundred she was paid from the grocery store, Mom lived comfortably on her eight hundred plus monthly income, worth about five thousand in 2015 dollars.

When I wrote to Mom, only sanitized versions of my lifestyle passed through the Jack censor. Of course, I never associated my check to her with poker winnings. Nevertheless, she quickly sensed that there was some sort of flaky stuff going on. Following an eye-opening visit to me in California by Ester and her husband, Mom pretty much got the big picture. But for some reason, she didn't seem particularly surprised or upset. Her main comment was "Jack, are you becoming a Mormon?"

Things changed dramatically throughout 1968, when all hell broke loose. Many young men were being drafted and sent to fight in Vietnam, mostly against their will. Students could obtain deferments, but leaving school resulted in a formal draft letter from their least favorite uncle.

Most nonstudents had no alternatives besides going underground or leaving the country. Only a few rich kids with the right connections, likely due to big contributions to their local congressperson, could avoid combat duty by joining the National Guard; that option was closed to the poor and the middle class.

A Texas newspaper carried a small article announcing that a kid named George Bush was commissioned in the Air National Guard. His father was a member of the US House of Representatives. Later we learned that he was selected as a pilot despite his low-aptitude test scores and irregular attendance.

I was lucky enough to have been born in 1940, a little too early to be drafted.

January of 1968 marked the Tet Offensive; about seventy thousand North Vietnamese troops moved the battle from the jungles to the cities. The offensive lasted for weeks and proved to be a major turning point in American attitudes toward the war.

In March, Senator Eugene McCarthy nearly defeated President Lyndon Johnson in the New Hampshire 1968 presidential primary election. Soon after, Senator Robert Kennedy finally took a strong antiwar stance and entered the race. Johnson, beset by the war's widespread unpopularity, announced that he would not run for reelection.

Martin Luther King, who had been a solid supporter of Johnson and his Great Society program, had come out very publically against the war in 1967, pissing off many in the power structure, including Johnson and FBI head J. Edgar Hoover. One year later, in April of 1968, King was assassinated. Widespread riots in the cities ensued.

In June, I watched Robert Kennedy's late-night victory speech on TV after he won the California primary. It seemed certain that he would be our next president. A few minutes after he left the stage, my TV screen became confused chaos. What the hell was going on? Kennedy had been shot in the head and died a few days later.

In August, the Republicans nominated Richard Nixon to be their presidential candidate; Nixon, who had lost a close presidential race to John Kennedy in 1960, claimed to have a secret plan to end the war.

The Democratic National Convention became famous for the violent Chicago police action against antiwar demonstrators who strongly favored McCarthy over Johnson's vice president, Hubert Humphrey.

Many of the people I knew continued to party, explore community building, engage in casual sex, experiment with drugs, and so forth but with a higher level of foreboding in the background. For some, the dishonesty and viciousness of the government came to justify counterculture behavior that most participants would not have considered in normal times. The more extreme activities were often associated with LSD or even bombings of government buildings by the Weathermen.

A few weeks after Robert Kennedy was murdered, Gene and I were again doing our favorite ten-mile round-trip run on Black's Beach. Thus far in our discussions, Gene had been curiously noncommittal on the subject of Vietnam. By then I had read a lot of background material and pressed Gene for his views.

"Gene, tell me if I'm wrong. It appears that the government and mainstream press have both given us a distorted picture. In the 1950s, the United States apparently provided large-scale military support to the French in their attempt to make Vietnam a part of their colonial empire. The French were ultimately defeated and a peace agreement signed in Geneva calling for elections to unify Vietnam. The United States realized that North Vietnam prime minister Ho Chi Minh would easily win an election, so they managed to sabotage the peace process and create a separate South Vietnamese government."

Gene remained quiet for a long time, then sighed, and said, "Jack, I'm going to tell you some things that I probably shouldn't. The reason I'm opening this can of worms is that I am becoming progressively more disgusted and disillusioned by the stuff I'm seeing, both public and private. But first I must have your word of honor that you will not repeat any of this. To do so could put me in danger."

I started to make a joke but thought better of it. "You have my word; my lips are sealed."

Gene went on. "When I accepted the job at IPS, I had little idea of the specifics of the work, as I honestly told you and Marie. What I didn't tell you was that my boss, currently known as the Colonel, is also a long-time friend of my father, George Stanford. Both have histories with military and intelligence organizations; the specifics are not important now.

"The Colonel, under a high-level order from the executive branch, is in the business of collecting information for a secret history of the US involvement in Vietnam. As part of this effort, he is quietly snooping into intelligence areas for which he may not have actual authority.

I was somewhat taken aback. "Executive branch? You mean Johnson wants a history book written?"

Gene produced a small smile. "Actually, Johnson doesn't know anything about IPS or its actual activities. The orders come directly from McNamara. I don't think anyone else close to the administration knows either. How far the Colonel is prepared to stretch McNamara's orders to essentially spy on our spies, I can't say. But I can tell you this. Johnson has systematically lied, not only to the public but also to Congress. The deceptions were already well in place during the 1964 election when he successfully painted Goldwater as a warmonger. When elected, Johnson 'out-Goldwatered' Goldwater. The last thing Johnson wants is an accurate history, but McNamara is doing this secretly."

I had a flood of questions. "Why is the Colonel taking it upon himself to expand on his orders from McNamara? How can this possibly be kept secret from military brass, a group unlikely to cooperate in any history lesson? What about the secretary of state or national security advisor? Surely they would get wind of this and tell Johnson."

Gene replied, "McNamara has ordered that analysts rely on existing files in the Office of the Secretary of Defense. No consultations with the armed forces, the White House, or other federal agencies are to occur so as to keep the study secret from even highly placed officials. But on his own, the Colonel has devised a whole series of cover stories that allow him to extract information from intelligence agencies without revealing the existence of McNamara's history.

"As to the Colonel's motivations, I can only speculate based on his offhand comments as well as the strong opinions that my father has expressed over the years. Remember Eisenhower's farewell speech warning of the severe dangers of the military-industrial complex to our freedoms? Well, my father is a close friend of Eisenhower and had some influence over his address to the nation.

"My father often pictures the military and intelligence community as a mixed bag consisting of 'true patriots' and others. He labels people in the others category with things like 'cowboy,' 'idiot,' 'chicken hawk,' and even 'psychopath.' Without the close personal connection between the Colonel and my father, I would never have been taken into the Colonel's confidence."

I was stunned. "This totally blows my mind. Why in hell are you telling me all this? I'm just a twenty-eight-year-old poker player who has only recently become more interested in world affairs."

Gene answered carefully, "For now, just accept my explanation that I need someone to talk to for my own sanity, someone I can trust without reservation. To be honest, I do have ulterior motives in taking you into confidence, but the disclosure of these motives must be placed on hold until other events unfold. In the meantime, I hope you will deepen your studies of the US government and its policies. You are apparently able to support yourself with less than twenty hours per week of effort at poker. Use your free time productively. Believe me: you won't be sorry. And for God's sake, stay away from Sandstone."

Why did Gene even care about my Sandstone visits? I supposed it was just part of his mentoring strategy as a surrogate big brother. Oh well, I thought, Sandstone would just have to get by without my friend Johnson. No big loss; he spent most of his time sleeping anyway.

Under strong encouragement from Gene, I had been taking weekly karate lessons from a master named Hiroshi Hashimoto, who ran the gym with his partner, Lester Ingber, in Solana Beach. Lester was a brilliant, eccentric physicist with a black belt, an old friend of Gene's.

By this time, Gene had reached the lofty level of fifth dan black belt. I, on the other hand, was way down on the list; call me Mr. Pink Belt. Eventually, however, I did gain some skills and even did some sparring in body armor, which allowed full-power techniques with some measure of safety. Of course, I would get my ass kicked against any genuine expert.

Hiroshi was both funny and demanding, a student of the Funakoshi tradition. If his energy got low, he would complain that it was because he had missed his sushi. He seemed somewhat disappointed in me, claiming that I had excellent potential to advance to black belt. But I was only moderately motivated.

In the Funakoshi school, it was considered unusual for a devotee to use karate in real physical confrontations more than once or twice in a lifetime. Practitioners must never be easily drawn into a fight. One blow from a real expert could cause serious injury. Those who misuse what they have learned bring dishonor upon themselves.

Later I would find my karate training, even at the pink belt level, to come in handy.

Chapter 10

My discussion with Gene about IPS and the Colonel had caused me a lot of worry and self-doubt. It was now crystal clear that the government had been lying from the beginning about Vietnam. Furthermore, our mainstream media had swallowed this crap hook line and sinker. What were the implications of this explosive new knowledge from Gene? People were dying needlessly in Vietnam. Good friends were active in war protests. What was I doing? Not a thing! Was I in any physical danger from the spooks? Would I still be playing poker for a living when I was fifty? Was I just wasting my life? And so on and so forth.

My poker game suffered as a result. At Bicycle Bill's I drew a ten-high pat straight just to the left of the dealer "under the gun" and checked it. An old guy known as Pizza Pete opened the pot for $6 from mid position. The dealer called, and I check-raised an additional $40, more than doubling the pot. Pete hesitated for a while and then reraised all he had—another $130.

Pete owned several pizza joints and had plenty of money to burn. Nevertheless, he played so tight he squeaked, and I knew his play well. His actions spoke to me loud and clear—flush or better. But my guilty unconscious self decided to call anyway. Sure enough, he showed me an ace-high heart flush. As tight as Pete played, he probably would never have reraised with a lower hand, not even with just a lower flush. I knew this as well as I knew my friend Johnson.

My screwed-up poker play basically started a two-week losing streak, which sent me even further down in the dumps. I took a needed break from card rooms over the next several weeks and attended one of the many community functions popular in the counterculture, some sort of pot-luck evening with plenty of the former. That's where I met Mandy. She was twenty-one and petite with brown hair. Some would describe her as cute rather than pretty. For one thing her breasts were very small—maybe in the lower ten percent of the female population, at least according to my recently acquired expertise. It didn't matter to me. I was immediately taken with her, in spite of my depressed state.

But it was hard to stay depressed with Mandy; her effusive smile and bubbling personality always gave me a lift. Mandy was studying in the Art Department at San Diego State University, located in the east part of the city. She supported herself with part-time work as a nurse's aide at Scripps Hospital. We started to see each other two or three times per week.

My poker skills returned with a vengeance; I was soon averaging about $25 per hour, about $130 in 2015 dollars. On my card playing nights, Mandy would come to my group house at around eight or nine, hobnob with my housemates until she got tired, hop into my king-size bed, and be fast asleep well before midnight. She was charming and intelligent, and my housemates were quickly taken with her. Ava even evolved into sort of a big sister figure to Mandy. I would return by two in the morning, take a quick shower, and join her in bed.

Human sleep occurs in several alternating stages, ranging from light to deep, labeled stages one through four. In addition, the dreaming state exhibits rapid eye movements and loss of muscle activity, the latter normally preventing sleep walking. I soon learned that Mandy's first period of stage-four (deep) sleep lasted about two hours; afterward she would typically enter rapid eye movement (REM), the dreaming stage. I could read her eye movements under her eyelids by employing my handy-dandy book light. If I felt especially sneaky, I would mentally insert myself into her sweet dreams like some superhero on a white horse. Hi Ho Silver! Who was that masked man?

In the mornings we had leisurely breakfasts in Del Mar or Solana Beach, the adjacent coastal community just to the north.

One weekend we walked down the steep bluff trail behind the famous Salk Institute to Black's Beach, nearly deserted as usual. I presented Mandy with a self-promoting version of my beach runs and other heroic-sounding accomplishments as we leisurely walked north. If she was put off by my unabashed immodesty, it didn't show.

In the distance we could see two figures standing near the waterline, but from our location no gender determination was possible. As we got closer, a couple, apparently in their early twenties, came more clearly into view. My scientific training allowed me to make a rapid, astute observation that may have escaped ordinary males—the girl was missing her clothes.

Later Black's was to become a famous nude beach, but at that time the few visitors were normally clothed. Another observation was that the guy was wearing a bathing suit. This picture evoked several silly ideas that passed quickly through my consciousness. Was he more modest than she? Did he have some reason to hide his dick? Could the "he" actually be a disguised "she"? All nonsense, of course. What was my unconscious up to, anyway?

They introduced themselves as Laura and Jason. Laura had just graduated from Stanford with a major in economics and a minor in dance. She was a striking beauty with black hair down to her waist. We talked for a while about work and play, and Laura asked Mandy how much she earned at Scripps Hospital. "About five dollars per hour," replied Mandy.

Laura smiled. "Listen, how would you like to make three times that much doing something that's a lot more fun? Have you ever heard of the Body Shop?"

The Body Shop was located near the intersection of Interstates 8 and 5, a few miles north of downtown San Diego and an easy taxi ride from the naval air station with its hordes of sailors. IDs were checked carefully at the door by a rough-looking bouncer who probably chewed on nails for breakfast. Inside was a U-shaped stage surrounded by twenty or so high chairs. Booths lined the walls in front of the stage. The girls entered the stage from the top of the *U*, chose a song from the jukebox, and danced on the stage. In one corner was a small bar.

Mandy was at first reluctant to become a professional dancer. For one thing she was shy about nudity; for another she didn't believe she had the right body type to attract customers. When she expressed this, Laura laughed heartily. "Are you kidding? You look so young and innocent. Sure, some men go for big boobs, but for many men you are a dream come true."

I later discovered that Laura often showed such wisdom well beyond her years.

As predicted Mandy was hired in a flash and became an instant hit with the customers. She would enter the stage in a short dress, put on her song, and begin to dance. The seated customers would produce dollar bills; mostly ones but an occasional five would appear, and she would collect these at the end of the first round. The crowd would then become impatient, anticipating the second dance routine.

In the second routine, Mandy removed her dress, revealing all, including her lush brown patch of pubic hair. The house did have rules, however, strictly enforced by the city. There was to be absolutely no touching and no showing of spread labia, known fondly in lofty academic circles as a *split beaver*. The police regularly monitored the performances with undercover cops dressed like businessmen, lawyers, or whatever. Technically, I suppose a girl could risk arrest if she shaved before her dance and failed to keep her legs fully locked.

Come on, Supreme Court; give us a more definitive "beaver ruling" so we can be more creative with our modern dances.

I left Bicycle Bill's in Point Loma just after midnight in good spirits, up $125 for the evening. Ruthie asked me to join her for a drink, but I declined. "Can't tonight. Let's take a rain check."

I headed for the local fast food Mexican outlet and ordered twelve chicken tacos to go. The Body Shop was only fifteen minutes away; I arrived at half past midnight, in plenty of time to enjoy multiple dance routines.

I found an empty booth back from the stage and ordered a straight-up Manhattan from a girl I recognized but whose name I didn't know. She served me and happily accepted my offer of a taco. Soon after, a bevy of pretty, smiling girls came to get their tacos; most knew that I was Mandy's boyfriend, so they were friendly and trusting. A new song came on.

Riding on the City of New Orleans
Illinois Central Monday morning rail
Fifteen cars and fifteen restless riders
Three conductors and twenty-five sacks of mail

This was Mandy's trademark song, so I moved quickly to an empty chair next to the stage. Friend Johnson was enjoying a special erotic bonus from watching Mandy perform in public for the first time, but then the later performance got even better. Laura and Mandy came to the stage and danced together in an exceptionally provocative manner.

Mandy gave me a big smile as she picked up the ten-spot in front of me. Fortunately for the dancers, the undercover police had apparently gone fishing. The crowd went wild.

When the Body Shop closed at two, Mandy and I left in our separate cars and met at the southwest corner of my king-size bed in La Jolla. Before falling off to sleep, I again heard the lyrics in my mind:

Dealin' card games with the old men in the club car
Penny a point ain't no one keepin' score
Pass the paper bag that holds the bottle
Feel the wheels rumblin' 'neath the floor

The *City of New Orleans* described in this song is an overnight train between New Orleans and Chicago. The emergence of Al Capone and other mobsters following Prohibition in 1920 turned Chicago into a bustling center of black entertainment. Chicago gangsters promoted jazz music to facilitate their gambling, alcohol, and prostitution rackets. Black musicians regularly came from the south, riding to Chicago on the *City of New Orleans.*

A few days later, I decided to go back to the Crystal Pier Cardroom, mainly for a change of scene. I was doing moderately well but feeling the adverse effects of thick secondary cigarette smoke that permeated everything, especially in cold weather when the doors were closed. A grouchy guy was sitting on my left; he was middle-aged, overweight, and a bit over six feet. He had placed his ashtray right next me, and his cigarette emitted a curling column of smoke that seemed tuned to my sensitive nose. When I politely asked him to move it, he refused. I fumed internally but said nothing. When he left for a bathroom break, I gleefully extinguished his cigarette with my Diet Coke.

He returned to the table, and on seeing his dead fag, he whacked me hard on the side of the face with no warning. Mammals, be they humans or rats, exhibit fight-or-flight responses when threatened. In this case it was fight. I jumped from my seat, faked a left to his face, and then used my right to hit him just below the belt with everything I had. The wind left him in an audible rush. I followed with a short left chop to his neck. Don't ever hit someone in the jaw with an unprotected hand; your hand is more likely to break than his jaw.

Down he went like a sack of potatoes hit by a runaway truck. I resisted the impulse to kick him in the head. Jake, the card room owner, came over at once to attend to the fallen gladiator, and he even apologized to me. No police were called. After that incident some fellow poker players began to refer to me as "Jack the Boxer," or simply "Jack Box." But, if the truth be told, my fighting skills were limited to a few karate classes that Gene had organized for me. Anyone really good would have kicked my ass from here to Sunday. Fortunately, most people didn't know this.

Chapter 11

One Sunday morning I was sitting in the family room of my group house in La Jolla. Ava and Bob were away, but my newest housemates, James and Mary, were sharing a late breakfast with me. James, a real estate agent, was thirty-three. Mary, a nurse working at Scripps Hospital, was twenty-nine. Ava, Bob, and I had selected them from the applicants who responded to our ad in a local newspaper. The ad had included words like "Come join us in our beautiful hillside home near the beach in La Jolla…Send us a one-page letter describing yourself and the kind of living environment you seek."

We received thirty-eight responses and quickly rejected the seemingly illiterate, destitute, sex crazed, and sociopathic. We scheduled interviews with six who seemed pretty good; James and Mary were our top choices.

Gene called unexpectedly. "Feel like a good run tomorrow morning at eight? The tide will be high, so I recommend Torrey Pines Park."

"Gee, Gene, why so early? You know I'm used to sleeping until ten or so. And anyway, tomorrow is Monday. Don't you have to go to work at IPS?"

His voice took on an unusual quality. "I could explain further, but my answer would seem paradoxical."

What? And then I remembered our code word. Evidently, Gene had something important to tell me.

The next morning we met in the parking lot at the top of the bluff near Torrey Pines Golf Course. For once I had gone to bed early, so I felt pretty rested, even if it was a bit too early for my tastes. We headed into the south end of the park and onto one of the winding beach trails with panoramic views of the Pacific Ocean.

I was anxious to hear what Gene had to say, but he calmly engaged me in small talk for the first fifteen minutes or so. Squirrels and rabbits scurried here and there, not the least interested in our discussion.

Finally Gene got serious. "Over the past few months, the Colonel has somehow become involved in adjudicating disputes between the CIA and the FBI. Apparently, this is unrelated to his work for the McNamara project. The stuff he has discovered is mind-blowing. Let's start with J. Edgar Hoover. The Colonel has placed him solidly in his sociopath category—manipulative, cunning, grandiose self-image, and so forth.

"More specifically, in the past Hoover not only failed to pursue organized crime figures but denied they even existed. But the reality of organized crime became all too clear when the Senate committee headed by Senator Kefauver forced Hoover's hand in 1950. Many high-profile crime bosses testified with television cameras rolling, embarrassing the hell out of Hoover. But this is all in the public record."

My question was an obvious one. "How did Hoover keep his job?"

"Well, Jack, that question has been asked over and over during the forty plus years that Hoover has been director. The short answer is that he has blackmailed two generations of politicians. He uses FBI surveillance agents to obtain defamatory information, much of it sexual, on prominent persons to be used for political purposes. When a new president is elected, Hoover will pass along gossip to the president, thereby raising troubling questions in the president's mind. Just what did Hoover know about him? In such presidential cases, Hoover is a veiled blackmailer. This may have happened with John Kennedy with all his screwing around.

"In other instances—for example, with Martin Luther King—the blackmail was overt. He used illegal wiretaps to find that King was

apparently involved in an extramarital affair. Hoover then wrote directly to King, implying that he would expose him unless he killed himself
or maybe just dropped out of the public eye, I'm not sure which."

I had so many questions I didn't know what to ask first, but Gene stopped
me. "There's more," he said. "While Hoover was forced to acknowledge the
Mafia and other organized crime figures by the Kefauver committee, he
hasn't really focused on them unless put under pressure from above. There
is some reason to believe that Hoover himself is being blackmailed by organized crime. According to several of the Colonel's sources, the Mafia re-
strains or maybe even controls Hoover through his homosexuality, which
seems to be pretty well established. Hoover's longtime lover boy is the associate director, Clyde Tolson. There is even a rumored picture of Hoover
giving Tolson a blow job, but the Colonel couldn't verify it. Nor does he
really know the full depth of the Hoover-Mafia connection."

"Hell and damnation," I said. "Is that all?"

"No, there's still more, and it's even more relevant to current events.
The Colonel found a specific directive from Hoover to his agents, and
here I quote verbatim. They are to 'expose, disrupt, misdirect, discredit,
or otherwise neutralize' the activities of certain movements and their
leaders. The tactics they employ include discrediting targets through
psychological warfare, smearing individuals and groups using forged
documents, and planting false reports in the media. The name given
to this FBI activity is *COINTELPRO*, an acronym for *Counterintelligence
Program*.

"The FBI targets include perfectly legal antiwar and civil rights activists, as well as genuine criminal groups, but apparently excluding
Hoover's Mafia associates. Hoover managed to get several professors
fired from universities run by chicken-shit presidents. He has completely fucked the Constitution."

"Are you implying that Hoover was involved in King's murder?" I
asked.

"No," Gene replied. "At least, the Colonel has found no evidence for
that. King had many powerful enemies, powerful enough to pull off his

killing without being caught. Maybe James Earl Ray really did act alone, but that seems to me to be the least likely scenario."

For several minutes he was deep in thought. "On the other hand, if the Hoover-Mafia connection is real..." His voice faded, and we remained lost in disturbing thoughts for the remainder of our run through the park.

A few weeks later, Mandy and I joined Gene and Marie for dinner at the Chart House, located right on Cardiff Beach just north of Solana Beach. We enjoyed a spectacular sunset view with crashing waves in the foreground. I ordered a twelve-ounce filet mignon medium rare; the others choose assorted fish dishes. It was the first meeting of Gene and Marie with Mandy. As agreed, all talk of politics was off-limits. In any case Mandy knew nothing of my running conversations with Gene. Later I came to understand fully that Gene had shared little of substance even with Marie.

Marie was at first a bit cool toward Mandy, this pretty young thing who danced nude for money. But Marie soon warmed up in response to Mandy's genuine personality. Marie was curious about Mandy's dancing job at the Body Shop—especially about her feelings toward the customers. "You have all these lecherous old men, sailors, and whoever else ogling your body. Doesn't that make your skin crawl?"

Mandy responded, "No. Not at all; we see all kinds of customers. Some are crude; some are even a little scary. Most are really nice. I don't mind if they are turned on by me. I truly believe that most are just lonely. If I add a little happiness to their lives with my dance routines, that's a good thing; it makes me happy too."

Looking at Marie, I could see the wheels turning. Perhaps she had never looked at life in such a charmingly innocent manner. I imagined her thinking that such naive innocence could lead to either joy or grief, depending on the circumstances.

But Mandy had a surprise for us, and it ran quite counter to her perceived innocence. "At the Body Shop I get paid at three times the hourly rate I was making as a nurse's aid. I'm my own boss in a sense, and the Body Shop is my client. I can quit at any time and go back to being a nurse's aid if I choose to suffer the income loss. Forgive me, but maybe in your world it's hard to relate to someone whose economic survival depends on such closely calculated trade-offs. I'm acting in my own best interests as I see them."

Holy Johnson's ghost! Just then I could have kissed Mandy from head to toe with multiple round trips. She really hit this one out of the park. Marie, for once, was at a loss for words.

As we said good night, Gene gave me a serious look and said, "I'll not be running with you during the next two weeks; I'll be out of town."

Partly for a change of scene, I decided to visit Bob's Cardroom on Fourth Street in a seedy downtown section of San Diego. The place was dirty and the tables well-worn; hey, a little slumming wouldn't hurt. While I didn't know the players well, they didn't know me either. This situation required a quite different approach on my part, a little like some young buck challenging the established alpha male in a herd of horny water buffalo.

I played aggressively against the tight players with pat hand bluffs and against loose players with moderate hands like a two pair and a small three of a kind. I was not only playing well—I was lucky. As they say, the cards were running all over me.

By eleven at night, I had run my initial hundred dollar buy to well over five hundred. I didn't know the exact amount; overtly counting your chips was socially unacceptable. In more graphic poker language, it could really piss people off.

Then three seats to the dealer's left, I was dealt a dream come true: a monster hand of four eights. Four of a kind is very rare in games without wild cards. In California draw poker, the joker is only wild when used with aces, straights, and flushes. In my years of card room play, I had never had four of a kind beat. My main concern was that no one else might have much of anything and my monster hand would be wasted.

An old guy with a two-day growth of gray beard opened under the gun, just to the dealer's left. I flat called. I didn't want to lose this guy or anyone else for that matter. I sent a silent message to the poker gods: will someone else please raise? Sure enough the dealer, a slimy-looking dude with slick black hair, raised $40. On his left, Gray Beard reraised another $90. It was my turn; I tried my best to look like a sick and wounded duck. I flat called the $130.

At that point Black Hair pushed in his entire stack—about $600. Gray Beard's face looked like some light bulb had been turned on; he quickly folded. As I called the final raise, I vaguely remembered some guy standing behind Black Hair when the previous hand was dealt. My own light came on, but it was too late. Damn it all to hell!

Black Hair showed four queens and took the pot with an evil smile that seemed to say, "Don't ever fuck with us, kid. You may be good, but we have the means to take your chip pile no matter how well you play." It was a no-brainer; the guy standing behind Black Hair had slipped him a cold deck just before he dealt.

Generally, a cold deck is a stacked card deck that is switched with the deck actually being used in the game, benefiting the dealer making the switch. The stacked deck has been arranged in a preset order, designed to give a specific outcome when the cards are dealt. The term itself refers to the fact that the new deck is often physically colder than the deck that has been in use; constant handling of playing cards warms them enough that a temperature difference may be noticeable to experienced players. Black Hair had apparently acquired advanced training, maybe even getting a PhD in cold-decking from the lofty University of Crooked Gambling, Prostitution, and Peeping Toms.

From then on whatever went down at Bob's Cardroom would have to take place without my generous contributions.

For a few days, I suffered from sucker's remorse, but my net loss of $100 was not earthshaking. I returned to my favorite spots, Bicycle Bill's and Crystal Pier. Several weeks later, Gene called. He seemed in good spirits. "Back from my trip and ready for a long beach run," he announced. Perhaps we can discuss the famous 'barbershop paradox' proposed by mathematician Lewis Caroll of *Alice in Wonderland* fame."

This arcane reference was way above my pay grade so I decided to try to one-up Gene with silly nonsense. "Yes, my barber has just discovered an apparent paradox in Einstein's field equations; I think maybe general relativity has a fundamental error."

"Oh, for Christ's sake, Jack," he said, laughing, "can't you ever embrace just a little subtlety? I'll meet you tomorrow behind the Poseidon Restaurant at Del Mar Beach."

As we headed south parallel to the train track on the bluff, Gene came quickly to the point. "I'm sure you appreciate how weird this whole thing with IPS and the Colonel has become. I have somehow come to gain explosive knowledge of US intelligence agencies that I'm not supposed to know even with the highest possible security clearance. The Colonel and I know things that not even the president knows."

The Amtrak train passed us on the bluff fifty feet above. A flock of seagulls leisurely moved aside, generously allowing us to pass without paying a toll.

He continued, "Officially, my recent trip was to Washington, but I also spent a week in Europe on an unofficial project that I want to discuss with you in-depth. You keep asking why I am passing on all this sensitive information to you. I'm now ready to answer, but first let me emphasize just how critical your complete silence is to our welfare. Even Marie cannot be informed." He became silent to allow an older couple to walk out of earshot before continuing. "Jack, do you have a passport?"

Chapter 12

The 1968 election featured Richard Nixon, Hubert Humphrey, and third-party candidate George Wallace, a vocal advocate for segregation of public schools. Wallace's position was popular in much of the Deep South. His running mate was General Curtis LeMay, a name that would later boil to the surface in my briefings with Gene.

Many in the antiwar movement skipped the election, feeling they had no candidate to represent their views. In November, the popular vote totals were Nixon 43.4 percent, Humphrey 42.7 percent, and Wallace 13.5 percent. The Electoral College vote was not as close, but who knows who would have become president had the Chicago police riots at the Democratic convention and their aftermath not occurred?

Gene put his mysterious proposal to me in stages, probably because he didn't think I could digest too much too fast. "What do you make at poker these days?" he inquired as we ran south along Pacific Beach parallel to the long boardwalk filled with the weekend crowd. It was the week before Christmas, a beautiful sunny day, air temperature sixty-five degrees and water temperature sixty-two degrees. Perfect for running but too cold for surfing without a wet suit, at least for this candy-ass.

"About twenty-five dollars per hour after card room fees is my average over the past six months," I replied.

Gene made his proposal. "I'm offering you a part-time job at thirty dollars per hour plus expenses. You get paid for travel hours, but there are no fringe benefits. I expect to use your expert services maybe sixty to eighty hours per month."

"Expert at what?" I said. "I know nothing about spooking. Sorry, I'm not into manual labor. I'm sure to be incompetent at contract killing. My karate classes are more likely to get me killed rather than the other way around. Plus, I've already turned down a job offer to be a sexual surrogate servicing horny nuns. OK, just kidding."

Gene was patient with my sick humor and replied, "I'll explain in more depth as we go along. In essence you are to be a sort of recording secretary, or maybe *personal historian* is a better term. You are a good choice for several reasons. First, is your ability to keep your mouth zipped. Second, our beach runs provide the perfect cover for exchanging information. Third, your poker career is a good cover for trips you will be taking to Europe. And most important of all, you are a close friend that I trust without reservation. Did you get your passport yet?"

"No, it should arrive in the next two weeks. Your choice of pronoun indicates that I will be working for you personally, not IPS or the Colonel. Is that right?"

"Yes," he replied. "You will not be apprised of what the Colonel knows or doesn't know. I will be your only contact."

My head was spinning. "Could this evolve into a dangerous job?" I asked.

"Probably," he replied with a smile.

All I could think to say was, "I accept."

My relationship with Mandy continued to be very positive—three nights a week plus some time together on the weekend seemed just right. Somewhere along the line, we came to a mutual understanding that we were in a special, but nonetheless open, relationship. She was my "significant other" and vice versa. In theory, we were free to sleep or even wake up with other people. However, I stayed exclusive beyond the first six months or so of our meeting; as far as I knew, she did the same.

Scripps Pier on La Jolla Shores is closed to the public because it contains research projects and equipment used by the Scripps Institution of Oceanography. I often frequented the beach nearby for volleyball games, bodysurfing, and beach runs. I met Gene near the pier late one morning in early 1969, and we began running on the beach south toward the La Jolla Shores parking lot. After the first half mile, we passed a young woman jogger, and Gene said in an unusually enthusiastic and friendly voice, "Well, hi, Dawn, good to see you; meet my running pal, Jack."

We slowed our run to match her pace. Dawn was of medium height and slim with small breasts. Her short brown hair was wrapped naturally around her face. She wore baggy white shorts and tank top. Perhaps her most striking feature was her skin, which showed no evidence of sun exposure; she was white as snow. She also seemed quite young and naive: bouncing around, very talkative, and full of energy. My initial impression was "What a cute little pixie."

It turned out that Gene hardly knew her; they had just conversed during a few earlier beach runs. Dawn seemed quite taken with me, patting my arm and batting her eyes, even with no special encouragement on my part. As a result of this unexpected attention, I became curious about her age. High school girls were way off-limits, even in my world of flexible proprieties. I questioned her indirectly, asking where she grew up, worked, and so forth. It turned out that she had just recently come to California from the Midwest, was living nearby with some friends, and was looking for a secretarial job in the San Diego area. She had actually just attained the ripe old age of twenty-two. Bingo.

When she finished her run, I stopped with her in front of the lifeguard tower next to the parking lot. Gene looked at me, rolled his eyes, said good-bye, and continued his run along the beach. When Dawn realized I was stopping with her, her attention to me became even more pronounced, so much so that friend Johnson was becoming electrified. "What are you doing now?" she asked provocatively.

"My house is just at the top of the hill. Why don't you follow me in your car, and I will fix us a nice lunch?" We arrived at the house, and I was happy to see that my four housemates were all away. I fixed us a very simple lunch of tortillas topped with melted cheese, onions, and pepperoni slices. She declined my offer of a beer.

We sat on the couch with her on my left. I immediately put my left arm around her, and we kissed, first lightly and then more deeply. She was turned toward me but kept her left leg on top of her right, an awkward position for both of us. While we kissed, I reached over with my right hand and pulled her left leg on top of me. Her breathing became noticeably faster. Johnson, unfairly suppressed by my running shorts and the weight of her leg, experienced simultaneous pain and pleasure.

I removed my left arm from her shoulder and slipped it into the back of her running shorts and underneath her panties until I felt her cheeks and crack. She offered no resistance. I then reached down deep underneath her ass and felt first a puff of pubic hair and then her swollen labia. I lightly rubbed her clitoris; by this time her breathing was loud and fast. She was so turned on she seemed ready to explode.

It seemed to be time for us to undress and really get down to business, so I started to extract my hand from her shorts. "No, please don't stop," she moaned. OK by me; I could wait. I carefully put my finger inside her vagina, moving it in and out for a time before returning full attention to her clitoris, rubbing it slowly at first and then faster and faster. Soon after, her body stiffened, and she emitted a partly muffled scream. Her orgasm lasted for more than seven seconds.

Johnson begged to be let out of jail and allowed entrance to this luscious wet beaver. But when I tried to remove her shorts, she demurred. "Please, I can't," she said. "I am a Christian."

"Oh" was all I could think to say. I backed off with my advances, and we then engaged in some friendly discussion of her faith. While I was ultra frustrated, it just didn't seem right to try to change her mind about completing our lovemaking or to question her about just what was or was not allowed. She just seemed so sincere about her Christianity and general naïveté about life in the real world. She left before four in the afternoon; I didn't expect to see her again, at least not at my house.

Two weeks later I again ran into her on the beach, but this time it was late afternoon. Again she was all over me with her enthusiastic flirting, touching, compliments on my looks, and so forth. But she offered no mention of earlier events; our new interaction seemed to be a replay, as if we had never had the earlier sexual encounter. But then she offered a confession. "I stopped by your house twice in the past two weeks, but you were not home."

I assessed the new situation as some sort of unspoken bargain between us in which I would play with her private parts and bring her to orgasm with my magic finger but we would not actually have intercourse. Evidently, this would allow Dawn to satisfy her compelling sexual desires but remain, in her own mind at least, true to her Christian faith. Burning questions about whether tongue could replace finger in this enterprise or whether her small mouth might be coaxed to liberate my frustrated psyche were not yet answered. I did know one thing, however: I experienced a compelling desire to enjoy Dawn fully naked and to penetrate her with whatever body part I could manage, be it finger, tongue, or perhaps even long-suffering Johnson.

Again she followed me home. We were still dressed in our running shorts in my small kitchen; she was helping me prepare an omelet with cheese, five different vegetables, and hot salsa on top. As we carried out the task of dividing the omelet into two parts and putting them in separate plates, we bumped into each other. I quickly lost all interest in food. I pulled her to me and began kissing her ears, her cheeks, and her lips. She responded in kind, and I got down on my knees and pulled down her running shorts, leaving them on her ankles. Staying on my knees, I began rubbing the inside of her legs moving slowly from bottom to top. When I reached Dawn's pink panties, I began rubbing between her legs; I heard her moan. Encouraged by this sweet sound, I pulled down her panties and pulled both shorts and panties from her ankles, spread her legs, and buried by face in her wet muff while she remained standing. My tongue worked its magic faster and faster until she exploded with amazing intensity.

Afterward, she tried to put on her panties and shorts, but I kept them away from her. "If you won't let me make proper love to you, I'm at least going to enjoy your naked bottom half for a while; we'll have a seminude dinner together."

"But what if your housemates come home?" she whispered.

"No problem," I said. "We can eat in my bedroom."

After we finished our dinner, I suggested a joint shower; Dawn readily agreed. As we adjusted the water temperature, I could see she was fascinated by my full erection, almost as if she had never seen one before. I wondered briefly if she was a virgin but dismissed the thought; she was, after all, twenty-two years old. But maybe her earlier lovemaking had occurred exclusively in the dark or under bedcovers. It didn't matter; I soaped up my horny cylindrical friend, took her wrist, and moved it to the strategic location. She grabbed the anxious Johnson and began slowly moving back and forth over it as I took one of her nipples in my mouth. My breath rate increased like I was finishing the fastest 10K run of my life; I came quickly.

I loaned Dawn one of my T-shirts that was just barely long enough to cover her beautiful rear end and put our running clothes in the washing machine. Just then my housemate Bob came home, and I introduced him to Dawn before she had a chance to flee to the privacy of the bedroom. She had probably never been in the presence of two men wearing only a T-shirt. I could see that Bob was quite taken with her.

As he engaged her in friendly conversation, she seemed to relax a bit and enjoy his obvious attraction to her. Bob was sitting at the kitchen table, and Dawn brought him a drink from the refrigerator. Before she could sit down, I grabbed her from behind and began tickling her while raising her T-shirt so that Bob could get a good look at her brown public patch. Dawn screamed and her face turned a bright red, but I kissed her gently on the lips, and she calmed down quickly. Dawn and Bob continued talking for another thirty minutes or so as if nothing had happened, but I imagined that both of them were turned on by her unexpected pussy display.

Dawn left at about nine in the evening. I kissed her good-bye, but no mention was made of another date. It was all up in the air. After she left, Bob insisted on a blow-by-blow description of the day's events. "OK, Bob, if you insist on twisting my arm." But if the truth be told, I enjoyed the telling almost as much as the original events.

Bob, an experienced clinical social worker, was especially complimentary about my handling of Dawn's religious quandary. Thanks to Bob, I felt a dime of pride that more than canceled out a nickel of guilt.

Chapter 13

In March of 1969, former president Eisenhower died in Washington of congestive heart failure. Gene and his father, George Stanford, attended the funeral at the National Cathedral. I never found out if the Colonel also showed up. If he did, he probably traveled under one of his many assumed names.

That summer Earl organized a reunion for former and current members of Astro's Guidance Analysis group. We met Sunday afternoon in Presidio Park overlooking Old Town near downtown San Diego. The site is where the San Diego Presidio and San Diego Mission were founded in 1769. These were the first European settlements in what is now the western United States. The park covers about forty acres of hilly, wooded terrain with sweeping views of the city and Pacific Ocean.

It had been five years since I was laid off by Astro Dynamics; I was now twenty-nine. Earl and Jim both remained in their old jobs. I recognized Earl's wife, but Jim was accompanied by a moderately attractive but slightly plump woman of maybe thirty-five with thick glasses. She turned out to be Jim's third wife. I had missed entirely wife number two; maybe I should call her the "midwife." Audrey, wife number three, turned out to be a super sharp attorney who worked for a New York law firm. By necessity, they had a part-time relationship, but this arrangement seemed to suit both of them just fine.

The reunion was great fun. Kovac was full of funny stories about his rapid moves between several jobs, first heading back east for two years and then returning to Los Angeles, where he currently held a managerial position with a small company. Somewhat surprisingly, he was happily married to the same woman he had moved in with when he was canned by Astro in 1964. They had their little two-year-old girl with them, a real cutie; a second child was obviously on the way.

Kovac removed a football from his car, tossed it to me, and said, "Jack, it's a good thing you showed up. Now we can demonstrate to these peons how we tore up the Astro football league."

Yes, I thought, except for those damn mail room guys who treated us like a bunch of Pop Warner kids.

I entertained them with poker stories but downplayed my more exotic and erotic adventures. Club Snooze was another favorite topic that produced ongoing laughs. As the stories continued about those present as well as those absent, I became aware that no one had said a thing about Nancy.

When I broached the question, several looked away, and Earl answered. "I'm sorry, Jack. I thought you knew. Nancy died last year—some sort of liver failure."

I was deeply saddened. Nancy's alcoholism was a major flaw in her character, but she had a heart of gold. I flashed to an image of my dad singing one of his favorite Irish ballads:

The more I kissed her, the more I liked her
The more I kissed her, the more she smiled
Soon I'd forgotten my own poor mother's teachin'
Nancy whiskey soon had me beguiled

Gene and I met for a run one overcast morning at Moonlight Beach in Encinitas, located four miles north of Del Mar. The beach was empty except for several flocks of noisy seagulls. We ran north toward Carlsbad, another one of the series of charming beach towns between La Jolla and Oceanside, spanning twenty-four miles.

Gene expanded on his job offer. "You will keep a confidential written record of all my disclosures to you. Everything will be in your own handwriting; no documents of any kind will be passed to you. You will be very careful with accuracy; make sure to distinguish facts from speculations. When I tell you the Colonel's sources have claimed something happened—let's say X—that doesn't make X true. If I say X is pretty well established, it just means there is an excellent chance that X is true, but it's not proven. You will, of course, have absolutely no evidence to back up anything you write about. In the case of gray areas, do not hesitate to use caveats like 'My impression is...' We will have to work out a secure place for short-term storage of your records. On my recent trip to Europe, I arranged for secure long-term storage."

"Why can't I just get a safe-deposit box?" I said.

Gene looked exasperated and sighed. "Jack, we are potentially dealing with the most powerful groups in the United States if not the world. Safe-deposit boxes in the United States are not really safe once the stakes get high enough."

"OK, what's the long-term storage? It's in Europe, you say?"

"Listen very carefully," said Gene. "And train yourself to remember every detail that I pass on to you. On my recent trip, I opened an account in Zurich at Credit Suisse, the second-largest Swiss bank. I met with Marco Oliver, a high bank official with whom my father has had business dealings for many years. Marco has all your details. He has set up a private security box in which you may deposit your reports and just about anything else. You do not, however, have the right to extract anything from the box.

"In addition, you may withdraw funds from my numbered account up to a maximum of ten thousand dollars per month but only in person and only in US cash. All you need is the account number and your US passport. You are not yet required to declare cash when you reenter the United States, so the cash should cause you no problems this time. Be aware, however, that the law is about to change. Soon you will be required to declare anything over five thousand."

My pulse quickened beyond its normal running pace; fantasies of becoming some sort of international playboy, a new 007, or whatever were in high gear.

Gene continued, "Switzerland's tradition of bank secrecy dates to the Middle Ages. This arrangement is about as good as it gets for us. It also facilitates criminal activity, especially tax evasion by wealthy Americans and Europeans, but that's not our problem. The main thing is—your reports will be safe.

"You will visit Credit Suisse with your reports and anything else I may give you as needed. I envision approximately one visit every two or three months. You will also submit an invoice for your hours and travel expenses to the security box. Just tell Marco how much you are owed, and he will give you US dollars from my account. In the short term, it's on the honor system, but I have no worries that you will abuse it."

I thought to myself, yesterday, I was a small-time poker player. Today I seemed to be some sort of player on the world scene, although I knew almost nothing about the game I was in. One thing was for sure: my pond had suddenly grown a whole lot larger. I'd better keep a good lookout for sharks.

I gave some thought to the short-term storage issue. I first purchased a small, inexpensive safe that I assumed would be easy pickings for professionals. I made copies of several personal documents, including my passport and birth certificate. I placed these documents plus two-hundred in cash in the safe. For good measure I added several pieces of fake jewelry that looked expensive to my untrained eye. I then hid the safe under a pile of dirty clothes in my closet.

I briefly considered adding a smart-ass note to the safe contents that said something like "Ha Ha, I fooled you, assholes!" But I thought better of it.

I never used one of the electrical outlets in my bedroom, so it seemed like a good candidate for spook mischief. I removed the outer plate and inner box and disconnected the wiring. The resulting hole in the wall was big enough for me to insert a cylindrical cardboard container containing several sheets of rolled-up paper. I then replaced the plate and purchased a cheap stereo system and small end table. I placed the system on the table and plugged it in, but in truth its only power came from backup batteries. I had to use my Phillips screwdriver every time I accessed my hiding spot—a minor inconvenience, but it seemed that a secret Jack box had been born.

On our run a week later, I described my "fake-out" safe and Jack box to Gene. He said, "OK, your grade is B-. Good enough to fool the semi-professionals but not the real pros. I'll think over other options."

As we finished our run, Gene carefully looked around us and asked, "Where are your car keys? Never mind; I see you have pockets. Take this and put it away quickly."

I put the thick envelope in my pocket in one deft motion, just like any James Bond wannabe would do.

Gene smiled. "Your first assignment is to enjoy a London vacation. The only downside is you must go alone—absolutely no girlfriends. I want you to become familiar with London's casinos. Visit several; maybe play a little small-stakes poker. Nothing serious; remember, you are just there to establish a cover story. If anyone ever gets curious, your trips to Europe's casinos will explain nicely your cash income as well as visits to Switzerland."

"No girlfriends? Suppose I'm accosted by some sex-starved British babe. What could I do? My hands would be tied."

Gene remained patient. "Just don't fly over with anyone. Keep your mission in mind. Keep your eye on the damn ball. Or maybe I should say stay out of ballrooms."

My "mission"? Wow, now I really felt like 007.

I waited until I got home to open Gene's envelope and count the twenty-five crisp hundred-dollar bills. Mandy and my housemates were informed that I would be gone for a week or so—off to London to check out new poker opportunities. Otherwise, I was purposely vague about my travel plans, but Ava questioned me further.

"Listen," she said, "I know a pretty young schoolteacher named Elizabeth whom I met when she came here on an exchange program last year. She lives in a little town near Oxford, less than an hour or two from central London, depending on how you get there. I can write to her and see if she is interested in having you over to visit." She beamed. "I will, of course, give you my highest possible recommendation. Just give me your hotel details, and she can write or call you there if she's up for a Jack-like adventure."

This seemed like a real long shot, but I replied, "Oh, Ava, you are so good to me."

A week later I flew from San Diego to New York. After a three-hour layover, my 11:00 p.m. flight left for London. Six hours later I landed in the early morning local time at Heathrow Airport and caught the train to Paddington station in central London.

My hotel room near the north end of Hyde Park was only a short Tube ride from Paddington. The small room was about the size of my walk-in closet in La Jolla. Thankfully, it did have its own tiny bathroom with mini shower. Good thing I was in shape; any fat guy would have been forced to stay dirty. I was sleep deprived and a bit nauseated from inhaling secondhand cigarette smoke on the flights. Of course, the airline had put me in the so-called nonsmoking section as requested. Sure. Thanks for nothing.

Since there was no hurry, I spent the next two days getting over jet lag and clearing my assaulted lungs with runs through Hyde Park and short trips on the London Underground, otherwise known fondly as the Tube—"fondly" to us visitors at least.

In the late afternoon of the third day, I walked to the Baker Street station. I took careful note of the words engraved at the edge of the platform: "Mind the Gap." Using my athletic skills, I deftly hopped over the two-inch gap and caught the Bakerloo line south to Piccadilly Circus. I then transferred to the Piccadilly line north and got off at the first stop, Leicester Square.

London weather has a bad reputation, but this day was mild and sunny. After a short walk, I bought a ticket at the Ambassador Theatre for the evening's performance of *The Mouse Trap*, the famous whodunit play that had been running since 1952. I found a small sidewalk restaurant, ordered a glass of wine, and finished a forgettable meal of fish and chips wrapped in newspaper in time to return to the Ambassador.

OK, enough of these play days; it was time to fulfill my *mission*.

After gambling was legalized in the early 1960s, the Clermont Club was the first London casino to be granted a license. It was located in Berkeley Square near the west end of Hyde Park. From the Baker Street station, I took the Jubilee line south to Green Park; it was a short walk to the club.

I never got through the front door. "Sir, this club is for members only," I was advised by an elaborately uniformed doorman.

I felt a little foolish. After all, my hero 007 was never denied casino entrance. "I'm sorry; this is my first time in London. How do I become a member?"

"Sir, you must be nominated by a current member or some other person of stature." Blast, I fumed, no wonder we kicked out bloody King George in 1776.

I suppressed my scorn at this upper-class snobbery. "Do all casinos require membership?"

"Membership policies vary between casinos, but all require that you establish membership at least twenty-four hours before entering for the first time. And sir, can I offer you some additional advice?" He looked me up and down with disdain. "All clubs require that you be smartly dressed, including a proper jacket and tie."

Damn, this was more complicated than I had imagined, but I did manage to identify three clubs whose standards were sufficiently low to possibly accept me. I filled out the applications and extended my hotel reservation to accommodate the delay.

A letter was delivered to my room on Wednesday. It was written on pink stationery; the return address was some place I had never heard of.

Dear Jack,

Ava sent me a nice introduction. I'd like to invite you to our small village this weekend. The locals are reenacting a famous battle in the countryside; it should be great fun. We don't have an extra bedroom, but you are welcome to sleep on our living room couch.

Cheers,
Elizabeth

All three of my casino applications were approved. I spent several days surveying poker games but could never get even close to the quality of information required by a professional player. I especially needed to know how much money the casino was taking from the pots. Another problem was the rules; small rule changes in poker can cause major shifts from skill games to games of chance, thereby ensuring that only the casino can win in the long run. The devil is in the details. I could see that it would take me many months of study to determine if I could actually make a living in London.

Fortunately, that was not my mission.

Chapter 14

The invitation from Elizabeth was a marginal call for me, but why not? Maybe this reenacted battle would be interesting. Also, her village was close to Oxford; with its long intellectual tradition, Oxford University would certainly be worth a visit.

After getting directions on the phone, I showed up at Elizabeth's village on a Friday afternoon. Elizabeth and her housemate, Victoria, lived in one-half of a two-story block building that seemed to be hundreds of years old. The other half served as the village schoolhouse where both Elizabeth and Victoria taught small children.

Both women were young and attractive in their own way, Victoria with red hair and glasses and Elizabeth with short black hair and a lively smile. They fixed me a simple dinner, and we all went to bed early, me on the couch as advertised. I was stoked; here I lay, the honored guest of two famous queens.

The next day we attended the mock battle involving a thousand or so participants wielding fake wooden swords in the scenic countryside. A big truck with a sound system was perched on the highest hilltop, the announcer providing a running commentary of the battle. Real ambulances were kept busy caring for injured players who had forgotten that this was only a simulated battle.

That night I took Elizabeth out to the local pub for dinner. After we loosened up from our second round of drinks, she said, "Ava had a lot of good things to say about you, but you seem a lot more reserved than I expected."

"You're right on the money," I replied. "This is my first time of out of my country. I'm feeling uncomfortable with your social conventions. You British are friendly but also seem quite reserved. I'm afraid of coming across as some sort of ugly American or crude cowboy."

"Actually, I was hoping for a nice Californian who would be decidedly non-British. Do you want to sleep with me or not?"

Wow, she got down to business with no beating around the bush! And she really was quite pretty. It seemed that the cultural barriers were vastly overrated. Three cheers for the bloody British.

"I just don't want Victoria to know anything; she's pretty traditional. Wait an hour after we go to bed. Then come up the stairs; my bedroom is on the right. Don't knock; just come in."

I followed directions at first, but my memory failed me at the top of the stairs. Which room was hers? Well, I had a fifty percent chance of being right. I opened the door on the left to find Victoria sitting up in her bed reading a book. Her mouth dropped almost to her belly button, but no sound came forth.

For once in my life, I was quick to minimize the damage. I walked over to her bed and said, "I've come to kiss you good night. It's just the way we do things in California." I kissed her on the cheek and left; she looked to be in shock and never said a word, not even the next morning. Elizabeth and I spend an hour of giggling foreplay, followed by explosive five-play, all the while trying to stay queenly quiet, before I returned to the downstairs couch. I slept like a royal baby.

When I returned to my house in La Jolla, I regaled Bob and Ava with my British adventures, from the snooty casino doorman to the two queens. Ava laughed. "I'm going to write Elizabeth right away to get her side of the story. I wonder if Victoria ever figured things out."

I soon got back to regular poker playing but limited my play to three evenings or about twenty hours per week at Crystal Pier and Bicycle Bill's. But I almost never missed Friday nights when the card rooms were full. Mandy also danced about three nights per week but not necessarily the same nights. When our evenings matched, I would show up at the Body Shop at about half past midnight, after the card rooms closed.

I never bothered to visit the Body Shop on Mandy's nights off. Was it my imagination, or did the girl's attitudes and the general ambiance of the place become much less friendly when Mandy was absent? Or was I getting just a little jaded?

The girls were required by law to be clothed when serving drinks between dance routines. I'm not sure of the purpose for the law; maybe having beer spilled in your pubic hair was a health hazard. All the dancing and repeated taking off and on of dresses and panties seemed to create big appetites, but Taco Jack came only about once per week. I was forced to triple my supply of girl-friendly tacos on the special Jack nights because the girls seem slighted when they missed out.

As 007 often reminds us, you never want to piss off a naked girl.

On our next running session, Gene asked me if I had a tax accountant. "What do you mean?" I replied. "I don't have a job, and poker players never worry about income taxes."

"Well, Jack, the law requires that you pay taxes on income, even gambling income. In your new position as my recording secretary, you will be required to obey laws, even tax laws. I'm giving you the name of a good accountant. Every year he will figure your tax liability; you must then happily send your tax payments to our friendly uncle. Based on what you have told me, I have estimated your 1968 tax liability. Since you didn't plan for this expense, I'm advancing you the money.

"In future years you will be responsible for your own taxes. I want you to stay as clean as possible to avoid unnecessary scrutiny. My accountant contact will also put you in touch with a trusted real estate agent; he will direct you to appropriate tax shelters. You are on the verge of the unimaginable—actually becoming respectable. Obviously, none of these people know anything at all about our activities; make sure to keep it that way."

The accountant and real estate agent both turned out to be helpful. DeSilva, the real estate agent, was a short, wiry guy of about sixty with a huge grey and black mustache. "I recommend that you buy some residential houses in middle-class areas of San Diego," he said. "The market has been suppressed since the Astro layoffs. You can buy houses in the Claremont area near Astro for peanuts. With bank loans and my special finance program, you can get a decent rental house with only a minimum down payment."

I thought to myself, landlord my ass! My image would be mud. Christ, 007 would be disgusted.

"Sorry deSilva. Becoming a landlord is the last thing on my mind. I'd have to make repairs, unplug toilets at midnight, and collect rents—all kinds of crap."

"Hold on, kid," deSilva said. "I'm told you're a smart guy, so listen to the whole deal before you jump the gun. I have conveniently set up a full-service management company to deal with repairs, tenants, and pretty much everything else. You choose the house, we buy it, and I take my real estate commission in the form of a promissory note. We get you a ninety to ninety-five percent loan through my banker friend; all you need is about fifteen hundred dollars down. On a house selling for thirty thousand, that's twenty-to-one leverage."

DeSilva looked smug. "I'm predicting a twenty percent increase in prices over the next four years, in which case your house that's initially thirty thousand will be worth thirty-six thousand. Your initial equity of fifteen hundred will have grown to seventy-five hundred, a return on investment of four hundred percent. Of course, I have oversimplified by not accounting for expenses, but given the tax savings, it's pretty much a wash."

I tried to find an error in his analysis, but it seemed solid. Of course, leverage would work the other way if house prices went down. But in that case I could just let the bank have the crappy little house and walk away from the bank loan. I couldn't have cared less about my credit rating, or in basic poker speak, I didn't give a rat's ass.

Was it really this easy to make money in real estate? The whole scheme depended on access normally available only to the financially well-off. A guy like deSilva and a friendly banker to smooth out the rough spots were essential. The creative banker could magically transform deadbeats into good credit risks. The system generally worked to allow the rich to become even richer, but ordinary Jacks like me could perhaps scavenge a few unpicked bones in the process.

I found a small three-bedroom house in Claremont near Mesa College. It was perhaps twenty years old and needed work, but it backed up to a steep hillside, providing a private backyard and a nice ambience. Proximity to the college guaranteed renters, and deSilva's boys were ready to clean up if the students trashed it.

My offer of twenty-eight thousand was accepted. DeSilva's banking friend even filled out the loan application for me. All I had to do was come up with sixteen hundred in cash, and the house was mine.

On our next run, I relayed my dealings with deSilva to Gene. He approved of my house, particularity my attention to its rental potential near the college. "Good move, Jack. You may yet become a genuine capitalist, but let's move to another subject. I'm going to enlighten you with some background on our new arrangement.

"My father, George Stanford, and the Colonel were midlevel officers under the command of General Eisenhower in 1944. They played small parts in planning Operation Overlord, the code name for the Normandy invasion. You were probably too young to remember any of this, but I vividly recall my excitement at the time.

"The amphibious assault involved about seven thousand ships and other vessels. Nearly one hundred sixty thousand troops crossed the English Channel on the sixth of June in 1944. More than three million Allied troops were in France by the end of August. American and British troops moved toward Berlin from the west while Soviet troops attacked from the east. Germany finally surrendered on the seventh of May, 1945, shortly after Hitler committed suicide.

"My father retired when the war ended and started his defense business. Ike, as many called him, became good friends with my father in the years that followed. When Eisenhower ran for president in 1952, my father was a big contributor to his campaign. I don't know as much about the Colonel's history with Eisenhower. Even if I did, I wouldn't tell you, but I can say that he was an important intelligence operative during the Eisenhower administration and beyond.

"Eisenhower coined the term *military-industrial complex* in his farewell address, warning against lack of oversight of secret government organizations that could undermine the freedoms we enjoy. While he didn't single out the CIA or NSA, they certainly qualified as examples of his concern. Perhaps now you get some sense of the reasons behind the Colonel's access to all kinds of government secrets."

I was feeling more and more like a little fish in a huge ocean; forget the puny pond metaphor.

Chapter 15

It had been more than six weeks since my last poker game at Bicycle Bill's. I returned one Friday at about five in the afternoon. All seats at active tables were taken when I arrived, so I put my name on the waiting list and pulled up a chair across from Ruthie, seated at the only empty table.

"Jack, where have you been? We missed you. I even checked with several players from Crystal Pier, but nobody had seen you there either. Hey your hair's a bit longer; I like it."

I was always glad to see Ruthie, high on emotional intelligence, not to mention pleasing on the eyes. She was suitably impressed by my London trip and laughed heartily at my uncensored stories of British queens and casino doormen. She tilted her head, winked, and said, "Come on. I'll buy you a drink while you wait." She knew I never started drinking this early; such bad habits could lead to serious wallet disease. What was up?

We ordered gin and tonics at the bar across the street. "But, bartender, hold the gin in mine."

She turned serious right away, "Did you notice the tall, well-dressed man with white hair and scarf sitting next to Jersey Joe? That's Fast Eddie Wilcox. I'm sure you've heard of him. He's been playing here almost every day for the past several weeks and has really cleaned up. My old boyfriend once had some shady dealings with him. Watch out; I just wanted to warn you."

Ruthie's friendly warning brought back an unpleasant memory of an old encounter I had with Blackie Francis. Word around town was that Blackie was the top player in San Diego. He was a small, quiet, introverted man of about fifty, with a permanent two-day growth of black facial hair. He could be easily mistaken for a skid row bum. Several years back, when I had first moved up to no-limit games, I had foolishly tried aggressive play against Blackie. To make a long story short, he cleaned my clock. If I didn't know better, I'd swear that the fucker could actually read minds.

In both personality and appearance, Fast Eddie and Blackie were complete opposites. Eddie was tall and typically wore a fancy scarf, elaborate shirt, and expensive shoes; he was both distinguished looking and gregarious. Many considered Eddie's game to be a close second to Blackie's.

For the past year, most customers had thought of me as the top player at both Bicycle Bill's and Crystal Pier, a big fish in two tiny ponds. How did I fare citywide? It's hard to say precisely, but somewhere between five and ten is my guess. In any competition with Eddie, I would be the underdog.

So Fast Eddie had, in a sense, invaded my home territory. Was this going to result in one of those classic showdowns like the famous gunfight in the movie *High Noon*? Or Ali versus Liston, or Wyatt Earp versus the Clantons, or 007 versus Goldfinger? Oh goody. What fun to wallow in such delusions of grandeur. But in reality most head-to-head contests among professional poker players tended to be eliminated by natural selection. The rare professional who directed his main efforts towards some other top player would likely lose out in the long run.

My goal as a professional poker player was to maximize my winnings against opponents of varying abilities. Thus, my strategy was directed mostly toward weaker players. By analogy, the most successful lion is especially good at identifying the weakest wildebeest and catching it. Strong wildebeests are to be avoided as they are quite capable of injuring lions. Similarly, the most successful poker player is not necessarily the best player judged by head-to-head competition against other professionals.

As soon as I sat down, Eddie said, "You must be Jack; I can tell from your dirty-blond hair and brown mustache. I hear you're one hell of a card player and a pretty tough guy too; you really kicked some punk's ass over at Crystal Pier. Remind me to keep my ashtray away from you."

I was lost for words; I hadn't expected Eddie to know me from a bottle of bourbon. But I wasn't fooled by his superficial friendliness. This guy had been around many blocks many times. Nice to meet you, you fancy shark.

As the game progressed Eddie talked almost nonstop as he collected more and more chips. He played aggressively, especially against me. Rather than confront Eddie's challenge, I went into my semi defensive mode. My experience with Blackie had taught me a valuable lesson: you are here to feed your wallet, not your ego. When Bill's closed at midnight, Eddie cashed out as the big winner—maybe $400 compared to my puny $60. Everyone else in the game lost.

I stepped up my visits to Bicycle Bill's to four nights per week. Eddie was there every time and continued his aggressive play against me. I continued to play cautiously against him but was selectively aggressive against others. I mostly ignored Eddie's distractive chatter while observing him closely. After a month or so, I began to get a good feel for his play.

Like most top players, he looked for profitable chances to check-raise before the draw. One hand in particular was the turning point in the competition between Eddie and me. I was dealt a pat spade flush under the gun. It was checked all the way around to the dealer. Please poker god, let him open the pot. Sure enough he opened for $5. He seemed to have a weak hand; probably he was just trying to steal the ante. I knew Eddie would also see it this way, so I flat called. As I had hoped, Eddie put in a $20 raise. The dealer folded quickly.

I then meekly reraised a very paltry $30 more. I guessed that Eddie was now chomping at the bit. He figured me for a weak hand and had successfully blown me off a number of pots; he was sure he could do it again. But when he reraised another $150, I went all in—an additional $350. Eddie then smelled a rat but called anyway with his piddling three fives, an incredibly bad call based on his entire misreading of my play. His usual gregarious demeanor took a hike in the Amazon rain forest when I showed down the flush. He gritted his teeth and angrily called for $500 more in chips.

After that, Eddie's aggressive play against me worked mostly in my favor. Whenever I won a big pot from him, he would complain, "That fucking Jack is so lucky; he always holds over me. I hope he gets cancer of the dick." But when two players are of equal ability, the one playing defense usually wins, like a counterpuncher in boxing.

Eddie would often try to hustle some sort of side bet from other players. "I'll bet you a hundred dollars that I can toss this card and hit the far wall," he would say, or "I'll bet you I can drink a beer in three seconds." He would propose these contests and others designed to boost both his income and reputation.

He continued in his talkative ways, relating all kinds of blarney; some of it might even have been true. He claimed his IQ was 160. He also said that he never paid for restaurant meals; he just faked trips to the bathroom and walked out.

The last one I could easily believe. The scam would be easily accomplished by this superficially distinguished-looking con man who acted like he had *mucho* bucks to burn. Did Eddie's name-prefix "Fast" originate with his quick restaurant escapes? I never found out, but it sure fit.

Gene called me as I ate a quiet brunch in the family room of my rented La Jolla house. "I've read your draft paper on the apparent paradox in Einstein's field equations. Meet me tomorrow at Moonlight Beach. Let's aim for the low tide at noon."

Well, at least Gene still had his sense of humor. We started with light stretching to warm up while engaging in small talk. He listened with obvious interest to my adventures with British queens, casino doormen, and Fast Eddie and then smiled and said, "Nice going. But now you need to focus on your real job; get ready for another flight to London. For right now, I want you to repeat to me everything of substance that I have told you about my father, the Colonel, the FBI, and so forth."

As we ran south toward Cardiff and Solana Beach, we noticed a lonely dolphin in the breaking surf close to shore. I repeated everything I could remember. Every minor error or inaccurate interpretation drew an immediate correction from Gene. When I finished, he said, "OK, now tell me the story once more, this time without errors."

After we finished this tedious exercise, Gene got even more serious. "As you know, for the past six months or so, the Colonel has been in the middle of conflicts between the FBI and CIA. He's basically acting as a peacemaker, but in the process he has discovered all kinds of explosive information.

"The Colonel is particularly concerned with a well-funded CIA program of terrorism directed at Cuba, called Operation Mongoose. This program includes sabotage and bombing of oil storage, railway bridges, power plants, and so forth. Mongoose was authorized by President Kennedy in 1961, even before the Bay of Pigs debacle. Mongoose activities also include numerous attempts to murder Fidel Castro; they continue to this day."

My head was spinning at the implications. The Cuban missile crisis of 1962 was still fresh in my mind; we had come far too close to nuclear war with Soviet Union. But the Soviet missiles had since been removed from Cuba, so why was the CIA still trying to kill Castro? What would happen if they actually succeeded?

I couldn't remember just what an actual mongoose looked like. I did remember a small animal imported from Asia to the Caribbean Islands to kill rats and snakes. Unfortunately, the little critters caused too much destruction of native plants and animals to be useful. Was this failed history a bad omen for Operation Mongoose?

Again I was full of questions, but Gene held up his hand to stop me. "I don't have answers to the many obvious questions—only little pieces of the puzzle. But there's more, and it really stretches credulity. After the Cuban Revolution in 1959, Castro closed down all the mob-owned casinos and expelled the mobsters. Castro also shut down the prostitution rings so popular with many American businessmen. The Mafia really hates Castro and has plans in place to return to Cuba once Castro is removed.

"In 1960, the CIA recruited ex–FBI agent Robert Maheu to approach Chicago mobster John Roselli. Maheu passed himself off as representing international corporations that wanted Castro killed. Roselli introduced Maheu to Chicago boss Sam Giancana and Tampa mobster Santo Trafficante, the latter one of the most powerful mobsters running casinos in pre revolution Cuba.

"The CIA gave the mobsters poison pills to use to murder Castro. For several months, anti-Castro Cubans tied to the Mafia tried unsuccessfully to put the pills into Castro's food. Snipers were also trained at a secret CIA base in the Florida Keys with the mobster Roselli in charge at first. After the failed CIA-sponsored Bay of Pigs invasion, the assassination attempts continued at an even higher pace with a CIA officer, the so-called 'Wild Bill' King Harvey, taking charge of Roselli's efforts."

"Christ!" I exclaimed. "You're telling me that America's secret Cuba policy is being implemented by a decidedly unholy mixture of anti-Castro Cubans, the CIA, the FBI, and the Mafia. I've heard that politics makes strange bedfellows, but this is completely insane."

Gene looked more downtrodden than I had ever seen him. He replied softly, "Unlike the Colonel's revelations about Hoover and the FBI, this CIA-related information contains numerous names, dates, and other details. Over the next week, we will be going through this story over and over until you have it all down pat. We meet again tomorrow morning to begin your next lesson."

I said good-bye to Gene, showered at the beach, and drove my Chevy aimlessly out of the Moonlight Beach parking lot. I had no idea where to go. I was especially aware of the enormous weight on my shoulders but had absolutely no one to talk to. I was sworn to secrecy. At that moment I achieved a much deeper appreciation of Gene's relationship with me. He also needed someone to talk to.

I stopped at a little 7-Eleven convenience store to get a local newspaper. My movie choices included the James Bond flick *On Her Majesty's Secret Service* and *Bob & Carol & Ted & Alice*, a comedy about open relationships. These nicely represented the two sides of my lifestyle, but for the mood I was in, neither one sounded good. I drank a couple of beers at a local bar, ate a fast-food hamburger, and bought a ticket to the La Paloma Theater in Encinitas. *Butch Cassidy and the Sundance Kid* was playing, perfect for my escape from the disturbing reality of Gene's new information.

Chapter 16

Gene and I met for ten more running sessions over the next two months. Each time, Gene directed me to new sources of public information, including articles by investigative reporters from the *LA Times, New York Times*, and *Washington Post*. Also included were serious books by professors and ex-military thinkers.

"Here are some excellent sources, written by 'true patriots,' as the Colonel labels them. These sources seek the truth uncompromisingly, regardless of their ideological biases."

My rented house was a convenient walk to the beautiful UCSD campus in La Jolla. The new library site looked like an alien spaceship had landed in the middle of a huge grove of eucalyptus trees. With multiple reading assignments to keep me busy, I avoided the card rooms and the Body Shop entirely and put in a good sixty hours per week of study. Yes, I went back to school with a vengeance, but now I was being paid by the hour. Gene quizzed me over and over about plausible interpretations of the Colonel's revelations in the broader context of published material.

Given the inside information I had gained from Gene and the Colonel, much of the mainstream media seemed incredibly naive about the US government's secret activities. When I expressed this to Gene, he dropped still another bombshell. "We know that at least a dozen or so well-known media people are being paid under the table by the CIA. Some of these arrangements are probably justified; the media can possess information pertinent to national security.

"Unfortunately, since congressional and presidential oversight is missing, we don't know the degree to which reporters may be altering their stories due to CIA influences. Do the CIA and other agencies purposely plant false information to further self-serving goals? Or maybe they just aim to support America's superrich, who have investments in third world countries? That would be consistent with their past history. We don't know specifics, but what's to stop them if they decide to spread propaganda in the United States? Eisenhower understood this."

Everything needed for the Zurich security box drop-off was embedded safely in my overstuffed brain; nothing was written down. Since the little secret hiding place behind my electrical outlet was no longer required, I removed three pages from a pad of lined paper and filled them with neat, handwritten random numbers and spaces, a code that even

God's cousin couldn't decipher. The cheap safe that I had hidden in my closet remained in place. Now I owned two stashes of useless contents festering happily in my bedroom, ready to thwart evildoers.

In 1968 US soldiers had murdered four hundred or so unarmed civilians at My Lai, South Vietnam. Many were just lined up in a ditch and shot. The victims included women, men, children, and infants. Some of the women were gang-raped and their bodies mutilated. For a year or so, the army represented this event as a US military victory resulting in the deaths of enemy combatants. Just add them to the body counts regurgitated every night on the six o'clock news by the good old father figure Walter Cronkite and other trusted news anchors. But finally the secret leaked out, and several investigative reports put pressure on the army to take action.

In March of 1970, the army charged fourteen officers with suppressing information related to the incident, but in the end no one ever served real jail time. Widespread stories of the massacre further galvanized public opinion against the war. Later reports showed that My Lai was far from an isolated incident.

In late April, President Nixon announced that he had ordered US forces to cross into neutral Cambodia, which threatened to widen the war and sparked nationwide protests. These events constituted a broad spectrum of activity, ranging from constitutionally protected peaceful protests to riots that threatened private and public property.

In early May, the governor of Ohio dispatched armed national guardsmen to Kent State University to deal with a scheduled demonstration. Not surprisingly, events got out of control, and the National Guard shot thirteen of the students; four died. No charges were ever brought against guardsmen or public officials; the antiwar movement became even more energized.

In the mid 1960s, I had often visited the UCSD campus on weekends to join in pickup touch football games. One of my friends in these games was a physics graduate student named Keith. In the late afternoon of

May 10, 1970, Keith was walking through UCSD's Revelle Plaza when he witnessed a horrible sight. A student was on fire and running across the plaza. Keith heroically tackled him and attempted to extinguish the flames, but the student died a few hours later at Scripps Hospital. Keith suffered burns to his hands, but they were not life-threatening.

The badly burned student was George Winne Jr., the son of a US Navy captain. Winne was a former member of the ROTC and had no previous affiliation with any organized war protests. He had ignited gasoline-soaked rags in his lap next to a sign that said *In God's name, end this war.* Winne's act was inspired by the widely reported self-immolation of a Buddhist monk in 1963 protesting the persecution of Buddhists by the South Vietnamese government.

In late May, I booked the same hotel used on my first trip near the northwest corner of Hyde Park. Again I flew San Diego to New York to London. Two days of rest and running were on my agenda before serious business began. Early on the morning of the third day, I walked to the Baker Street station and caught the Tube on the Bakerloo line south to Chairing Cross. There I boarded the regular train for the two-hour ride to the Dover Priory station on Britain's southeast coast.

I took a short taxi ride to Dover Eastern Docks and purchased a ferry ticket. After a forty-five-minute wait, I caught the ninety-minute ferry ride across the channel to Calais, France. Then I walked across the footbridge into town and on to the Calais Ville train station in about twenty minutes. Fortunately, my only luggage was my Sierra Club-approved backpack, so I could move pretty fast. I just barely made the train to Paris, where I switched to the Zurich train in the afternoon.

I finally arrived at the Zurich station at half past nine in the evening, tired and thirsty for a tall beer. My thoughts drifted to the genre of civil engineering. Maybe someday the Europeans would dig a tunnel under the channel; it would probably cut travel time in half.

I was booked at the Hotel Alexander, a short taxi ride from the station. The hotel is located in the financial district, where the headquarters of major global companies, including Credit Suisse, are everywhere. Gene had arranged my meeting with Marco Oliver in advance. Oliver left a message at the hotel to meet him for a late lunch at the Ristorante Orsini near Paradeplatz Square. His note said, *It's not a long walk, but it is better that you take a taxi to avoid getting lost since you are unfamiliar with Zurich.*

Oliver, about forty-five and of medium height, wore an expensive suit in sharp contrast to my jeans and running shoes. He was tanned and fit. He looked like he worked out regularly—not anything like the fat old banker I was expecting. Oliver was formal in his manner and speech but also quite helpful. If he disapproved of my somewhat hippie-like

appearance, it didn't show. He apologized for not picking me up at the hotel. "Mr. Stanford advised against it—a privacy issue." I wasn't entirely sure if he meant Gene or his father, George, but I let it go.

The Credit Suisse building was a short walk from the restaurant. We went straight to his fancy office. Oliver was a major contact for high-networth customers of the bank. From the looks of his office, he might have owned the whole damn bank. We sat down on his leather couch, and he carefully went over bank procedural issues. At the end, he added, "Here is my private number. Please do not hesitate to call me collect at any time. If I am not available, my private secretary will take your message. In most cases I will be back to you in less than four hours—faster if you call in the Zurich daytime."

I entertained a fleeting thought: I wished that snobby casino doorman could see me now. "Thanks, Mr. Oliver. I have documents to put in the security box, but I'll need one or two days to get them ready." Oliver got me a taxi back to the Hotel Alexander, where I began to write down everything I had learned from Gene and indirectly from the Colonel.

It took me three days, but finally I was satisfied. I placed the seventy-three pages of neat handwritten text in a large brown envelope and caught a taxi to Oliver's office at Credit Suisse. His secretary came with a large metal security box. I placed my envelope in the empty box, and Oliver handed me a key. "The box can only be opened when both keys are used," he said as we walked into a fortress like room with numerous security boxes in the walls. "As per Mr. Stanford's instructions, you are not authorized to remove anything. Thus, I will accompany you every time you access the box. Now, I believe you have an invoice for me."

Greedy thoughts bubbled down to my toes and up to my brain and back. This was my first payment as Gene's recording secretary. I handed Oliver my invoice. "I've kept a close accounting of hours worked since the beginning of my arrangement with Gene. I have four weeks at sixty hours per week plus another hundred hours of piecemeal time and six hundred dollars in travel expenses. At thirty dollars per hour, the total comes to ten thousand eight hundred dollars."

Oliver accepted the invoice like it was a dirty diaper. "I'm not concerned with the accounting details—only the total. But Mr. Stanford has authorized a maximum of ten thousand dollars per month." He opened his desk, removed a metal box, and counted out 100 crisp hundred dollar bills like it was chump change. He handed me an empty oversize envelope and a receipt for ten thousand dollars to sign, which also listed the remaining eight hundred owed to me. "Today is the fifth of June; you may pick up the additional eight hundred any time after the fifth of July, plus payment for additional hours."

I decided to fly back to London rather than endure the long train ride. Over the next three days, I visited the three casinos with such low standards that they had actually accepted me as a member. I played stud poker since I couldn't find an actual draw game. Serious stud players remember all cards dealt and base their strategy on this information. The best film example is from *The Cincinnati Kid*, a 1965 flick with Steve McQueen as the kid and his nemesis Edward G. Robinson as the crusty old veteran. I had never had reason to acquire such memory skills since stud was illegal in San Diego.

I just fooled around in several small stud games, managing to blow off three hundred or so; my goal was only to establish a presence. The

casinos did have excellent food, so dinner every night was a guilty pleasure—a big improvement over the usual fish and chips rolled up in
British newspaper. In order to enter even these low-end casinos, I had
to wear a jacket and tie, which I had purchased at a small shop. I had to
ask the salesman to tie the tie. When I left Astro, I tossed out all my ties;
I honestly couldn't remember how to operate the damn things.

While eating at the casino restaurant on my last night, I sneaked off
my tie and put it in my pocket just before cutting off a piece of my me-
dium-rare filet. I wanted complete freedom for my Adam's apple. Free
at last! But before I could fully swallow even one luscious morsel, I was
busted by the casino tie police. "Sir, you must put your tie back on if you
wish to finish your meal."

I recalled getting busted at Club Snooze and the infamous ballroom.
At least I didn't get booted out for sleeping in the dining room.

I had one minor problem. I had brought several thousand dollars to
Europe and obtained another ten thousand from Zurich. After expenses, I still had nearly seven thousand over the new five thousand dollar
limit on how much undeclared cash could be brought into the United
States. I securely packaged seventy US$100 bills and mailed them to
Mandy together with a note that said, *Join me in La Jolla Friday night? In
the meantime, please take good care of my little green men.*

Chapter 17

It was September of 1970, I opened a beer can with my handy-dandy *church key* as the instrument was called. The original openers used on bottles looked similar to old-fashioned keys used by monks to open the church and keep their private beer safe. The name was adopted by many tools used to open beer containers.

I switched on my new color TV to watch the first Monday night football game featuring the New York Jets and Cleveland Browns. This event was a big deal for me; color TVs were not sold in large numbers until 1965 and did not exceed black-and-white sales until 1972.

With the nice pile of little green men obtained in Zurich, I was feeling pretty flush. My first purchase was the TV, now set up in the family room so my housemates would have full access. Bob retrieved a beer from the refrigerator and joined me. Bob was a forty-plus clinical social worker, tall and thin with a large nose and beginning to lose his hair. Nobody would ever call him good-looking, but many women loved him just the same. He projected an open, friendly, and empathetic manner. When women talked, he really listened. He was a good and trusted friend; I always enjoyed his company.

Bob said, "Nice new toy; great reception. But I wonder if Monday night football will last; it seems like we're already saturated with Sunday games. By the way, did you ever get together again with that little pixie, Dawn?" I knew he was really attracted to her even though their age difference meant that the chance of his hooking up with her was below zero. Maybe the little pussy peek incident that I had engineered for his benefit was not the best idea.

Keith Jackson was providing the play-by-play. Howard Cosell and Don Meredith were the color men. Jets quarterback Broadway Joe Namath was famous for his guarantee of an upset victory over the Baltimore Colts in Super Bowl III the year before. The announcer informed us that the game was sponsored by Marlboro cigarettes, Ford, and other familiar names.

The game was still in the first quarter, and I had just finished my beer when the phone rang. It was Gene's wife, Marie. "Jack, I need to talk to you privately; can we meet for lunch tomorrow? And please don't tell Gene."

"This is a bit strange," I said. "You want to meet with me behind Gene's back? Am I supposed to sneak around in dark places with my friend's wife? People will talk."

"Don't take this the wrong way," she replied. "This has nothing to do with romance. If I were going to have an affair, you would be at the bottom of my list, assuming you even made the list."

"Thanks for the compliment," I muttered. "How about we meet at Mike's in Del Mar at half past one? I'll be up late tonight, and I'm planning a long beach run in the morning."

She had already secured an outdoor table when I arrived at Mike's restaurant overlooking the Pacific Ocean. It was typical Southern California—a beautiful sunny day. Marie looked luscious in her loose-fitting black dress.

"I already ordered a wine; want to join me?" she said.

"Too early for me," I replied. In fact, I could not remember Marie ever drinking at lunchtime. Even at her rarely attended wild parties, she never had more than two or three drinks; something unusual had to be afoot.

She placed her hand lightly on my arm. "First let me apologize for what I said yesterday about my silly imagined affair list; I trust that your formidable ego remains intact. It's just that you are more in like my brother or cousin; any hanky-panky between us would be *mucho* incestuous."

I smiled my best enigmatic smile and tried to mask a tiny twinge of guilt brought on by my memory of the pool party.

Marie got down to business. "Have you noticed how strange Gene has been acting lately?"

"Well, Marie, in fact, he has seemed quite preoccupied; I assume he is overworked and has a lot on his mind." Marie, of course, didn't know anything about the Colonel's blockbuster revelations. "I actually haven't seen much of Gene in the past month, but we did a ten-mile run at Black's Beach on Friday. He was really pushing himself, like he needed to dump extra stress."

Marie was silent for several minutes and then replied, "It's much more than just the usual job stress. He's become quite secretive, nervous, and…well…less interested in sex, or much of anything else, for that matter. And yesterday morning I found this in the mail," She handed me a bill for three hundred-twenty dollars for four visits to Dr. Avery Blackwell, a psychiatrist with an office in La Jolla. "When I asked him about it, he just blew me off—said it was just a few minor issues he needed to work out with the shrink. The Gene you and I know is about the most mentally stable person there is; this whole thing is way out of character. I'm really worried; I asked you here to see if you might try to get through to him and find out what's really going on, for God's sake."

"Marie, if he won't talk to his wife, what makes you think he'll talk to me?"

"Jack, you're his best friend; all I ask is that you give it your best shot."

I obviously couldn't say no. We finished our meals while mostly engaging in small talk and agreed to meet again after I had a chance to interact with Gene.

That night I had a dream. Marie was sitting across from me at a table in some seedy bar. She smiled, stood up on her chair, and slowly pulled up her dress until her generous brown patch came into view. My God, she had nothing underneath! She pulled her dress over her head and tossed it aside as she smiled and stepped onto the table.

She then began a little dance as she moved toward me. I tried to reach for her, but my arms were hopelessly pinned to my sides. I even strained to get my face between her legs, but before she got close enough, loud clapping and cheering emanated from a big crowd that had surrounded us, enthralled by Marie's dance. Then out of the crowd marched Gene with a scowl on his face. He snatched Marie from the table and carried her into the crowd.

When I awoke, I again flashed on Exodus. Covet you neighbor's ass? Don't even think about coveting.

I called Gene's office number; he answered after the second ring. "Hi, Gene, it's about time for us to journey on another paradoxical run. Low tide is at eleven tomorrow morning; La Jolla Shores good for you?"

Gene showed up at the beach in his gray T-shirt, blue shorts, and black running shoes. At thirty-six he was in excellent shape, a six-foot-two bundle of muscular energy. When he talked, his blue eyes flashed high intelligence, and believe me, women picked this up quickly. Perhaps his only shortcoming from some female perspectives was his black hair with a few strands of premature gray, slightly receding and worn at medium length in contrast to the cooler long hair of the late 1960s. Long hair would likely be frowned on in the intelligence community. He often made creative jokes about my own long, sun-bleached, blond hair with contrasting brown mustache and sideburns.

Gene could easily keep up his usual pace of seven minutes per mile for ten miles. I was six years younger and a former track team guy, so I had to slow down from my ideal six-minute pace to talk easily with Gene. I relayed my experiences with Marco Oliver in Zurich in detail. Gene had several questions about my written record and seemed satisfied with my answers.

As we turned around at Scripps Pier, I changed the subject. "You have seemed a bit unhappy and distant—in a different world lately. What to talk about it?"

He didn't reply for several minutes; I imagined a conscious computer analyzing all the implications of my question. What motivated it? What was he prepared to tell me and when? And on and on until the majestic computer that was Gene calculated the correct answers and produced the output: "Marie got to you, didn't she?"

I was silent and thought, damn, I spent all this time planning on how to keep my promise to Marie to keep quiet about her involvement, and our little game was lost in just two minutes.

"For the life of me, I don't know how you win so often at poker," he said. "I can read you like a book."

I was silent for several minutes and then replied, "You may have said that as a joke, but your observation has a serious side. Perhaps my transparency is easily explained; my unconscious self is highly uncomfortable with being even a little dishonest with you. Deep down, I guess I really wanted to be found out.

"For essentially the same reason, seasoned poker players advise their friends never to play if they feel guilty about something. The unconscious tries to erase the guilt by throwing money into the pot. It seems like Freud has been vindicated."

Gene considered this. "I think many of Freud's ideas are complete crap—penis envy, dream interpretations, and so forth—but I concede that you may have a good point about the unconscious, although the idea didn't originate with Freud."

"We are drifting away from the original topic," I said. "I want to know what the heck gives with Gene Stanford. Why are you seeing a psychiatrist?"

Gene hesitated for a minute or so. "The Colonel and I have a new project leading to even more explosive revelations. Lately I have really been feeling the weight of this knowledge. Dr. Blackwell, my psychiatrist, has helped some, but I can talk to him in only the most general terms. Are you familiar with term *cognitive dissonance*?"

"No, never heard of it."

"Dr. Blackwell explained it to me as mental discomfort experienced when someone holds two or more contradictory beliefs at the same time. We humans strive for internal consistency. When inconsistency or dissonance is experienced, we can become psychologically distressed. That, in a nutshell, is my problem."

"I suppose that makes sense," I replied, "but your nature as a scientist is to seek the truth no matter where it leads you. The solution seems simple: just choose the correct ideas or beliefs and drop the bad ones. Bingo, no inconsistency. Problem solved."

Gene looked aggravated. "If only it were that simple. We all have basic beliefs that start being implanted early in childhood. In my case I grew up in a super patriotic military family. I chose a career based on my desire to help keep America safe and strong. I had long assumed that most in military or government service shared those beliefs. But, since joining IPS, I am discovering things that call this idealized picture into serious question."

"You mean the Hoover-CIA-Mafia connections and all that stuff? Is there more?"

Gene nodded his head. "A lot more, but first I have some more homework for you. Let's talk again in a week or so after you have completed your reading assignments. Don't worry about reporting to Marie. I'll explain my cognitive dissonance issue to her in very general terms. I should have done so sooner."

The next day I hiked from my house over to the UCSD library and looked up publications on cognitive dissonance. Several things stood out. Dissonance may be so uncomfortable that the afflicted person will go to great lengths to reduce it. He or she will actively avoid situations and information that would likely increase it. What did this imply about Gene's future? Would his work with the Colonel just make his mental problem progressively worse? I had no idea.

Chapter 18

I spent most of the next several weeks in the UCSD library learning about nuclear weapons policy in the Cold War environment as Gene had instructed. Our planned meetings were delayed because Gene was often away on trips to Washington and places unknown.

After a long absence from my chosen profession, I dropped in one evening at Bicycle Bill's. Fast Eddie was in his usual mode of nonstop stories, offering bets on almost anything and winning big. I played for two hours, but my heart just wasn't in it, so I cashed in. Eddie actually seemed disappointed to see me go. Maybe he had thoughts of rescuing his bruised ego at my expense, or maybe he just enjoyed the challenge of facing me—maybe a little of both. At about nine in the evening, Ruthie and I walked down the street to the bar; she sensed that something had changed.

'I'm doing consulting work these days—not so much time for poker," I said, downplaying my London casino cover story. I didn't fully appreciate it at the time, but this evening essentially marked the end of Jack Box's career as a professional poker player. My job with Gene made my card room experiences seem trivial by comparison. As in my transition away from Astro seven years earlier, a new life lay ahead.

One morning Bob and I were having a late breakfast in the family room. Bob went to answer our front doorbell. An attractive woman of about thirty-five with a flushed face and seemingly out of breath had come a-calling. She was dressed in workout clothes and pranced in like Rudolph the Red-Nosed Reindeer, bouncing from place to place with more energy than ten barrels of monkeys. After a brief hello, she disappeared with Bob into his bedroom.

About ten minutes later, she bounced out of the bedroom and out our front door, yelling over her shoulder, "See you in two hours." I heard her car leave our driveway, or maybe it was her sleigh. A little later, Bob emerged, looking totally drained. "Oh, Jack," he said, "That woman is beautiful but she wears me out; maybe I'm getting old." He hit the couch like a cadaver tossed in its coffin.

From his prone position, he gave me a briefing. Susie was a happily married aerobics instructor. She loved sex, and her energy level was off the map. Possibly her husband was unaware of the full spectrum of her exercise routine. Susie had promised Bob that she would return from her aerobics class in two hours for another quickie. Bob hurried back to his room to catch enough rest to be ready for the pending storm. I felt just a bit sorry for him; hopefully I wouldn't have to call for an ambulance after her upcoming visit.

With the additional money due me in Zurich and my new hours working on Gene's studies, I had plenty of bucks to spend or, better yet, invest. I picked up the phone. "Hey, deSilva, my uncle from Antarctica died and left me a whole warehouse full of penguin guano. I'm looking to buy more of your tacky little houses. Got any tips on how to proceed?"

DeSilva laughed. "You seem pretty good at selecting our product. Unlike most of my investors, you also have plenty of free time to shop around. Here's an action plan that can help both of us. Drive around several well-kept middle-class neighborhoods. Find some nice quiet streets and maybe some little jewels on cul-de-sacs. Give us a list of areas and houses. My boys will leaflet the neighborhoods with offers to buy houses outright, as is, with no commission. If we get too many takers, I'll just buy the extras for my own inventory, assuming I like your choices."

"No commission? How can you make money this way? Somehow I don't see you as running a charity."

DeSilva explained, "Simple. You just pay me six percent up front. As before, I'll take promissory notes. Remember, we expect to buy below market because we're not all that particular about the houses we get, as long as they meet our general criteria. Often these are divorce situations, and the owners want to move their houses quickly with no up-front expenses. Of course, I also expect you pay me for ongoing management."

I followed deSilva's plan, focusing on houses on quiet streets with minor charms like private backyards. A week later I had compiled a detailed list. "I'm placing an order for six houses," I told him. How nice it was to have contacts with the upper class; it gave me such opportunities for easy money. This crony capitalism made poker playing look hard.

I arranged a quick round-trip flight to Zurich to visit Marco Oliver, this time skipping London entirely. I presented him with a new invoice for work plus travel expenses coming to a little more than eight thousand dollars. Oliver counted out the green men from his favorite goody box. Counting the cash I had brought with me, I had about ten thousand. I had no new documents to feed the security box. Following my earlier strategy, I mailed five thousand directly to Mandy.

I flew out of Zurich directly to New York. When I arrived at the immigration deck, an official questioned me about the five thousand in cash I had declared. A full search of my luggage revealed an additional $153 that I had forgotten all about. I was let go with a stern admonition; the $153 was confiscated. It dawned on me that this event might alert the IRS; I told myself I'd better make sure to contribute generously to Uncle this year.

Over the next two months, I used a little over nine thousand for down payments on six new houses. As with my first house, deSilva took his six percent off the top in paper. His banker friend arranged the six 95 percent loans, filling in all kinds of vague and misleading answers on my loan applications. I just held my nose and signed.

In March of 1971, I met Gene in the parking lot of Los Peñasquitos Canyon, just off Black Mountain road, about seven miles inland from Del Mar. Its name means "little cliffs," appropriate to its beautiful canyon views. A stream runs through the forest of live oaks for about five miles. Gene had suggested the new running venue in celebration of my pending retirement from the poker business. We shared our adventure with friends well adept at keeping secrets—the birds, bobcats, deer, and coyotes.

Gene got to the point quickly. "A lot has happened since I last saw you. Before we get into anything classified, let's go over some recent history. For some time the United States and the Soviets have largely adopted the doctrine of mutually assured destruction, or MAD, as named by mathematician John von Neumann, well-known for inventing game theory.

"Here's the basic idea. The actual use of sufficient nuclear weapons by opposing sides would cause complete destruction of both attacker and defender. Such threat is then an effective deterrent in which neither side, once armed, has any incentive either to initiate conflict or to disarm. But in his book *On Thermonuclear War*, Cold War strategist Herman Kahn argued that MAD, when pushed to extremes, becomes absurd. These ideas were parodied in the film *Dr. Strangelove*."

"Yes, I saw the movie several years ago," I replied. "I've thought about it a lot during your latest reading assignments. I can see several fallacies in MAD right off the bat. One is the assumption that both sides will behave rationally. You made essentially the same mistake at the poker table. In the movie all it took was one psychopathic general to end the world on his own initiative. In real life, that might be unrealistic, but the possibility of accident or miscommunication is very real."

Gene approved. "Your assessment is right on the money. But let me ask you another question. How many nuclear warheads do you think we need to deter the Soviets from attacking us? Or a similar question—how many warheads do the Soviets need to send America to the bottom of the third world?"

I thought about it. "Well, if you equate one warhead to one city destroyed, I would guess no more than a few hundred. That's also roughly the number of US cities with populations greater than one hundred thousand."

"Good, Jack; you've been doing your homework. Nobody really knows the answer, but it could be much lower. Maybe you only need ten well-placed nuclear bombs to devastate America for the next hundred years. Suppose you take out New York, Washington, Chicago, Los Angeles, and the San Francisco Bay Area. Millions of survivors would have radiation sickness, and there would be few doctors left to care for them. Think of all the expertise in our technological society that would be erased instantly. Kill too many engineers, and your society collapses.

"And how many warheads do we actually have? Here I will pass on the classified figures. The United States has about thirty thousand and the Soviet Union about fifteen thousand. Why does either side need so many? You can only kill people once."

I had no answer to this. It seemed that the military was just playing some version of the well-known parlor game "my dick is bigger than yours."

As we continued our run across a small footbridge over the stream, several girls on horseback approached us. We moved off the trail to let them pass; the girls smiled and waved. They were quite pretty and animated and their horses big and healthy. The forest was beaming with life; several crows flew into a nearby tree. I saw a deer in the distance. A beautiful, vibrant scene lay before us, in sharp contrast to our morbid discussion of death by nuke.

Mandy and I had dinner that night at the Market Café in Solana Beach. The restaurant was decidedly downscale in appearance, with worn plastic table covers and garish Mexican paintings on its dingy walls. It looked to be transported right out of Tijuana, but the water was wet and perfectly safe. My favorite waitress, Isabel, was her usual friendly self. She served us Negra Modelo in huge glasses. The tacos and rellenos were excellent. I briefly pondered that the director of my recent dream about Marie in the starring role might have chosen the Market Café as his stage. But, why did my mind flash on Marie when I was having such a good time with Mandy? As psychiatrists and poker players will tell you, such secret messages from the unconscious can be interesting.

After dinner Mandy and I returned to my house in La Jolla to find an unscheduled party in progress. My housemates, Bob, Ava, James, and Mary, were all there, along with a dozen or so of their friends whom I didn't know. Music was playing; some people were singing along, and some were dancing. The environment was friendly and inviting; Mandy and I joined in without much forethought. Some were smoking joints, but Mandy and I stuck with wine.

During intervals between dances, we all introduced ourselves. I became engaged in a serious conversation with Gabriella, a pretty Italian girl with long jet-back hair. Vietnam, always lurking in the background during these years, came up. She was a UCSD graduate student in philosophy, no less, working under Marxist philosopher Herbert Marcuse.

I would have loved to impress Gabriella with inside information from Gene, but that was out of the question. Once I had attempted to read one of Marcuse's books but found it impenetrable. If it had been science, I would have tried harder, but with philosophy my motivation was limited. On the other hand, I had attended one of his talks in the UCSD quad and listened to an interesting discussion about free speech. Is speech really free when only a few plutocrats have genuine access to substantial numbers of citizens through the mass media? This seemed to me to be a critical question in any so-called democracy, but the issue seemed largely ignored in most circles.

I asked Gabrielle for a brief summary of Marcuse's positions.

She obliged. "As you may know, Marx believed that capitalism exploits people. Laborers become alienated; this ultimately dehumanizes them to functional objects. Marcuse adopted this view and expanded it. People identify with their commodities; they find their souls in their automobile, hi-fi set, and home. Under capitalism humans become extensions of the commodities they buy."

An old adage came to mind: *Under communism man exploits his fellow man. Under capitalism the reverse is true.* California conservatives were up in arms against Marcuse, not for any specific actions but just because of his ideas. Governor Ronald Reagan pressured UCSD to fire Marcuse, essentially finding him guilty of "thought crime," as depicted in George Orwell's novel *Nineteen Eighty-Four.* But in this case, university administrators actually displayed some guts and resisted Reagan.

Not surprisingly, Bob was closely engaged in conversation with Mandy; after all, he did have impeccable taste. Eventually our small talk led to an animated discussion of Mandy's job at the Body Shop. Mary and Gabriella seemed especially curious.

We were all sitting in a circle, and Gabriella turned toward Mandy. "I'd really like to see your professional dance routine. Why don't you just get in the middle of our circle here and show us your stuff? I want to see it all." The circle occupants responded with laughter, loud clapping, and supporting comments. "Yes, yes. Do it."

Mandy was clearly embarrassed; she really didn't want this. I was about to rescue her with some lame excuse, but then Gabriella upped the ante. "Come on, Mandy. If you agree, Mary and I will join you."

Mary looked shocked. This latest offer was news to her, but she kept quiet. Ava then piped up. "OK, count me in too." Mandy's resistance disappeared. I retrieved my tape of *City of New Orleans*, popped it into the cassette player, and we were off to the races.

As soon as she heard her signature song, Mandy was transformed. She entered the circle and began her dance with her usual enthusiasm. The three amateurs in waiting were uncertain if they should join Mandy right away or wait. They turned to me, veteran Body Shop customer number one, to tell them how the pros did it, but in the end they did whatever they wanted.

Each woman did a provocative number in turn. In the first round, Mandy and Gabrielle removed their shoes and danced in their dresses; then they slyly removed their panties. Every once in a while, the dresses would somehow rise high enough to show just a little bit of bush. Mary and Ava were more modest.

In the second dance round, to the delight of all us dusty old men, all four dancers ended their dances naked. They were rewarded with standing ovations. I kept Johnson under control long enough for some scientific study. Mandy was petite with brown hair and small breasts; Gabrielle had a medium build, black hair, and large breasts. These two entertainers provided an interesting contrast, but each was beautiful in her own way. Our favorite nurse Mary was of medium height and build, blond top to bottom, and also very beautiful.

I found Ava very interesting even though she was a little overweight and, at age forty, sagging in the usual places. She had been my good friend for several years, but I had never had the pleasure of observing her naked. She sported a huge patch of red pubic hair, perfectly matching her hair on top. From the lecherous look on Bob's face, I suspected they would have quite a hot night together. Forget the energetic aerobics instructor—for this night anyway.

After her dance Mandy looked for her dress and panties, but I had them hidden. I had suddenly gotten the impulse to play Tarzan to Mandy's Jane. I offered her clothes, but when she approached, I threw her naked body over my shoulder, turned to the crowd, and bit them good night. This time I was the one to receive a standing ovation.

Later, as we lay next to each other, Mandy said, "Wow Tarzan, that was as good as it gets. I'm glad you didn't invite Gabrielle to join us in a threesome."

"What! That never occurred to me. Even if I wanted it, I would have asked you first."

She smiled. "Yes, I thought so. But did you notice Gabrielle's attraction to me? I think that's why she wanted to see me dance. She probably would have happily joined us in a threesome if invited."

It had never even entered my mind, but I finally got it. Gabrielle was lesbian or perhaps bisexual. And all the time I thought maybe she was hot for me. Evidentially my recent experiences with women had overinflated my self-image. Good God, Johnson, you ain't nothing but a hound dog's schmuck.

Chapter 19

The following Monday night, Bob and I hopped in my 1962 Chevy and headed for a local theater where the first Ali-Frazier fight was to be shown on a closed circuit broadcast. The fight was taking place live at Madison Square Garden in New York. Earlier we had purchased advanced tickets for fifteen dollars each. Ali won the heavyweight title in 1964 but was stripped of it for refusing induction into the armed forces in 1967. In Ali's absence, Frazier became champion.

Joe Frazier had an outstanding left hook; he was a tenacious competitor who attacked opponents with ferocity. Ali had remarkable speed and dexterity for a man of his size; he could float like a butterfly and sting like a bee. Both men were undefeated. The fight was interesting from a narrow sports perspective, but there was a lot more to it. The event transcended sports, becoming an extension of strife within the country. Ali had become a symbol of the antiwar movement during his government-imposed exile from the ring. If you backed Joe Frazier, you seemed to be favoring conservative America and were possibly even a war supporter.

The theater crowd got about as loud and disorderly as I had ever experienced it to be. Crazy dudes were up and down faster than the nudes in Sandstone's Jacuzzi. Bob and I cheered Ali on, but Smokin' Joe dominated the later rounds, knocked Ali down in the fifteenth round, and won a unanimous decision. Frazier was a great champion, but the political climate dominated the fans' choices—no fault of Smokin' Joe.

The next week Gene and I met again at Los Peñasquitos Canyon Preserve. As we headed out of the parking lot to the forest trail, Gene had some dramatic news. The Colonel and IPS had become new directors of an ongoing project to compile a classified history of the Cuban missile crisis. The project had been secretly initiated in the executive branch, possibly by McNamara in 1967 while he was still secretary of defense. President Nixon was apparently unaware of the project. IPS participation in McNamara's Vietnam War history was winding down.

Gene began with some background. "In the 1960 presidential election, Kennedy attacked Nixon from the right, claiming that the Eisenhower-Nixon administration had allowed a dangerous missile gap to grow in the Soviet Union's favor. But in fact, the nuclear balance was overwhelmingly to America's advantage as Kennedy well knew from intelligence briefings while still a candidate. The US nuclear arsenal consisted of intercontinental ballistic missiles, long-range bombers, and missile-equipped submarines. All told, the United States enjoyed about a nine-to-one ratio of warheads over the Soviets.

"Despite America's overwhelming nuclear preponderance, Kennedy ordered the largest peacetime expansion of military power—specifically, a colossal growth of its strategic nuclear forces. Beginning in 1961, this included deploying intermediate-range Jupiter missiles in Italy and Turkey, right next to the Soviet Union. From there, these nuclear missiles could hit Moscow and Leningrad in just a few minutes. So here is your first exam question, Jack. What are the military implications of placing missiles so close to the Soviet power center when you already have an overwhelming military advantage?"

I knew Gene would not let me get by with some superficial answer, so I took a long time to answer. "Well, the obvious thing that comes to mind is that we are locked in an arms race with the Soviets, so we just keep adding more and more weapon systems in order to stay ahead. My dick has to grow faster than your dick. But I see problems and paradoxes with this viewpoint."

"OK, go ahead," said Gene.

I flashed on the critical difference between my casino and small card room experiences. "Hitler's annexation of Austria in 1938 and invasion of Poland in 1939 were essentially zero-sum games with a clear winner and loser. When I play poker in San Diego, I'm charged only a small hourly rate—pretty close to a zero-sum game. In contrast, cutting pots, as practiced in casinos, is not zero-sum for the players. If the cuts are large, no player can ever win in the long run. It seems to me that while some conventional wars can approximate zero-sum games, nuclear wars are never going to; everybody always loses."

Gene interrupted me. "Hold on; you have forgotten something. If one side has overwhelming nuclear superiority but is worried about the other side catching up, doesn't it make sense for the strong side to completely destroy the weak side at the outset, effectively winning the game once and for all?

"In fact, the Berlin crisis of 1961 caused a number of military planners to consider a preemptive strike against the Soviets. The fictional general Jack Ripper was not entirely fictional. If successful in wiping out Soviet nuclear capability, could this not have been an action close to zero-sum?"

I replied, "But to continue our discussions of last week, the Soviets might still deliver sufficient power to send America to the bottom of the third world. You can't guarantee taking out all the missile silos, bombers, and submarines, even in the best-case scenario. Also, what would be the long-term implications of killing millions of innocent people?

"Let's forget the moral implications, which don't seem to concern some of our leaders so much. If we initiated nuclear war, America would be correctly labeled a mass murderer, subject to all kinds of revenge terrorism and suffering conventional, biological, chemical, and nuclear attacks in the long run. In fact, I would even anticipate substantial retaliation by ordinary US citizens against their own government if their children were killed and their lives ruined."

Gene nodded. "Fortunately, the kinds of arguments you just expressed prevailed, and no preemptive strike took place. But now look at the picture from the Soviet side. Imagine yourself as Khrushchev; what do you see?"

I closed my eyes. "I see missiles newly deployed in Turkey just a few hundred miles away. Given America's overwhelming nuclear superiority, this action makes sense only as part of first-strike planning. Maybe there's a way out. Suppose I put nuclear missiles in Cuba? Kennedy will crap in his pants. Chances are we can then trade Cuba's missiles for Turkey's missiles."

Gene approved but added, "The Cuban missile crisis demonstrates with shocking clarity the dangers created when one or both sides fear preemptive strike. But it gets much worse. With the invention of intercontinental ballistic missiles, or ICBMs for short, launch on warning has become an integral part of the doctrine of mutually assured destruction, that is, MAD. Under this strategy, a retaliatory strike is launched upon warning of enemy nuclear attack, while its missiles are still in the air and before detonation occurs. Obviously, this raises stakes beyond all reason. All it takes is some glitch in a computer or radar system to start a war on false warnings."

I was shaken by Gene's boldface picture even though I already knew parts of it. "The implication of your summary is that many of our political and military leaders are psychopaths."

Gene shook his head. "No, I would say that, as individuals, most of the people involved are making informed decisions that appear rational in the short run. For example, one can argue that Khrushchev's decision to put missiles in Cuba was a rational response to the real threat of a US first strike. We may not agree with the benefit of hindsight, but his actions are consistent with his limited knowledge. Maybe the appropriate descriptors are *mob mentality* and *groupthink*. In this case, the mob consists of both Americans and Soviets. It's the mob that has become psychopathic, even if most of the individuals who make up the mob are sane."

Gene had one more bomb to drop into my overstuffed brain. "The Soviets still fear US first-strike capability. The Colonel recently obtained an interview with a high-level defector. According to this guy, Soviet scientists are conducting research on a new system to be called the 'Dead Hand' to provide them with fail-safe deterrence. It will automatically trigger the launch of Soviet ICBMs if a nuclear strike on its soil is detected by seismic, light, radioactivity, and overpressure sensors."

I reflected on this new bombshell. Essentially, the Dead Hand would be a computer with eyes and ears; the new computer would be in charge of the world's fate. If the Dead Hand were implemented, the fictitious doomsday machine from *Dr. Strangelove* would no longer be fictitious.

That night my sister Esther called with some real bad news. Mom's car had been hit by a drunk driver on her way home from her job at the grocery store. "She's got a concussion, broken nose, and extensive bruising all over her body. She's still in a coma."

I was terrified. "Come on, Esther, what does the doctor say about her chances? Give me the full story; what about the coma?"

"Jack, I just don't have more information. We're all on pins and needles. Are you coming?"

Bob was browsing our refrigerator in his usual search for something healthy as I relayed the news. "This kind of thing is really tough; all I can do is to wish you and your mother the best and a good outcome."

I called Mandy and told her I was off to Florida the next day. Thankfully, nobody tried to comfort me with foolish statements like

"These things happen for a reason." True, the reason was obvious: some asshole was driving drunk.

I flew to Atlanta and changed to an Orlando flight. I rented a car and arrived at the hospital near Cocoa Beach in the early evening. I was prepared for the worst—maybe Mom was already dead.

I entered her hospital room to be greeted by my brother and sister and their spouses. I was quite taken aback; they were all smiles.

In the bed, Mom was sitting up. Her face was mostly covered by bandages, but she managed a weak "Hi, Jack, nice of you to join the party." It turned out that she had come out of the coma just after my plane had left San Diego.

The drunk driver had fled the scene, but some Good Samaritan had recorded his license plate. The bastard was arrested but immediately freed on bond. His father owned a local car dealership; their family was rolling in the green stuff. It was unlikely that the playboy prick would ever see jail time.

Mom left the hospital in one week; she had improved dramatically. We had plenty of time to catch up. She had an occasional boyfriend but didn't seem to have any interest in remarrying. She was really enjoying the three grandchildren generously provided by Daniel and Esther. Mom quizzed me about my plans, if any, to contribute to this urchin population, but I tried to change the subject. Parenthood was the last thing on my mind.

My attempt at this sneaky diversion didn't work. "OK, Jack," Mom said, "Let's get down to brass tacks. Esther has given me most of your story. You don't have a regular job. You waste your time playing poker. Your girlfriend runs around naked. If Conner were alive, he would probably be in shock. Good Lord, he might have even returned to the Church for confession. Lucky for you I am far more broadminded. What's this girl's name? Oh yes, Esther told me, it's 'Mandy.' Just what the heck is going on?"

"Mom, that's too many questions all at once. In the first place, my poker profession is temporary. I have already started a consulting career and my poker days are limited. And Mandy doesn't run around naked. She's a professional dancer in a club where the environment is very tasteful."

Mom laughed. "Sure it is. Let's get serious. Do you love this girl? Are you going to become a Mormon and have a dozen wives? You're thirty years old. Just what do you plan to do with your life?"

"Yes, I love Mandy, but I don't see us as ever getting married and contributing little scouts to your troop of grandchildren. I prefer to remain free, as least for the next few years. Mom, you just said we should get serious so consider this. Surely you appreciate the enormous pressures on Dad to support three children on his meager salary, not to mention the period when he was laid off? I don't want to set myself up for that kind of desperate life.

"Then there is the Vietnam issue. The dishonest, barbarous behavior of our government has spilled over into other areas, causing reevaluation of many social conventions; it's a counterculture revolution. My attitude, as well as Mandy's, about human relationships has been influenced by these global events, perhaps far more profoundly than you can appreciate. For one thing, we're much more experimentally inclined than your generation."

Mom thought this over for awhile. "OK, Jack, I do appreciate what you are saying, but you have exaggerated Connor's trials and tribulations. In spite of the stress and hardship, he was genuinely delighted with his family. He loved us without limit; we were his whole life. You go on with your experiments if you must, but I think that eventually you will come to value my generation's more sober choices. In the meantime, keep me up to date, and remember how much I love you. I only want you to be happy."

Mom and I hugged and said goodnight.

With plenty of free time, I looked up my old high school buddy Sam. In high school Sam was tall and thin; he had placed fourth in the class-A state championship 880 yard run in 2:03. He had put on a lot of weight—mostly muscle, it seemed. He looked pretty formidable even in the full light; forget the dark alleys.

Sam had entered the University of Florida in Gainesville upon high school graduation in 1958. He partied nonstop with his fraternity and flunked out after one semester. Sam then joined the army for a four-year stint and obtained training in electronics there. He also took up regular weight lifting. He had a good job and seemed to be happily married. We had great laughs recalling the sophisticated woman Sam had wanted to pick up in our high school years. "I still say I would have had her tucked snugly in my bed if you hadn't stopped me," he said half-seriously.

Sam loved country music. "Look," he said, "I have to work late tomorrow, but why don't you meet me for some live music at the Redneck Mother Bar and Grill at nine?"

I got the address, showed up at half past eight, and found an empty table near the jukebox. I ordered a local beer and selected "LA Freeway" by Jerry Jeff Walker while I waited for the band to begin their gig. The lyrics nicely matched the bar's ambiance. Jerry Jeff sang,

Pack up all your dishes.
Make note of all good wishes.
Say good-bye to the landlord for me.
That son of a bitch has always bored me.
Throw out them LA papers
And that moldy box of vanilla wafers.
Adios to all this concrete.
Gonna get me some dirt road back street.

A buxom waitress with sparkling blue eyes served my beer and said, "Where you from, handsome? You sure ain't from here."

"California," I replied. "Just visiting my mom."

Some rough-looking drunk with snakelike eyes at the next table overheard and said, "California, huh? Lookie the blond hair. Is this kid a he or a she?' The other two guys at his table laughed. The taunts continued, "Hey, queer, where's your lover boy?" and on and on.

I knew I should have just left, but I simmered as I remembered the guy who cold-decked me in Bob's Cardroom with his sneering snake eyes. I also flashed on the drunk who nearly killed Mom, now out on bail. But I kept control, finished my beer, and got up to leave. At that point, Snake Eyes grabbed me by the shoulder and spun me around. I put my hands up to my eyes like I was about to cry and said in a quivering voice, "Please, I don't want any trouble, sir. Maybe you would like me to give you a blow job?"

Snake Eyes smirked and relaxed his defenses just a little. My flashing elbow caught him square in the face. I backed up and executed a perfect leaping kick to his balls. Down he went like he had been hit by a freight train. His head smashed against a chair, and he quickly folded into a wimpy fetal position.

He lay crying on the floor, screaming, "That little queer kicked me in the balls!" His two friends approached me sporting broken bottles. My heart was racing; these guys could do serious damage to me. I backed away toward the door, ready to run faster than I ever had run before, but a voice behind me said, "Relax, Jack; I can finish up here, or maybe you would prefer to castrate one of these punks by yourself?"

The menacing presence of Sam was enough to persuade my attackers to gather up Snake Eyes from the floor and limp home to their redneck mothers, or whatever.

When I reflected on the incident, I pondered the implications of my limited karate skills. As a black belt, I might even have killed Snake Eyes and ended up serving serious jail time, especially if the bastard had local connections.

Sam and I retreated to his living room and traded old stories until two in the morning. We agreed to get together again soon. The next day I bid good-bye to Mom, Daniel, and Esther and flew back to San Diego.

Chapter 20

After my redneck encounter, my motivation for karate training found new life. I made a triumphant return to the Solana Beach gym after missing three weeks of lessons.

My instructor, Hiroshi Hashimoto, and his partner, Lester Ingber, welcomed me back and asked about my mother's health.

"She's doing great; thanks. We were lucky. Unfortunately, the drunken kid that hit her and fled the scene got immediate bail. He will probably never serve jail time. His father owns a local car dealership."

Lester was dressed in his karategi, the familiar white karate outfit with black belt. He shook his head. "I often see it in my classes. Some rich kids grow up in such overprotected environments that they don't do well in fair competition. So they spend their efforts using their money and wealthy contacts to rig competitions in their favor. Here I include the ability to avoid penalties for crimes or using contacts to avoid the draft as categories of competition."

Lester looked me in the eye. "You seem to have behaved honorably in Florida; however, I do not believe the Funakoshi School has ever suggested the offer of a blow job as a means to distract an opponent." He laughed. "Who knows? Maybe you have broken new ground in the martial arts."

Mandy came to my house for a simple dinner; I grilled some burgers and topped them with extra veggies to promote our good health. "Hey," she said, "why don't we catch a movie? I hear *The Last Picture Show* is really good. It takes place in a small Texas town in the early fifties; it's supposed to be an Academy Award contender."

We hopped in my Chevy and headed for the theater in downtown La Jolla. For aesthetic reasons the director shot the movie in black-and-white. This approach was unusual for filmmakers at the time, but the dark comedy *Dr. Strangelove* had employed a similar strategy several years earlier. It worked for me.

Later as we lay in my king-size bed, I popped a question. "How'd you like to come to London with me next week?"

She squealed like a little pig riding a roller coaster, jumped on top of me, and seriously messed up my hair. We kissed with much gusto and things progressed nicely. When we finished our enthusiastic love making, the first thing Mandy said was "London! Jack, baby, did you really mean it?"

Gene and I met again for a run at Moonlight Beach. He was genuinely pleased that my mother was recovering nicely from the car crash.

I couldn't resist relaying my macho experience at the Redneck Mother Bar and Grill. Gene shook his head. "I'm glad you're OK, but you should have left the bar sooner. Suppose your friend Sam had been late. Your modest karate skills might not have saved you from the two guys with broken bottles. You rolled the dice and got lucky, much like the United States and Soviet Union in the Cuban crisis.

"After the Cuban missiles were discovered by American U-2 flights, the Joint Chiefs of Staff were unanimously in favor of a full-scale attack and invasion of Cuba. Their idea was to kill two birds with one stone— get rid of the missiles and Castro in one operation.

"The Joint Chiefs believed that the Cuban missiles would seriously alter the military balance, but McNamara strongly disagreed. An extra forty nuclear warheads in Cuba would make little difference to the overall strategic balance. The United States already had approximately five thousand strategic warheads, while the Soviet Union had only three hundred. Adding forty more in Cuba would not mean much for military purposes.

"All agreed, however, that the missiles would affect the political balance. Kennedy had explicitly promised the American people less than a month before the crisis that if Cuba should possess a capacity to carry out offensive actions against the United States, we would act. Kennedy could be crucified by the enthusiastic cold warriors for not looking tough."

I raised several questions. "So both the military and many of the civilian advisors were willing to risk nuclear war to get rid of missiles that were of questionable military value? They apparently expected the Soviets to back down. As I recall from mainstream press accounts, the military wanted to act swiftly before the Soviets had the chance to arm the missiles. Is that right?"

Gene replied, "That's right. Except the Colonel now has good information from high-level Soviet defectors that blows the strategy proposed by the military right out of the water. The critical information, which Kennedy and his military apparently did not know, is that the

Soviets had already deployed tactical nuclear missiles to Cuba. These battlefield weapons are short-range, intended for use against an invading army. Their warheads have explosive capacity nearly matching that of the Hiroshima bomb. Had a local Soviet commander fired one of these, it would have been the start of a general nuclear war."

A fundamental question entered my mind. "But were the local Soviets really in full command of the nuclear weapons? Didn't their use require Khrushchev's approval?"

Gene replied, "In theory, the strategic weapons that could reach Washington and much of the US mainland were under Khrushchev's control. We now know, however, that in addition to these nuclear-armed ballistic missiles, the Soviet Union had deployed one hundred tactical nuclear weapons to Cuba. The local Soviet commander there could have launched these weapons without additional codes or commands from Moscow.

"The US air strike and invasion that were scheduled for the third week of the confrontation would likely have triggered a nuclear response against American ships and troops and perhaps even Miami. Once American forces were attacked, there is no question that we would have responded with overwhelming nuclear force. The resulting war could easily have led to the deaths of a hundred million Americans and more than a hundred million Russians. The country we know would have ceased to exist."

My next question was "Do field commanders always follow orders? This would seem to be the essential question with so much at stake."

Gene said, "The issue of command and control is critical in any kind of interaction where there is risk of nuclear exchange. The United States viewed the shooting down of our U-2 spy plane to be a serious escalation of the crisis. It was decided that if a U-2 were shot down, the United States would attack. Khrushchev had reasoned just as we did: he did not want to provoke an attack. Therefore, he had issued orders to the Soviet commander in Cuba: 'Do not shoot down US planes.' But some Soviet soldier did it anyway. Fortunately, Kennedy backed off on the immediate attack plan.

"Arguably the most dangerous moment in the crisis involved a Soviet submarine that, unknown to the United States, was armed with a nuclear torpedo. Running out of air, the submarine was surrounded by American warships dropping depth charges and desperately needed to surface. An argument broke out among the captain and two of his officers as to whether they should attack the US ships. They were unable to communicate with Moscow to get orders—yet another instance where command and control has broken down. Finally, the captain decided not to attack but just come to the surface peacefully; some insiders now call him 'the guy who saved the world.'"

"Fortunately," Gene remarked, "the submarine captain was not the Soviet equivalent of US Air Force general Curtis LeMay, who pushed hard to bomb Cuban missile sites. He opposed the naval blockade that led to a peaceful resolution. After the end of the crisis, he suggested that Cuba be invaded anyway, even after the Russians agreed to withdraw the missiles. LeMay considered the peaceful resolution of the Cuban missile crisis to be the greatest defeat in our history."

A lot was going through my mind. "Let me summarize the information you have conveyed in our last two meetings. The United States put missiles in Turkey, only a few minutes' flight time from Moscow. Given the overwhelming advantage of the US nuclear weapons systems, the apparent motive, at least from the Soviet perspective, was to retain a first-strike option. This act in itself was very dangerous because it increased the chances of war by mistake. I have to conclude that this action was carried out by officials with extremely poor judgment at best; maybe the label *pathological* applies here."

Gene said, "Go on. What about the Soviets' response?"

"Well, Khrushchev was apparently quite traumatized by the Turkey missiles for understandable reasons. He also wanted to deter future US attacks on Cuba, both the overt kind like the Bay of Pigs and the ongoing terrorist activity perpetrated by the CIA and Cuban exiles. So he took a big gamble by sending missiles and nuclear warheads to Cuba. He really upped the ante. I would say poor judgment on his part but not totally crazy."

Gene said, "What about the US response?"

I replied, "It was a huge overreaction driven much more by expected political fallout than military considerations. The obvious practical solution was to make a deal with the Soviets to trade Cuba's missiles for the missiles in Turkey. This deal would have stabilized the situation, a win-win case with reduced chances for accidental war. In the end, both Kennedy and Khrushchev came to their senses and overruled

their nuttiest advisors. The Turkey-Cuba deal was, in fact, ultimately struck, but only after we came within a hair's breadth of nuclear war. The risks were totally unnecessary and incredibly stupid.

"As for the Jack Ripper act-alike, General Curtis LeMay, I nominate him for the medal of dishonor, 'Psychopath of the Decade.'"

Mandy didn't have a passport, so we delayed our London trip for several weeks. One morning she called me all excited. "My beautiful little passport just came in the mail. In order to be away for ten days, I've done some body trading with the other girls at the Body Shop. I'll be dancing five days this week.

"Jack, I'd really like it if you would come at least two or three times; it really turns me on to see you there watching me with your big smile and evil eyes so intent. And I don't mind at all that you watch the other girls wiggle their tushies at you, as long as they don't forget that you are my man."

What could I do? "Never piss off a naked woman" was my motto. "I'll be there tonight at about nine with a big load of tacos in hand. Those tushies need their nourishment."

I showed up as planned. My tacos and known relationship with Mandy always made me popular with the girls, and hey, let's be honest, all the five-dollar notes that I left on the stage didn't hurt either.

For a while I sat at the bar and struck up a conversation with an interesting guy with a large bushy beard. He had been involved in the free speech movement at Berkeley in 1965. It turned out he had grown up in Florida as I had. "So what part of Florida?" I asked.

"Cocoa Beach; I went to Cocoa High School," he replied.

"That's crazy." I said. "I went to Cocoa High School—graduated in 1958." We were actually in the same 1958 class but didn't recognize each other in 1971, what with his beard and my long hair and mustache. Here we were, two apparent strangers sitting in a bar in California. I tried to attach some profound significance to this strange coincidence but came up short. Oh well. I went back to the stage chairs to watch Laura dance, and boy, could she dance. Her waist-long hair and perfect body flew through the air, seeming to defy gravity. Eat your heart out Isaac Newton.

Mandy had never flown; she was both excited and scared. I must admit that I was charmed by her innocence in worldly affairs and general sweetness. She had only minimal interest in politics or science, but she loved art, an area in which I was a dunce. We had great fun together, but deep conversation between us was rare. All relationships have their trade-offs, I thought.

We flew San Diego to New York and on to London. After Mandy's initial nervousness regarding the flight, she surprised me with a question.

"I saw the way you looked at Laura when she danced; do you ever fantasize about sleeping with her?"

"What a question," I replied. "The answer is no; however, I did imagine discussing Einstein's field equations with her nude in a hot tub. But what brought this on? Are you planning a surprise birthday party for me where Laura pops out of a cake and joins us in a threesome? Or maybe the Body Shop wants to hire Johnson and me to join Laura on the stage for some real live action after you have drugged the undercover cop."

Mandy laughed and shook her head. "Sorry I asked."

After catching up on sleep in our hotel near Hyde Park, we caught the Tube to Charing Cross station, Mandy's first experience on an underground rail, London or otherwise. She was fascinated by the whole experience, especially the wide variety of passengers of different ethnic backgrounds. As an experienced dancer Mandy easily minded the gap.

We exited the station. It was then a short walk to Trafalgar Square and the National Gallery, which houses one of the largest and best collections of paintings in the world. Mandy was in hog heaven. After an hour or so, I got just a little bit bored of looking at one painting after another, but Mandy's enthusiasm made for a fun four-hour visit.

The next day we grabbed the Tube to Tower Hill station for a fascinating visit to Her Majesty's Royal Palace and Fortress, more commonly known as the Tower of London. This historic castle is located on the north bank of the River Thames in central London. Our charming tour guide filled us with fascinating castle stories and related British history.

On the third day, we walked from our hotel through Hyde Park to Buckingham Palace, the official residence of the queen. We then caught one of the red two-story tour buses and spent most of the day hopping on and off like good tourists are expected to do.

"Mandy, I must leave you for a day. But you now know your way around pretty well. With the Tube, it's easy to get anywhere in London. Why don't you visit more museums? Art is really more your passion than mine."

"Jack, why won't you tell me where you're going? Have you got some girlfriend over here? Better yet, take me with you. You're normally so honest with me; this secrecy gives me a bad feeling."

"Come on, Mandy, we already covered this ground. As I told you, my consulting work requires complete secrecy. You know that companies doing technical work keep details to themselves; otherwise competitors will steal their advances."

"I can't see why you can't even tell me what city you're flying to." She pouted for a while but finally let it go.

In preparation for this trip, I had completed my recording of Gene's latest revelations before leaving the United States. I made a quick round-trip flight to meet Marco Oliver in Zurich. My new report was placed in the security box under Oliver's watchful eye. I handed him my new invoice, and again he pulled out my favorite little box and counted out five thousand in Benjamins.

The $100 bill was the largest denomination that had been printed since 1969, when the denominations of $500, $1,000, $5,000, and $10,000 were retired to pasture. Damn, I wished I at least had one of the $1,000 bills with Grover Cleveland's picture; it would have really impressed poker players and naked dancers.

Mandy and I played tourist for several more days in London before flying back to San Diego.

Chapter 21

In June of 1971, the *New York Times* published the first of nine commentaries on a top secret document—seven thousand pages long—officially called *United States–Vietnam Relations, 1945–1967: A Study Prepared by the Department of Defense.* Shortly after, the *Washington Post* began publishing its own series of articles.

The study, labeled the *Pentagon Papers* by the media, had been copied and released by Daniel Ellsberg, a military analyst employed by the Rand Corporation. McNamara had created a task force for the purpose of writing an encyclopedic history of the war. He wanted a written record for historians, evidently to prevent policy errors in future administrations.

Gene called me a week later to arrange one of our so-called paradoxical beach runs. As we started north from the Solana Beach lifeguard station, Gene began. "The release of the *Pentagon Papers* may have set in motion a whole series of unpredictable events. I've never seen the Colonel so damn agitated. Of course, none of this so-called secret material is news to us. In fact, the papers represent a highly watered-down version of actual events. If the whole truth were appreciated by the general public, we might have a real revolution. Nevertheless, the Colonel is anxious to step up the pace of our information gathering. He's afraid of a severe crackdown on security; we may have only a little time left."

I responded, "As I understand it, only parts of the *Pentagon Papers* have been released. Also, this history was written by the Department of Defense, so I assume it's got to be biased."

Gene replied, "Yes, but in one sense that's what makes it so powerful; the government is admitting to a whole series of lies. But let's first start with some non classified history. The US government tries to sell the idea that the Viet Cong represent an uprising against an elected government. In other words, the Viet Cong are portrayed as terrorists sent by North Vietnam to cause trouble in the South. Amazingly, essentially the entire US mainstream media, including those who now oppose the war, have swallowed this lie hook, line and sinker. Our media regurgitate this crap even though the actual facts are available to anyone willing to dig for them.

"Vietnam has China on its northern border. Over a period of more than one thousand years, the Vietnamese tried to stay free from Chinese intervention and colonial rule. The Vietnamese don't want to be ruled by the Chinese."

I interrupted, "So, according to the *Pentagon Papers,* the main goal of the US incursion into Vietnam is to limit Chinese expansion. Let's suppose that this is a worthwhile goal. Given the historical conflicts between Vietnam and China, it seems to me that some sort of peaceful alliance between Vietnam and the United States might have been achieved easily—one that would guarantee Vietnamese independence from China, France, the United States, or anyone else. In other words a win-win solution. Am I missing something?"

Gene smiled. "You're getting ahead of my story; let's wait and see how realistic your peace plan might have been.

"During the mid to late 1800s, about the time of the American Civil War, the French conquered Vietnam and turned it into a French colony. The Vietnamese attempted to regain their freedom and engaged in armed resistance for many years. Eventually the underground struggle in favor of sovereignty and against colonialism was taken up by different clandestine communist organizations. In 1930, several groups overcame their conflicts and were able to form a union called the Indochinese Communist Party under a guy named Ho Chi Minh.

"By the time World War II broke out, the communists still controlled the best-organized and strongest anti-French underground groups. As an effective nationalist organization, they attracted many people who were not communist but shared the desire to kick the French out of their country. This began a fusion of communism and nationalism that would develop much more deeply during the Japanese occupation of Vietnam and later the effort by the French to destroy the Vietnamese independence forces."

Again, I interrupted. "This seems to be a key point. The typical Vietnamese farmer has little or no idea of what communism is all about. This farmer has never heard of Marx or Lenin. After all, many Americans are probably just as ignorant. Most of the so-called Vietnamese 'communists' are fighting for their homeland, not for some abstract idea that hardly anyone understands."

Gene went on, "That's right. The Viet Minh were first formed to oppose the French, but when the Japanese invaded, the Viet Minh fought an effective guerilla war with support from the American Office of Strategic Services, or OSS. In return, the Viet Minh helped rescue downed pilots and provided intelligence information to OSS agents."

"OSS? Wasn't that the precursor organization to the CIA?" I asked.

Gene replied, "Yes. In this limited sense, America and Vietnam were allies in World War II. By the end of the war, Ho Chi Minh was apparently a big fan of the United States, especially given our revolutionary beginnings. He reportedly had a picture of George Washington on his wall and kept a copy of the American Declaration of Independence on his desk.

"Apparently, Ho expected US support and recognition for his newly established government, the Democratic Republic of Vietnam. The Vietnamese Declaration of Independence of September 1945 begins, 'All men are created equal. They are endowed by their creator with certain inalienable rights; among these are Life, Liberty and the pursuit of Happiness.' At that time Americans were admired by the Vietnamese.

"Unfortunately, Vietnam was not to be left alone. For the next eight years, the French fought the Viet Minh in an attempt to reestablish their colony. Due to their superior firepower, they controlled the cities, but the Viet Minh controlled the countryside, and more and more of it as time went by.

"Beginning around 1950 and through 1954, the United States became France's sugar daddy, providing more than half of the cost of the war. The *Pentagon Papers* conclude that the US decision to provide France with massive aid set the course for future American policy, which was essentially to replace the French as a colonial power.

"The Geneva Conference was held in 1954 and officially registered France's defeat by the Viet Minh. It called for elections to unify combatants. The United States knew that Ho Chi Minh, a national hero, would win any such election, so they prevented it from happening. A South Vietnamese government was created by the Americans under the guise of democracy. The Viet Cong are essentially a later version the Viet Minh, specifically opposed to the South's government."

I responded, "You make it sound like the South had no broad Vietnamese support, but this can't be true. Surely, a substantial number of South Vietnamese oppose the Viet Cong."

Gene responded, "You are correct. But once you have a long history of war, people take sides depending on which side killed their friends and relatives. Also, there is a very substantial religious issue to consider. In South Vietnam the Buddhist majority comprises something like eighty percent of the population; the Catholics are a minority."

"How does religion affect the political alliances?"

Gene continued, "The first president of South Vietnam, Ngo Dinh Diem, was installed in 1955 with US support following the French withdrawal. Diem was a Roman Catholic who was biased in favor of Catholics in public service and military promotions, as well as in the allocation of land, business favors, and tax concessions. Some Catholic priests even ran private armies that looted villages and made forced conversions to Catholicism. Under Diem, the Catholic Church was the largest landowner in South Vietnam; the Vatican flag was regularly flown at public events."

The general picture seemed pretty clear to me. "From the start South Vietnam became divided on the basis of religious persecution along with its twin, unfair wealth distribution fueled by religious bias. We've seen the same dynamic repeat itself many times in other countries. But surely US government officials must have seen this as a recipe for disaster; what were they thinking?"

Gene answered, "Religious protests increased; a monk garnered worldwide attention when he set himself on fire with cameras rolling. Diem finally lost US support. He was assassinated in a coup d'état in November of 1963, just a few weeks before Kennedy's assassination. After Diem's assassination, South Vietnam was unable to establish a stable government, and several coups took place. The Diem coup d'état and its aftermath bolstered North Vietnamese characterization of the South Vietnamese as supporters of colonialism.

"The war has thus far resulted in the deaths of tens of thousands of American soldiers and more than a million Vietnamese, including many innocent civilians living in small villages. The United States has dropped more than ten million pounds of herbicide on Vietnam. Included are large quantities of dioxins. These chemicals are highly toxic and can cause reproductive and developmental problems, damage the immune system, interfere with hormones, and cause cancer."

"Oh boy," I said. "We are pursuing a chemical warfare campaign against Vietnam. The long-term implications are grim, even for the unborn Vietnamese."

Gene replied, "Yes, and don't forget that American soldiers are also being exposed. With these kinds of airdrops, the damage areas cannot be confined. A lot of future business for American VA hospitals is now being generated.

"Telford Taylor, a major in army intelligence in World War II, was the chief US prosecutor at the Nuremberg trials of Nazi war criminals.

He recently suggested that General Westmoreland and high officials of the Johnson administration could be found guilty of war crimes under the criteria established at Nuremberg."

I reflected on all this. The whole Vietnam exercise, draped in the mask of defense against communist evils, was nothing but a bright and shining lie.

We turned around when we reached Moonlight Beach in Encinitas and headed south back toward Solana Beach. Gene's tone was unusually hesitant. "I have to be honest with you, Jack. A lot of powerful forces could be unleashed, not so much because of the rather mild revelations of the *Pentagon Papers* but because of fear of much more damning releases. A lot of people will be looking to cover their fat asses. I'm afraid all of us may be at some risk. The Colonel is no wimp; when he gets nervous, we should all be nervous. All I can tell you is be careful."

That evening I worked up a simple code. The letter *A* was represented by 07, the letter *B* by 16 and so forth. I just picked the numbers at random for all twenty-six letters plus four punctuations marks, a total of thirty numbers. I then wrote in my code one page of an innocuous summary of my first London trip with emphasis on casino experiences, omitting any mention of my side trips to Oxford or Zurich.

The next morning I called my old friend Jim, who still worked at Astro. "Can we meet for lunch? I have a favor to ask."

Jim was a little pushed for time, so we met at a familiar place, the pizza joint just down the street from Astro Dynamics. I was only a little disappointed that they didn't seem to be offering topless go-go pizza anymore. The place was a lot quieter than I remembered. When I asked Jim about this, he answered, "Maybe all the girls with their twirling tassels got married or became real estate agents or something—who knows?"

I handed Jim a sheet containing my coded London trip report plus a short FORTRAN program. "Can you run this for me and get the printout on high-quality letter-size paper?"

Jim looked at my sheet and saw immediately that the program didn't seem to do much of anything useful. "Sure can do. But I have a sinking feeling you're not going to tell me what this is about. Maybe some scam involving your poker games? Or some joke? Or, better yet, something to do with impressing some chick?

"Thanks, Jim," I replied. "You are a wise man, not to mention a real wiseass. My beautiful girlfriend is not a 'chick.' She has nice fur, but not a single feather."

We spent the next half hour reminiscing over our past adventures. The next day I stopped by Jim's house and picked up the 107-page printout on high-quality letter-size paper. The first page would be fairly easy for spooks to decipher; the remaining pages were filled with random numbers on the interval 01–30, with nice, neat spaces so it read like 19, 07, 12, 09, 11, 14 and so on, making for 106 pages of random nonsense. My purpose was to allow some spook to easily decode the first page. I laughed as I imagined his frustration as he tried to make headway after that. I purchased a fancy binder and placed the nonsense report in the crappy little safe in my closet. For good measure I wrote the safe combination on a label and taped it to the underside of my toilet seat.

Chapter 22

In July, I again contacted deSilva with an order for three more tacky houses (well, "tacky" compared to my rented house in La Jolla), bringing my stash to an even ten.

DeSilva growled, "Don't get greedy, kid. You haven't paid last month's management fee or the payments on my notes. Are you sure you can afford more negative cash flow? Leverage is a great concept that I preach all the time, but with you maybe I've created a monster."

I laughed. "My check for sixty-five hundred is in the mail; that's fifty-four hundred for the new down payments plus eleven hundred for fees and notes. Don't worry about my finances, deSilva; I'm as flush as your toilet's best performance."

Wow, I said to myself after he hung up. What a load of bull. I was actually nearly broke—down to my last five hundred. But, I owned a lot more houses than most thirty-one year old guys. Well, let's be honest; the houses were actually owned by the banks holding my mortgages. I had only a small equity in each house.

A few days later, I left for Zurich via London to submit more reports and pick up another ten thousand from Marco Oliver. As usual I spent a few days in London in my fake poker-playing disguise. I even learned a little about stud poker—enough to get in trouble in serious games.

Shortly after my return to San Diego, Marie called to invite Mandy and me to dinner the following Friday. When I called Mandy to relay the invitation, she seemed to be in a sour mood. "No, I can't go; you know I have to dance on Friday nights. After all the time I took off for your London trip, I've used up my replacement options."

This seemed out of character for Mandy. Why did she say "*your* London trip," like it was entirely my fault? She seemed to have had such a great time; maybe getting back to her routine was too much of a letdown.

I showed up by myself at Gene and Marie's house with its fantastic view of La Jolla Shores. The sun was just above the horizon beyond the broad expanse of Pacific Ocean. After the usual small talk, we got down to a great steak dinner that the Stanfords' housekeeper and cook, Martha, had prepared. "How's your filet? Is it medium rare just the way you want it?" Marie asked.

The steak was perfect, and I finished my second glass of cabernet sauvignon. I sensed that Marie had something on her mind—something she had been holding back. I was not disappointed. "How's your relationship with Mandy going?" she offered as she feigned an innocent look.

When I replied, "Just great," too quickly, she raised a finger like a stern schoolteacher scolding a naughty little boy. "Come on, Jack, we have been friends too long for you to try to con me. Tell it like it is."

I looked over at Gene, who sported a wide smile but kept silent. Clearly he was enjoying his wife in action, making me sweat a little. I was lost for words, so Marie helped me along. "She's a real sexy girl with a sweet disposition; that counts for a lot. But, aside from sex, you have few interests in common. Mandy's main intellectual interests are in the art world. You have much broader interests in science, politics, and so forth, but your art appreciation sucks. I hesitate to say this because your ego has already run wild, but you are highly intelligent." Marie took obvious satisfaction in seeing me tongue-tied. "You see Mandy only two or three times a week. That schedule suits you just fine. But is that what she wants? What do you think?"

I was beginning to recover from Marie's surprise challenge and get my feet back under me. "OK, I'll come clean. Mandy has never actually complained about our part-time relationship. But she has recently expressed little quibbles like 'Our relationship doesn't seem to be going anywhere.' To which I reply, 'We have a great time together. Life is good. If it ain't broke, don't fix it.'"

Marie presented a victor's smile. "Let's see how long that lame excuse lasts."

Gene was ready to change the subject. "Jack and Marie, what do you know about warrants?"

Marie answered, "Somehow I think this is a trick question, but OK, I'll bite. A warrant is a document issued by a court that gives the police the power to do something. The cop comes to your door and says, 'I have a warrant for your arrest, you schmuck.'"

"Yes, that's one kind of warrant, but I doubt that cops normally refer to people as *schmucks*, which, by the way, is Yiddish for 'penis foreskin.' I'm interested in financial warrants, which entitle the holder to buy the underlying stock at a fixed price up to the date when it expires."

I understood the general idea. "So if I think some company—let's say IBM—is likely to go up in value over the next few years, I might buy a warrant that gives me the option of buying IBM stock at a fixed price. Suppose IBM is selling for $30 today and I buy a warrant that expires in five years with a settlement price of $40. If IBM does really well and its stock rises to $50 in the next five years, I can buy it from the company for $40 per share and immediately resell it for $50, pocketing the difference."

Marie jumped in. "That's too good, Jack. You're smart but not that smart. You already knew something about warrants, didn't you?"

"I confess. Once I got involved in using extreme leverage in real estate investments with your friend deSilva, I looked around for other vehicles providing leverage—a natural move for a professional gambler like me. Purchasing warrants is just another kind of leveraged bet."

Gene took on his professorial look. "OK so far. But first, only a few companies offer warrants. Your example of IBM is not appropriate; as far as I know, they have never offered warrants. Most importantly, right now, nobody seems to know how to price warrants."

Now I was really getting interested. "I spent a little time looking into the pricing issue but got stumped. My preliminary conclusion from running a few numerical examples was that warrants tend to be overpriced. If so, the main lesson for investors and poker players is *never buy warrants.* Case closed. But I have a feeling you're now about to enlighten us in some way."

Gene smiled. "I'm impressed, Jack; you know a lot more than I expected. I wonder if your warrant studies occurred during the hours I was paying you to do other things, but never mind. Let's see how well you can lay out the pricing problem."

I thought carefully. Gene was nearly always cordial. He never used his masterful intellect to ridicule us lesser mortals. On the other hand, his standards were sky-high. "Let's stick with IBM as the example since the actual stock is arbitrary," I said. "Today the stock sells for $30 a share. Let's say they are offering warrants for $3 that gives me the right to buy IBM for $40 anytime within the next five years."

Marie and Gene both nodded, so I continued, "The current $30 price essentially means that half the volume of bets are on the price going above $30 in the coming weeks and the other half are on the price falling below $30. This basically follows from the definition of a free market."

I was on a small roll. "If I buy a warrant under the conditions offered, I risk losing the $3 per-share warrant price plus the interest I might have made on this money over five years if I had never purchased the warrant. That's the easy part. The hard part is figuring my expected profit for the wide range of possible gains in the stock price. This issue is wrapped up in probability distributions reflecting predictions of how high the stock is likely to go over the prescribed time frame. Here is where I hit the proverbial wall."

Gene replied, "I have not fully figured out the pricing issue, but I have prepared some notes that I will gladly share with you. I'm far too busy on projects with IPS to spend much time on this, but you are more than welcome to use any of my preliminary work."

He then showed me a bell-shaped plot. "One may start with the assumption that price fluctuations follow a normal distribution." He went on for some time with more details. I gathered the notes for future reference and downed my third glass of cabernet sauvignon.

Gene had more financial wisdom to impart. "Did you hear that Nixon has just closed the gold window?"

Marie and I responded only with blank looks, so Gene expanded. "In 1958 a new international monetary system known as Bretton Woods became fully operational. Countries then settled their international accounts in US dollars that could be converted to gold at the fixed exchange rate of thirty five dollars per ounce. The United States was committed to backing every dollar overseas with gold. Other currencies were fixed to the dollar, and the dollar was pegged to gold. But after today, foreign governments can no longer exchange dollars for gold. We seem to be off the gold standard."

I responded, "Excuse me, but so what?"

Gene smiled. "No one can predict all the effects of Nixon's actions, but one thing's for sure: the long-term consequences will be huge. For one thing, gold prices will be going up—probably way up."

I couldn't know it at the time, but these events were to substantially influence the future of one Jack O'Malley.

In September of 1971, burglars broke into the office of Dr. Lewis Fielding, Daniel Ellsberg's psychiatrist. Ellsberg was the analyst who had passed on the secret *Pentagon Papers* to the media.

A few days later, Gene and I met for a run in Los Peñasquitos Canyon Preserve. It was early morning, the air was cool, and we were entirely alone on the trail except for several friendly deer and rabbits that magnanimously accepted our intrusion into their paradise.

Gene began right away. "The Colonel has discovered that the Fielding break-in was planned and executed at the highest levels. The motivation was to find information about Ellsberg's mental state. They needed something to discredit him. This could not negate the disclosures of the *Pentagon Papers,* but they wanted to discourage other leaks that were potentially far more damaging."

I interjected, "I see. It wasn't the *Pentagon Papers* that concerned them so much; that bobcat was already out of the bag. They wanted to send a message to potential leakers of the future."

"Yes," Gene replied. "Here are the details. In August, a secret meeting took place in a basement hideaway office in a building across from the White House. The group included former FBI agent G. Gordon Liddy, former CIA agent E. Howard Hunt, and Egil Krogh, the designated head of a group known as the Plumbers, a secret team of operatives charged with plugging information leaks.

"Hunt urged the group to carry out a so-called covert operation to discredit Ellsberg. Liddy claimed that the FBI had frequently carried out such 'covert operations,' a euphemism for burglaries or other illegal actions, in national security investigations. Liddy claimed he had even done some himself as an FBI agent. The actual break-in was apparently carried out by Hunt and Liddy, with assistance from others. Also involved with the Plumbers was John Paisley, director of the CIA's Office of Security.

"The Colonel has also learned that Hunt proposed drugging Ellsberg with LSD by dissolving it in his soup at a fund-raising dinner in Washington. The idea was to render Ellsberg incoherent by the time he spoke—that is, make him appear to be a burnt-out drug case—and thereby fully discredit him. The plot involved employing waiters from the anti-Castro Miami Cuban community. The plan was finally approved, but there was no longer enough lead time to get the Cubans in place. Thus, the plan was put into abeyance pending another opportunity."

We headed into the trail that followed the small stream through the live oak forest. Running conditions were ideal; the temperature was near sixty degrees and the surroundings beautiful. Gene said, "This is as good as it gets. Let's do a full ten miles today."

We came upon a small waterfall near the west end of the canyon. The tree line was sparse at this point, but since the day was cloudy, we were unconcerned with finding shade. We continued up a steep hill and came upon a pretty young woman who had fallen off her bicycle. She had twisted her ankle and suffered a few bruises but was otherwise OK. Her bicycle had a broken wheel, however.

We walked with her and alternated carrying her bicycle back to the far west end of the canyon where her car was parked. She was very grateful for our help, even slipping Gene a note with her phone number when she thought I wasn't looking. He just smiled and nodded.

I thought to myself, hey, I carried the bicycle half the time. How come I didn't get a phone number?

Gene and I continued our run in the opposite direction, returning to our cars at the east end of the canyon. When we parted, Gene said, "I don't think we've heard the last of the covert operations. See ya next week, and here's a present for you." He handed me the slip with the girl's phone number. I hesitated for just a moment before I tossed it away. Heck, she had chosen Gene over me. Anyway, 007 never rode bicycles; it might spoil his image.

Chapter 23

One night in October of 1971, Mandy came to my house in La Jolla in the early morning after finishing her dance routine at the Body Shop. I was deep in sleep, unaware of when she snuggled into bed. Mandy was still snoozing when I got up in the morning, so I went down to the kitchen to fix myself a coffee and enjoy a relaxed perusal of the *LA Times*.

Mary, barefoot and still in her pajamas, was fixing herself breakfast in the kitchen. Her blond hair was messed up like she'd just finished a wrestling match, but I found this even more attractive than her usual neat appearance. I joined her in the family room, and we engaged in a discussion of her career at Scripps Hospital. Up until then I hadn't appreciated that she had acquired substantial advanced training to become a nurse practitioner. I was quite impressed with her extensive medical knowledge; she probably knew more than many doctors. "The next time I'm in the hospital, I hope you're my nurse," I said.

After a while, she changed the subject. "I can't believe I let Gabriella and Ava talk me into taking off my clothes at our party. At the time it just seemed natural in the friendly and trusting atmosphere, but I feel a little embarrassed, just thinking about it."

I smiled. "Hey, I think you just nailed the issue with your choice of labels 'friendly' and 'trusting'. Our environment that evening encouraged freedom and experimentation; we all felt especially safe with each other. Even the Body Shop has managed to capture a tiny fraction of these kinds of feelings, at least on the nights when Mandy and her friend Laura are performing.

"And by the way 'Blondie', you looked absolutely beautiful in your dance routine. I'm sure you caused all the male observers to have sweet dreams over the following nights. It sure worked that way for me."

Mary returned my smile and winked. "Thanks Jack, you just made my day."

I returned to my bedroom to find that Mandy was just waking up. I rolled her over on her stomach and massaged the back of her neck. I then worked my way down her back, taking a long time to reach the bottoms of her feet. She turned over on her back and lay quietly with her eyes closed, not yet fully awake. She didn't seem especially receptive to more explicit advances so I went downstairs to fix her a coffee with cream and sugar.

A little while later we put on beach gear and headed for breakfast at Mr. T's in Solana Beach, grabbing a booth by the window. Candy, the friendly waitress, greeted us warmly, patted me on the arm, and brought us coffee. Mandy said, "She really seems to like you. Anything going on I should know about?"

I laughed. "No way, Jose. But I've been coming here to Mr. T's on a regular basis for several years. By now they know I like my eggs over medium, sourdough toast, crispy burnt bacon, and twenty percent tips."

After breakfast we walked a few blocks to the beach.

Mandy had been unusually quiet all morning, but now she spoke more forcefully. "We need to talk. We've always had an open relationship but never discussed just exactly what that means. In theory we are free to date and even sleep with other people, but under what conditions? Are we supposed to tell each other when this happens? Get permission ahead of time? Are extracurricular activities limited to a certain number of days per month? It's all up in the air."

I processed this for some time before answering. "You are absolutely right. I suppose I've avoided these questions because they're uncomfortable. The truth is that I would feel a little guilty sleeping with someone else without knowing you were OK with it."

I expected her to question me about my own recent sexual exploits, but Mandy responded with a different challenge. "And just how would you feel about me sleeping elsewhere?"

I was quite taken aback by this direct approach; Mandy was normally more subtle. "I'd be jealous, but not enough to try to stop you. We did agree to this kind of freedom, and I'm not a hypocrite. Are you trying to tell me you have recently slept with someone else?"

She looked at me intently. "No, I've kept my knees glued together. But I have recently become friendly with a fellow San Diego State graduate student named John. He's asked me out several times, but I've always said no. The other day he came to see me dance, and guess what? He's even more interested now. So I've been thinking—if we really have an open relationship, maybe I should accept. What do you think?"

I experienced a sinking feeling that my life was about to enter an unpredictable phase. All I could think to say was "If you want to try this guy, I won't try to stop you. Go ahead with my blessing. Afterward we'll see how we both feel."

I loved Mandy and, let's be honest; I really didn't really want her dating others. On the other hand, I had chosen maximum freedom for myself. True, I had reached the ripe old age of thirty-one, but I was still not ready to settle down with Mandy or anyone else. Vietnam, Gene's disclosures, and the entire counterculture seemed inconsistent with such constraints. On an intellectual level, I firmly believed in open relationships, but right then I felt like a poor lost soul.

After Mandy left the house, I grabbed my wet suit and fins and headed for the beach. The water temperature was sixty-one degrees, too cold for me to bodysurf without the suit. A good local swell had been created by a storm several thousand miles away. The six foot waves were long and smooth and came in sets of seven to ten. I caught one wave after another until it was nearly sunset, trying to distance myself from the day's depressing events.

That night I opened my third beer and sat down to watch the eleven o'clock news in our group family room. The news anchor was in the midst of describing Rancho Santa Fe, the super wealthy residential area just inland from Solana Beach. "...beautiful residences on lots of two to five acres or more are set back from the picturesque roadways winding through groves of eucalyptus trees."

I thought that was a pretty good description, but why was this stuff on the news? Then the guillotine blade fell, decapitating my relaxed mood. "...In 1954 George Stanford sold his company, Allied Military Systems, for three hundred million dollars...He was friend and confidant to many powerful leaders, including Dwight Eisenhower...Stanford is survived by his wife, Julia, and son, Gene.

"Police are calling it a probable hit-and-run accident. Stanford was walking his dog along a quiet residential street near his home early in the morning when he was evidently struck from behind by a speeding car..."

After gaining some composure, I called Gene's home and got Marie. "Yes, we're all in shock. As you can appreciate, Gene is not accepting calls right now; he's taking care of Julia. But I'll tell him you called."

I avoided the funeral since Gene was insistent that we downplay our relationship for security purposes. The following day I went to visit Gene at his home. When he answered the door, I gave him a brotherly hug and said, "Gene, I'm so sorry; I really don't know what else to say."

"There's really nothing you can say, but thanks for being such a great friend. Marie and I just have to go forward from here; my mother will need our full love and support. But, frankly, I'd prefer not to talk about it now; it just makes things worse."

On our beach run several weeks later, Gene briefly contradicted himself. "I'm not convinced that my father's death was an accident. He was standing several feet off the road when hit. The car, or more likely heavy truck, was going maybe fifty miles per hour on a two-lane backstreet. I've expressed this suspicion to the police, but they are noncommittal. My mother is thinking about hiring a private eye, but it's not clear he can do any more than the police."

Then Gene abruptly changed the subject. Talking about his father's death was probably too painful; better to discuss our project. "Today we focus on the CIA. Let's start with a brief history of CIA actions in South and Central America; it's mostly unclassified information. In 1954 a CIA-organized coup overthrew the democratically elected government of Guatemala. The reason for this US action was pressure from the United Fruit Company, whose land had been expropriated by progressive land reforms.

"This action was just one of many such interventions in which the taxpayer-funded CIA acted to protect a small group of US investors. As always, anti-communism was the excuse. Similar CIA-supported coups in the period 1954–1970 include Guyana, Ecuador, Brazil, Dominican Republic, Uruguay, Chile, and Bolivia."

I tried to summarize this history. "You could say that our CIA has been at war against the poor people of South and Central America for the past twenty years or so. The CIA has consistently put right-wing dictators in power, freeing US plutocrats to exploit these small countries for fun and profit."

Gene replied, "I partly agree, but I would modify your statement. The CIA was presumably carrying out the wishes of the executive branch, although they probably also initiated some of these actions on their own, perhaps forcing the hand of presidents concerned with reelection. In any case it might be more accurate to say that US political leaders have been at war with the poor people of South and Central America. Also, we don't know how well elected heads of government would have performed if they hadn't been overthrown. However, if democracy had been allowed to flourish, these countries would at least have had realistic opportunities to get good governments in the long run.

"And don't forget about the Iron Curtain. Between 1945 and 1949, the Soviets converted East Germany, Bulgaria, Poland, Hungary, Czechoslovakia, Hungary, and Albania into satellite states. Soviet-installed governments now rule these countries; the threat of communism is real."

"OK," I said, "so we are regularly setting up right-wing dictatorships, supposedly to prevent communist dictatorships. But, for the most part, the left-wing governments tossed out by the CIA were a long way from communism. The underlying goal seems to have been protection of American investments."

Gene nodded his head in agreement and went on. "The main point of my little history lesson is to reveal methods used by the CIA to achieve their goals, all in the name of so-called "national security." They employ bribery of military officers and propaganda campaigns against leftist third world governments. They create oppositional radio stations, engage in mass distribution of antigovernment leaflets, and anonymously submit newspaper articles painting progressive governments as communist."

I added, "It seems to me that George Orwell's novel *Nineteen Eighty-Four* anticipated the CIA. When you control the information, you control the society. As a result of the Colonel's probes, we now know that many in the mainstream media in the United States are paid under the table by the CIA. If their methods work outside the United States, they can work inside the United States."

Gene continued, "Now let's look at some of the CIA's domestic activities uncovered by the Colonel. Project MKUltra is the code name of a research operation for the behavioral modification of humans. MKUltra got its official start in 1953; it involves the surreptitious use of numerous methods to manipulate mental states and alter brain functions, including hypnosis, sensory deprivation, torture, and drugs like LSD. MKUltra involves research undertaken at universities, hospitals, prisons, and pharmaceutical companies. The CIA typically operates through these institutions using front organizations.

"In Operation Midnight Climax, the CIA set up whorehouses in San Francisco. The customers were given LSD without their knowledge. Using one-way mirrors, the fucking sessions were filmed for later viewing and study.

"LSD was eventually dismissed by the CIA as too unpredictable. But by 1962 the CIA and the army had developed a series of hallucinogens that were thought to hold greater promise as mind-control weapons.

"George White, the man in charge of Midnight Climax described his career in the following words: 'I was a very minor missionary, actually a heretic, but I toiled wholeheartedly in the vineyards because it was fun, fun, fun. Where else could a red-blooded American boy lie, kill, cheat, steal, rape, and pillage with the sanction and blessing of the All-Highest?'"

I was astounded. "Jesus. If you tried to put this crazy stuff in a novel, your editor would throw your ass out the door. It's just too far outside the normal person's reality framework to be taken seriously. Talk about truth being stranger than fiction."

Gene switched to CIA actions in Vietnam. "The current Phoenix Program seeks to attack and destroy the political infrastructure of the Viet Cong. Phoenix operatives kill or capture suspected VC as well as civilians who are thought to have information about the VC. Many are taken to interrogation centers and tortured in an attempt to gain intelligence on VC activities in the area. Few of the detainees interrogated survive; most are tortured to death. Those who survive the torture sessions are generally killed afterward; the number of Phoenix kills is in the tens of thousands."

I was feeling sick. The antiwar crowd had been criticized for exaggerating the US massacre of civilians as in the My Lai slaughter. But, in fact, the real situation was much worse than the protesters realized.

Gene went on, "Yes, unfortunately that's right. As you can see, the CIA has undertaken all kinds of illegal and immoral operations in the past; they have essentially no real oversight by Congress and a huge budget. It's not even clear that a president could control them if he wanted to. The Colonel and I are treading on very thin ice. To be frank, you are not entirely high and dry either."

Several weeks later I was awakened at five in the morning by loud banging and shouting. What was going on? Don't these bastards know I usually sleep past ten? I got out of bed in a grumpy mood, walked to the top of the stairs, and heard Bob say, "Who is it?" followed by a badass, harsh voice saying, "Police; open up!"

In marched half dozen bulky dudes with menacing scowls, some in uniform and some not. The head honcho, an overweight bald guy dressed in a suit, barked, "We have a warrant to search this residence."

He flashed a document so quickly that it could have been a recipe for peach pie for all we knew. "All individuals currently in the residence will assemble in the living room in exactly ten minutes. Be fully dressed and ready to exit the premises."

Bob, Ava, James, Mary, and I were forced to wait while the police carried out their search. After about forty-five minutes, Mr. Honcho read all our full names from his sheet and then said, "You are all under arrest for unlawful possession of narcotic drugs with intent to sell. You have the right to remain silent when questioned. Anything you say or do may be used against you in a court of law." And so on. The bastard gave us every single one of our Miranda rights.

We were hauled off to jail, booked, and after several hours, finally allowed one phone call each. Fortunately, I was able to get through to Gene at IPS.

"Damn! Just hang tight. I'll have my attorney down there within an hour. Just tell your housemates to button their lips until he gets there."

The attorney, Charles Thomas, came to the jail, and we were all out by four in the afternoon; no sleepless nights in the slammer—thank you, Gene and Charles.

Thomas took me to where my car was parked; I didn't go into the house. I followed him directly to his office in Del Mar. Thomas was about fifty with just a touch of gray hair worn at medium length; he was dressed more casually than I would have expected of a Stanford-connected attorney.

He quickly outlined the situation. "First of all, I am representing you alone. I did arrange bail for your housemates as a favor, but I'm not representing them. Evidently the police found small amounts of marijuana in several rooms plus a larger stash in the bedroom used by James."

"I thought the police needed probable cause to obtain a search warrant?"

"That's right. Apparently, they have a witness who claims to have purchased grass from James. That would be consistent with the large stash found in his bedroom."

"That bastard!" I couldn't help but shout. "I thought he was a legit real estate agent.

Let me be completely up front with you. First, had I known about this, I would have kicked his ass out in a heartbeat. Second, I'm not really into grass. Sure, when I'm at some party and someone hands me a brownie, I'll give it a try. Just like nearly everyone else I know."

"Anything else?" Thomas asked.

"Yes, just two confessions. Bob and Ava are not married, and I'm not a brother; we rented our house under false pretenses."

"What else?" he said.

"I sometimes engage in sex acts other than the lawful missionary position."

Thomas sighed and shook his head. "I'll get back to you in a week or so after I've talked to the district attorney."

On the way home, I stopped at both Roberto's Taco Shop and the local liquor store. I arrived home to find my domicile in turmoil. The police had totally trashed the place with their search; my housemates were busy cleaning up the mess. I decided to postpone any confrontation with James; I was too worn-out mentally and physically.

I went up to my bedroom. The bedcovers were in a pile on the floor and the mattress ripped open. My closet was a jungle. My little half-ass safe stood open. The 107- page document that Jim had printed for me was nowhere to be seen. Even my fake electrical outlet had been breached.

Chapter 24

As I cleaned up the horrible mess courtesy of the police raid, I noticed some folded scraps of paper under the lamp next to my bed. They were full of advanced math and crude handwritten diagrams. I had completely forgotten about Gene's notes on the proper pricing of financial warrants. The police had left the notes alone; maybe they were afraid of becoming infected with the dreaded math virus, known to have killed many potential scientific careers.

I briefly reflected. Was this was some kind of omen? So the next day I arranged for a safe-deposit box at the Torrey Pines Bank in Solana Beach where I stored Gene's notes and my passport and birth certificate. Who knows? Maybe I'd run for president someday.

Several days later, I was relaxed in our family room watching the nightly TV news when Bob appeared holding a letter and looking grim. "Bad news. This letter is from our landlord's attorney threatening us with all kinds of civil and criminal actions."

I read the letter. "Christ, our landlord must have gotten wind of the police raid in record time. If I read between the lines, the attorney implies that if we are gone quickly, no further action will occur. We'd better call a house meeting."

We couldn't start a full meeting until James finally showed up at eleven at night. Ava laid into him. "You messed us up royally. You were supposed to be a real estate agent; marijuana is not real property, not in anyone's book."

James apologized profusely. "I'm really very sorry. About a year ago, I started going down a deep financial hole; no houses sold in over six months. I started dealing grass on a small scale just to catch up. My attorney is working on a plea deal. Don't worry; I've sworn that none of you knew anything about my dealing."

Bob drafted an apologetic letter to our landlord's attorney assuring him that we would vacate the premises within two weeks. We also assured him the house would be left clean and tidy. Unfortunately, the police raid created a lot of minor damage that we had to repair.

I called deSilva and asked a favor. He laughed. "So the cops trashed your place? Welcome to the real world. Sure, my boys will do the repairs; they can start tomorrow. I'll just charge you my costs—no markup. You're also going to need a place to live. Why don't you buy something? No more need to dick around with landlords who don't appreciate your huge appetite for pussy."

After the events of the past few weeks, my so-called appetite was missing in action. But deSilva's suggestion to buy a real place to live had merit.

I called my old friend Jim from Astro; he had recently purchased a duplex in University City, a middle-class suburb just inland from La Jolla. "You're in luck," he said. "One side is empty, and I'm just now getting it cleaned up. You can rent it week to week. Buying a house to live in really is a big deal, not like one of your crappy little investment houses. You'll want to take your time looking around."

Jim sounded just like deSilva, I thought.

After the place was made ready, I moved my stuff into Jim's duplex.

I talked to Gene on the phone, and he hinted that we should all lie low for a while. "Good time for vacations," he said. "Got any plans?"

"Yes, as a matter of fact, I'm planning on a European train tour; I've applied for a Eurail pass that will give me unlimited stops over a two-week period. I'll probably do Paris, Berlin, and...who knows? I'm not planning ahead; I'll just see how it goes."

If I was going to buy an upscale house, I'd better get more cash from Marco Oliver. On this trip I flew directly to Paris, where I had booked a centrally located hotel. The Paris Métro was not as easy to use as the London Tube because of the language barrier, but I managed without much trouble.

After a few hours' sleep, I headed out of my hotel; the afternoon was overcast and the temperature in the low sixties. I walked a few blocks to the Champs-Élysées, one of the best-known streets in the world. The name means *Elysian Fields*, the place of the blessed dead in Greek mythology. I passed numerous cinemas, cafés, and luxury stores and made my way to the Arc de Triomphe, which honors those who fought for France in the revolutionary and Napoleonic wars.

I started the next day with a long run along the Seine River, which runs through central Paris. I returned to my hotel for a shower and light lunch and then headed for the Louvre, one of the world's largest museums, located on the Right Bank of the Seine. Once inside, I stopped to examine *La Liberté guidant le peuple*. The painting shows a woman holding the French flag in one hand and brandishing a musket with the other. The woman, representing liberty, leads the people forward over the bodies of the fallen in the French revolution of 1830.

An attractive woman of perhaps thirty with long blond hair seemed to share my appreciation of this famous painting. I took a step closer to her and said, "The guy on the left holding the gun looks a bit like Abraham Lincoln, but this painting's scene predates Lincoln's presidency. How can you explain that?" I silently congratulated myself on sounding so smart; this beautiful babe would probably be all over me, just like I was the real James Bond. Johnson gave his unequivocal approval; he was waking up fast in response to the events at hand.

The woman looked at me sideways, her manner dripping with disgust. She said something in French that I couldn't follow in detail, but I got the message: "Forget it, you horny American piece of shit."

Oh well, Johnson—nothing ventured, nothing gained.

I spent one more day sightseeing in Paris. Then I caught the night train from Paris to Berlin using my Eurail pass and paying a little extra for a spot in a six-berth couchette. The room consisted of three stacked bunks on each side—first come, first serve. I grabbed the upper bunk on one side. A young couple speaking German took two bunks on the opposite wall.

I opened my pack to remove a croissant sandwich and bottle of wine, enjoying a delightful French meal as the train pulled out of the station. I changed into my pajamas under the blanket supplied by the train and was soon fast asleep. I sleep like a baby baboon on trains.

I was rudely awakened the next morning by someone yelling in German. A red-faced guy in uniform was looking at me and demanding something. I briefly flashed back to my Club Snooze and ballroom sleeping experiences. But surely sleeping in Germany was not illegal—or was it?

I finally realized that the red-faced man was an East German guard demanding to see my ticket and passport. I noticed that my couchette mates, the West German couple, were fully dressed, but I was forced to deal with this asshole in my Mickey Mouse pajamas. He kept insisting that something was wrong with my passport, but I couldn't make out what the problem was.

He seemed ready to call for reinforcements to have me hauled away, but fortunately the German couple came to my rescue. They translated, "The guard is concerned that your passport expires next month. You must still have a valid passport when you leave Berlin."

I responded, "Please tell him that I will stay in West Berlin for only three days. After that, I plan to defect to East Germany and apply for a job with the train guard service. Soon I will be his friend and colleague."

My West German saviors looked confused at first and then ashen. Fortunately, they only translated the first part of my ill-advised rant, and the guard left to harass others on the train.

West Berlin was essentially a partly isolated enclave within East Germany. The East German Transport Police carried out inspections using sniffer dogs to uncover stowaways; passports and visas were processed at border stations, and the conditions of the tracks were poor so that trains had to keep speeds below about forty-five miles per hour.

I found Berlin to be delightful with its sidewalk cafes and historic significance. I followed most tourists in visiting Checkpoint Charlie, the main crossing point at the Berlin Wall. The stories of both successful and failed attempts to escape from East Berlin intrigued me to no end, like that of the girl who went on an extreme diet so she could fit in a moderate-size suitcase carried across the line by her boyfriend.

After three days in Berlin, I hopped on the train to Zurich, again choosing the overnight six-berth couchette. I headed for the Hotel Alexander, a short taxi ride from the station. Marco Oliver answered his exclusive phone on the third ring. I met him at his Credit Suisse office that afternoon.

Oliver had a pleasant surprise for me. "I have been authorized to settle all past money owed, including funds due from the new invoice you have given me. The total is $23,450. I am instructed to advise you to use your ingenuity—but to avoid breaking any laws—in figuring out how to transport these funds back to the United States." He counted out 234 hundred dollar notes plus one lonely fifty-dollar note. He even gave me an envelope to carry the money and a stick of bubblegum.

The next day I caught an early-morning train to Monaco on the French Riviera. Monaco, the second-smallest and most densely populated country in the world, is home to Monte Carlo.

After a day of rest and running along the coast, I dressed up for a visit to Le Grand Casino. I walked around the various tables for several hours, placing small bets here and there; half the time I didn't even know what the hell I was betting on. Frankly, the extravagant display of wealth disgusted me; I flew to London the next day.

I spent another two days touring the three London casinos with low standards, but I felt little enthusiasm. These visits were all just for show. On my last night, I caught the Tube to Leicester Square and walked to the Palace Theatre to see the new rock opera *Jesus Christ Superstar.* The musical is loosely based on biblical accounts, offering fanciful interpretations of the psychology of Jesus, Judas, and the other characters. The Christian community's response ranged all over the map from very positive to super negative. This controversy was somewhat interesting, but I mainly just enjoyed the performance.

When I arrived at customs in New York, I declared the entire bundle of cash, which I carried under my clothes in a money belt around my waist. Surprisingly, only a few routine questions were asked. Maybe I was looking more respectable these days.

A week after my return to San Diego, my attorney Charles Thomas called to say that he had reached a plea deal with the district attorney's office. I would plead guilty to some vague misdemeanor about being present where illegal drugs were used and pay a three hundred dollar fine.

"OK," I said. "But just out of curiosity, doesn't this mean that essentially everyone breaks this law on a regular basis? If the law were enforced uniformly, there would be more people inside the jails than out."

"Sure," Thomas replied. "That's why we need lawyers."

I called Gene at his home to let him know I was back and that my casino visits had been a great success. I suggested that we get together for a beach run, but he replied, "Yes, but I'll be a bit busy for the next week or so; I'll call you."

It was unlike Gene to be so abrupt with me. I was anxious for an explanation of the change in withdrawal limits in Zurich. Gene's demeanor added to my uneasy feeling that the whole operation was changing in a big way; my little part could end altogether.

I stopped by deSilva's little cracker-box office in Claremont, not far from Mesa College and the Blarney Stone Pub. DeSilva never wasted money on frills or appearance. He was sitting behind an ancient metal desk that supported his stocking feet; one sock had a large hole.

When he saw me, he put down the phone. "Hold on a second, Spike. Here, kid, take this. It's the latest multiple listing book; all houses listed for sale are in there."

He tossed a large paperback booklet to me; it was full of small pictures of houses with prices and other details summarized underneath each picture. I looked through it for several minutes while deSilva continued his phone conversation. The guy called Spike seemed to be deSilva's muscle for dealing with tenants who failed to pay rent.

"No, Spike, forget the rough stuff. Just use your menacing scowl. If that doesn't work, we'll just go legal on the deadbeats."

I waved good-bye and headed toward the coast. All my life I had wanted to live within walking distance to a nice beach. Maybe growing up in Cocoa Beach spoiled me. Also, I figured the beach areas were pretty much insulated from economic downturns for the simple reason that many others valued the beach just as much as I did.

The problem, of course, was cost. Going north up the coast, La Jolla and Del Mar were a bit too expensive. The next town was Solana Beach, where I found a fixer-upper listed for fifty-two thousand; the lot was covered with large trees and just a five-minute run to the beach.

I dialed deSilva's number. "I found a house in Solana Beach, but it needs work. I'm thinking of offering forty-five thousand; what do you think?"

DeSilva grabbed his multiple listing book and answered, "Good location, but don't forget your leverage lessons. Let's put in a full price offer with a seven thousand buyer credit towards repairs. That way, most repair costs get folded into the loan, and I get paid up front to do your repairs."

After some haggling back and forth with the sellers, I ended up with a four thousand credit for repairs. My down payment was thirty-five hundred after deSilva worked his magic with the friendly banker and took his commission as a promissory note.

The house itself was a modest three-bedroom, two-bath cracker box. The lot was fantastic, however: a half acre with large pine, oak, and eucalyptus trees on a quiet side street. I could easily imagine this as the perfect site for my future mansion, or whatever. Watch out, Hugh Hefner; here I come.

Chapter 25

I called Gene's home, and Marie answered. She seemed quite excited when I told her of my new toy, a house that I would actually live in. "Where is it? When can we see it? Can I offer suggestions for remodeling?"

A few days later, Gene and Marie met me at the house armed with color charts, carpet samples, brochures showing kitchen fixtures, and more. DeSilva even showed up. They all seemed to feel that getting me into my own home would keep me out of bars and ballrooms. Respectability, here I come.

DeSilva's boys repainted the interior in a light taupe color; Marie chose the thick new carpet to match. Both bathrooms and the kitchen were remodeled based on Gene's and Marie's recommendations.

The next day, I invited Mandy to come with me to shop for furniture. She seemed to enjoy our shopping jaunt but was unusually reserved. "So how did your date with John go?" I finally asked after it was clear she was not about to raise this particular subject herself.

"It was OK," she answered.

Was that all she had to say? She knew exactly what I wanted to ask, but I was caught up in her cat-and-mouse game. I wanted her to tell me without my asking, "Did you or didn't you?" But she was not going there. The proverbial elephant in the furniture store was not going to be acknowledged.

I decided to ask a different question. "Mandy, will you be spending tonight with me?"

She didn't answer for a long time. "No, Jack, I really have a lot of things to think about."

Well, that pretty much said it all. I loved Mandy, but if I wanted a chance to keep her, our relationship would have to become full time, much more like a marriage.

My perspective and lifestyle had evolved dramatically since my college graduation ten years earlier. The Vietnam War, the counterculture, and Gene's disclosures had shattered the naïve world view held by the old Jack. There was no turning back. Never again would I consider working in a conventional nine to five job, especially not one in the *military-industrial complex.* My soul was not for sale. I would not become another Willy Loman or Connor O'Malley. Marriage seemed like an alien institution. My freedom would be gone. The price was too high. I would rather be dead.

But, what about Mandy? What was best for her? Only she could decide. She pretty much knew that we would never be married; it would be highly unethical of me to pretend otherwise. If Mandy wanted a more traditional relationship, I could best express my love for her by helping our transition to go forward as painlessly as possible. On this high intellectual level, I didn't regret giving her the go-ahead to date John.

Yes, these were lofty thoughts but damn painful to carry out. The old empty feeling came over me once more; a chapter in my life was ending. I drove to my new Solana Beach house with my meager collection of personal stuff. I flipped on the radio; Bob Dylan's raspy voice resonated with my conflicted feelings.

Go 'way from my window
Leave at your own chosen speed
I'm not the one you want, babe
I'm not the one you need

You say you're lookin' for someone
Who's never weak but always strong
To protect you an' defend you
Whether you are right or wrong
Someone to open each and every door
But it ain't me, babe
No, no, no, it ain't me babe. It ain't me you're lookin' for, babe.

In May of 1972, Gene and I met again for a run in Peñasquitos Canyon. The day was overcast and cool—perfect for running—but Gene's mood was downcast. "A lot has changed since our last meeting. Aside from increased pressures on the Colonel, an entirely new issue has come up."

"Something to do with my payments through Marco Oliver in Zurich?" I replied.

"No, that's not it. I did relax the restrictions on your payments. You seem to have established an excellent cover with your casino visits. Declaring the cash you bring into the country should be no problem as long as you also declare it on your tax returns. How much federal tax did you pay in 1971?"

"Between deSilva's house shelters and your creative accountant, I had plenty of rich-man deductions. I paid only a couple of thousand. So what's the new issue?"

Gene was silent for several minutes. "I've restarted sessions with my psychiatrist, Dr. Avery Blackwell. I'm now going twice a week."

"I thought you came to terms with your cognitive dissonance problem. As you described it to me, the things you and the Colonel are finding out about our military-industrial system are totally at odds with the blind patriotism and naive views of America that you grew up with.

"Over the past five years, I have also experienced the mental stress of holding contradictory beliefs about America. But I now recognize more clearly that people and institutions generally do both good and evil, so maybe the contradictions are illusory."

Gene replied, "My current issues go well beyond the cognitive dissonance issue. What do you know about schizophrenia?"

I was puzzled. "Has it something to do with multiple personalities?"

"No, that's a common error. You are thinking of multiple personality disorder. Your confusion is due to the way these labels are often misused in the popular media. Schizophrenia involves a profound breakdown of thought processes. Common symptoms include delusions, such as paranoid beliefs, hallucinations, and disorganized thinking. Someone who has a schizophrenic delusion will continue with his or her delusion even when shown substantial contradictory evidence."

I replied, "You can't be serious. You're the most non schizophrenic guy I know. I'm betting you're more sane than your shrink, Blackwell. If he says you're schizophrenic, then it probably shows that he's a quack."

"Actually, I've developed a moderate level of confidence in Blackwell. And no, he has not diagnosed me as schizophrenic—at least not yet—but I do have some disturbing symptoms. To make a long story short, I have been hearing voices in my head for the past six months."

"What do you mean by voices?" I asked. "I could say I hear voices whenever I have an inner dialogue with myself. Probably everyone does this. Some of my friends believe it represents a conversation between the right and left hemispheres—one brain part talking to another. The neuroscientists say it's not so simple, but whatever it is, we all have it."

Gene explained, "My experience with the voices is nothing like the usual inner dialogue. I hear the voices as if they are entering my mind from somewhere outside, like telepathy. The effect is different from a creative idea, which I easily recognize as generated internally."

The whole thing seemed so far-fetched that I couldn't help being a little flippant. "What do these little ghosts have to say to you? Can they predict the stock market?"

Gene ignored my inappropriate joke. "The voices often speak coherently and even engage me in conversation. As far as I can tell, I am not responsible for the voices and have no idea what they are going to say next. I must say that the experience is highly intriguing—almost like having a new set of friends."

"Can you tune them out whenever you want?" I asked.

"Good question, but so far the issue has not come up. The voices, which seem to originate from two distinct personalities, only contact me for several minutes at a time and never more than once or twice in a day."

"Are they men or women?"

"As far as I can tell, they are gender-neutral. Sometimes the voices sound more real than other times; I may feel like they are sitting across from me. Other times, the voices are more like vivid dreams. We all dream and experience words and images. If bored, we can drift off and have a daydream. When we dream, all sorts of strange things can happen to us, but we still believe they're really happening. Hearing the voices is sometimes like that—a waking dream that I experience as real."

"And what does Blackwell say about all this?"

"He claims to have several other patients who also hear voices. For one thing, it's not uncommon for recently bereaved people to hear the voice of a dead person. But psychiatrists generally regard hearing voices to be auditory hallucination, a symptom of manic depression, schizophrenic disorders, and other psychosis. On the other hand, many people who hear voices are able to live with them and may even consider them a positive part of their lives."

I was really getting curious. "So what have they said so far?"

"For the first few months, the voices seemed to be just making friendly contact—a lot of small talk. But recently they have started passing information—in some cases secret information that I had already obtained from the Colonel."

My mind was racing, but "What the hell?" was all that made the journey from brain to mouth.

Gene was well ahead of me. "Hold on, Jack; I know what you're thinking. If the voices provide secret information, then maybe you think they are the actual source of all the stuff you have been recording for the past several years. Or maybe you even worry that the Colonel does not exist. Perhaps the whole ball game is just a hallucination that originated in my schizophrenic brain."

"Well, uh…"

"It's OK, Jack. Your doubts are fully expected based on what I have just told you. But let's look at the evidence. You can easily verify that the Colonel actually exists; Marie has met him several times. Most importantly, if you review the information that I have passed to you, it will become clear that you have received critical information about events way before they appeared in the media. The My Lai Massacre and *Pentagon Papers* are two such examples."

"OK, I'm convinced," I said, but I didn't feel quite so confident.

"Just the same, I want you to consider everything I tell you about the voices to be an integral part of your records. Don't leave out anything, even if it seems unimportant."

Gene and I finished our run and parted in the parking lot. I had a lot of new brain stuffing to process.

In June, the press reported that five men were arrested for breaking into the Democratic headquarters at the Watergate Hotel. The burglars included Bernard Barker, who had worked for the Cuban secret police under the vicious Batista dictatorship. Later Barker worked for both the FBI and CIA and was part of the US Bay of Pigs invasion of Cuba. The burglars also included former CIA operatives James McCord and Virgilio González.

In September, the five men, all associated with anti-Castro Cuban groups, were indicted by a grand jury, along with ex-CIA officer E. Howard Hunt and ex-FBI agent G. Gordon Liddy.

I recalled that Gene had told me that Hunt and Liddy were the main characters in the White House Plumbers, which was set up to stop security leaks and investigate other security matters.

During my student days at UCLA, I had met José Rivero, who had been a medical student in Cuba when Castro took power in 1959. We met quite by accident in the student cafeteria while trying to chat up the same girl. The girl got away, but José and I had struck up a friendship. He had supported Castro at first but later fled Cuba because he felt Castro had betrayed the revolution. Reflecting on Bernard Barker's past with secret police under the Batista, I recalled José's history lesson for me.

"Batista led a military coup that preempted the scheduled election of 1952. Back in power, he suspended the Cuban Constitution and revoked most political liberties. Batista partnered with the wealthiest landowners and presided over a stagnating economy that widened the gap between rich and poor. Batista's repressive government profited from the exploitation of Cuba's commercial interests by negotiating lucrative relationships with the American Mafia, which controlled the drug, gambling, and prostitution businesses in Havana. It also partnered with large American corporations that had invested considerable amounts of money. To quell the growing discontent among the populace, displayed by student riots and demonstrations, Batista established tight censorship of the media, utilizing his secret police to carry out wide-scale violence, torture, and public executions. Suspects who refused to talk had their wives raped in front of them and their balls cut off. These Batista guys were as brutal as it gets."

I reflected on all the negative publicity in our mainstream press surrounding Castro's quick trials and executions just after he came to power. How many were genuine victims and how many were guilty of heinous crimes? I had no way of knowing.

The 1972 presidential election featured Richard Nixon, the incumbent, versus Senator George McGovern, the peace candidate. The Watergate scandal had negligible effect on the election; at that time the majority of voters were unaware of Watergate.

McGovern flew thirty-five missions over German-occupied Europe during World War II and was awarded a Distinguished Flying Cross. But McGovern chose to not emphasize his war record during the campaign. As a result, top Republican figures were able to attack McGovern for being weak on defense and encouraging the enemy. Nixon asserted that McGovern was in favor of "peace at any price" rather than the so-called "peace with honor" that Nixon promised he would deliver.

On election night in November, I invited friends over to my new home to share our disgust with the outcome, which we knew well in advance because of the unanimous polling results. Bob and Ava, Trudy and Frank, and Jim and his wife came for an election wake with pizza and beer. Gene and Marie stopped by early for a short visit but then left to be with Gene's mother.

Mandy was missing in action; I really missed her. I imagined she was probably with her new friend John. Well, good luck to her; I hoped she would find what she wanted.

The Republican message proved to be a winning strategy. McGovern lost to Nixon; the popular vote was a disappointing 61 percent to 37 percent.

As it turned out, the election news was not entirely bad for the peace process. Because Americans were just plain sick of the war, Nixon's options were quite limited. In January of 1973, US military involvement in Vietnam mostly ended with the signing of the Paris Peace Accords. Nixon declared his so-called peace with honor; however, the war between North and South Vietnamese troops continued for another two years until the fall of the Saigon government in early 1975.

The Vietnam War cost fifty-eight thousand American and perhaps two million Vietnamese lives and ended with a victory for the North Vietnamese and Viet Cong. Saigon became Ho Chi Minh City. Later this deadly exercise in American imperialism would be aptly labeled "a bright shining lie" in a famous book of the same title.

Chapter 26

In March of 1973, Gene and Marie came to my house for a barbeque lunch. It was unusually warm for this early in the spring. As we sat in the shade of my large oak tree, I described my plans to fix up my backyard.

"I'd like to build a redwood deck under this tree and plant more bushes around the entire fence to create a private enclave. A large fountain and spa would add a nice touch. The yard could also use a few more trees; I'm thinking of eucalypti; they grow fast and don't need too much water."

Marie offered several suggestions, but Gene seemed lost in his own world. Could he be listening to voices? He was only thirty-nine, but he seemed to have aged a lot just in the past year.

After a while the old Gene came back to life. "Did you see the news a few weeks ago? The United States officially ended its adherence to the gold standard."

"I thought Nixon did it two years ago."

Gene replied, "Nixon called his action in 1971 temporary; now it's officially permanent."

I still didn't fully understand why this was important; Marie was equally in the dark. "Gene, you have been bugging me with this gold standard stuff for some time; maybe you should explain what it really means."

Gene switched to his professorial mode. "I'm not an expert, but my father, George, gave me regular financial lessons over the years. Until last month, most first world countries operated under the Bretton Woods system, set up in 1944. It was intended to govern financial relations among forty-four member countries; they were required to value their national currencies in terms of the US dollar. Under this fixed exchange system, only governments could alter the value of a currency.

"For example, suppose some country—let's call it Oz—has set two Oz dollars equal to one US dollar. If Oz wanted to devalue its currency, it might announce that from now on four Oz dollars would be equal to one US dollar. This would make its currency half as expensive to Americans and the US dollar twice as expensive in Oz."

Marie responded, "In that case we could profit nicely from an inexpensive vacation in Oz since my US dollar would be twice as strong."

I added, "If Oz devalues enough, you might even be able to buy the Wizard's palace in the Emerald City. But doesn't that leave us with one of those pesky paradoxes? What then determines the value of the US dollar itself? You're going to tell me *gold*, but then it just shifts the issue. What determines the value of gold?"

Gene replied, "You have a point, but first let me finish my basic lecture. As you suggest, the Bretton Woods system linked the US dollar to gold at thirty-five dollar per ounce, and the United States agreed to sell gold at that price to foreign governments at the so-called gold window. But now the price of gold in US dollars, the value of Oz dollars, and all other dollars are determined entirely by market forces."

"So where does this leave us?" asked Marie.

Gene answered, "The new world monetary system assigns no special role to gold; the US Federal Reserve can now print as much or as little money as it wants. There are substantial advantages to such an unconstrained system. The Fed is free to respond to actual or threatened recessions by printing money, but this new system also has risks. It leaves monetary managers free to do good things, but also allows them to be irresponsible by letting their printing presses go bananas."

We reverted to small talk for the next half hour or so, but I continued to process this new information. Suddenly my inner gambler jumped out of his unconscious box and interrupted the conversation.

"Christ, Gene, this new system opens a huge can of worms. Anyone with advance notice of devaluations can make megabucks buying and selling the right currencies. Just like in poker games, a few good players will take money from the poor and average players."

Marie added, "Well, that's the basis of free markets and capitalism, so what's new?"

Gene answered, "You're partly right, Marie, but the potential size of this new poker game is staggering. Jack's point is that huge wealth transfers are in the cards. In most cases, money will flow from the lower and middle classes to those able to exploit the new system—mainly people who are already rich. But a few middle-class actors will also benefit. If you expect your own currency to go down, you have several options that don't involve foreign money. You can buy hard assets like real estate and gold."

Oh goodie, I thought. My little houses are going up, at least when priced in US dollars, but maybe it's time to diversify and also buy some gold.

In late April, I was seated in my living room with my favorite oversize coffee cup and reading the *LA Times*. My eye caught an article on the newly established Chicago Board Options Exchange. Son of a bitch; they were now listing standardized, exchange-traded stock options.

With Gene's help I had acquired some understanding of warrant pricing, but I couldn't see how to profit from this knowledge since the warrants, issued by private companies, seemed to all be overpriced. But now the warrants were called options, and they would be traded in a free market without any involvement of the issuing corporations.

I got so excited that I called Gene at work with the news. "Here's the way it works. Suppose I own a thousand shares of IBM. I'm not expecting any big price move, so I want to hold my shares. On the other hand, I'd like to make a little extra money on my holdings, over and above the dividend."

At first Gene was irritated by my interruption at his work, but my story was beginning to pique his interest. "Go on," he replied.

"Suppose I contact some schmuck named Mr. Long Dong with this offer: 'I'll sell you an option to buy two hundred shares of my IBM stock a few months from now at a certain fixed price, called the *strike price.*' If the stock goes up far enough, we both make out. Dong gets my two hundred shares at below market, and I am happy that my remaining eight hundred shares have gone way up, plus I have the premium Dong paid for the option. All this happens through the exchange, so I never actually deal with this Dong in person.

"It gets even better. Dong can now freely trade the options on the exchange. If some other joker, Tinker Wong, thinks IBM is going way up next month, Wong can buy my options from Dong, provided they agree on price. But here's the kicker: nobody seems to know how to price these options."

"OK," Gene said. "Do you still have my old notes on warrants? Why don't you bring them over to my house on Saturday?"

Gene and I spent the afternoon going over his notes in detail. Although I still didn't fully grasp the advanced mathematics, I was able to gain an intuitive feeling for the option-price issue. To make a long story short, Gene and I were able to estimate fair option prices by calculating the areas under the extreme ends of bell curves. The curves depended on strike prices as well as the time when the option expired. I made notes for myself for future reference.

Gene and I agreed to meet in a few weeks for a run on our old favorite, Black's Beach.

I still had my old Chevy purchased new in 1962, so I went shopping. Eventually, I traded for a new Pontiac Firebird Trans Am, red with a black stripe on the hood; the interior was black vinyl. After obtaining a modest credit for my Chevy trade-in, I paid thirty-six hundred in cash.

I was really excited with my new car, but car trips were severely limited in the summer and fall of 1973 by long lines at gas stations. In the Yom Kippur War, Egypt and Syria had launched a military campaign against Israel in order to regain Arab territories lost to Israel in the 1967 Six-Day War. The United States supplied Israel with arms. In response, OAPEC, representing Arab oil countries, retaliated with an oil embargo. During one period in California, only people with an odd-numbered license plate could purchase gas on an odd-numbered day.

In August, I picked up Gene from his house in La Jolla on an early Saturday morning. We drove a mile or so north to the La Jolla Farms subdivision in my new Pontiac. We parked on the street and walked down the private road to Black's Beach.

I was quite taken aback by Gene's appearance and demeanor. He had acquired even more gray hair, so much so that he almost looked like a different person. His blue eyes seemed somehow less lively, lacking the overwhelming impression of raw intelligence that I had long taken for granted. He often seemed unsure when he spoke, sometimes forgetting simple things like names of people or locations.

As we headed north on the beach, I said, "Gene, you don't look so great. Are you sure you're OK for this run?"

With effort, Gene was able to reclaim most of his old self. "I'm not doing so well, Jack. But it's important that we get down to business. Our current arrangement with you as my paid recording secretary has only a very limited life. The Colonel and I may have to close down entirely in the coming months. Hopefully you will be able to make good use of your new investment skills to support yourself."

I had feared something like this, but nevertheless that old sinking feeling came over me again. "What exactly is going on?" I asked.

"As you know, IPS has gained top secret information about the activities of the CIA, FBI, NSA, and other government entities mainly because of our contacts with powerful people like Eisenhower, McNamara, and others. Now with Nixon in the White House, our whole operation is losing access fast. The Colonel thinks we will soon be put out to pasture, but he's determined to squeeze out some last bits of information before we're shut down.

"In particular, the Colonel has recently been looking into the Warren Commission report on the assassination of President Kennedy. As you know, a number of recent books have questioned the Warren Commission's conclusion that Oswald acted alone."

"Oh boy. Another can of worms," I said.

"Precisely," Gene replied. "Unfortunately, we have no definitive conclusions to offer at this point. There are hundreds, perhaps thousands, of witnesses who may have critical information. But how can you access their credibility? To make the case for conspiracy, one can cite numerous testimonies published in the recent books written by the critics. To support the Warren Commission's conclusions, one can challenge the veracity of such claims; just make the case that the witnesses or the investigators themselves must be mistaken or lying."

"Can you summarize what you do know?" I asked.

Now Gene became his old professorial self. "Suppose we simplify things by reducing everything to two basic questions. One: was the Warren Commission a comprehensive attempt to find the truth no matter what the outcome, or was it a cover-up? Two: did Oswald act alone, or was there a conspiracy?

"Let's address question one. We have already established that Hoover was widely criticized for being soft on organized crime. We don't know if the Mafia was blackmailing him, but the appearance, if not the reality, of substantial impropriety is crystal clear. The FBI was a main source of investigation for the Warren Commission. Might not any such investigation be steered away from possible Mafia involvement, which would end Hover's long career in an instant?

"Now consider the position of the CIA. They hired the Mafia to kill Castro through Operation Mongoose. They are continuing to support several kinds of terrorist activities against Castro using anti-Castro Cubans, many of whom hated Kennedy because of his failure to provide American air support at the Bay of Pigs invasion. Suppose it turns out that either the anti-Castro Cubans or Mafia were involved in the assassination; where would that leave the CIA?"

"Deep down in Hell's septic tank," I replied.

"Another thing," Gene said. "Allen Dulles was CIA director for twenty years. Kennedy fired him and Deputy Director Charles Cabell because of the Bay of Pigs fiasco, which Dulles had directed.

"Astoundingly, LBJ appointed Dulles as one of the seven commission members. Given his CIA access, one can argue that Dulles was the de facto head of the Warren Commission's investigations. In this sense the CIA was essentially investigating itself.

"Many conspiracy researchers have alleged a plot involving elements of the Mafia, the CIA, and the anti-Castro Cubans. These three groups were all in bed together at the time and had been together for several years in the fight to topple Fidel Castro. In 1963 Kennedy proposed removing the oil-depletion allowance—a huge tax break. The Colonel estimates that this would have cost Texas oilmen three hundred million dollars a year. These oilmen hated Kennedy with a passion; so here we have even more possible suspects.

"Tell me, Jack: what were your biggest concerns in the weeks and months after the assassination?"

I reflected on my memory of the fall of 1963. "First and foremost, we had just experienced the Cuban missile crisis. Anyone with even half a brain was scared shitless about nuclear war. The number one concern about the Kennedy assassination was that either the Soviet Union or Cuba was involved in a way that might lead to war. So everyone I knew hoped and prayed that the Warren Commission would eliminate this possibility. If there was a cover-up, in this sense we all participated."

Gene replied, "That's right on the money. In fact, Chief Justice Earl Warren didn't really want the job, but LBJ insisted that it was his patriotic duty to alleviate the nation-wide fears you expressed. Warren was determined that the commission report would be unanimous, so he compromised on some issues in order to get all the members to sign the final version. But there were other issues on everyone's mind."

We ran pass several nude sunbathers. I was so focused on Gene's story that I didn't even notice if they were men or women. I said, "Yes, everyone on the extreme ends of the political spectrum was scared that the assassin or assassins were from his or her own group. Kennedy was hated by the extreme right, so the right-wing crazies were obvious suspects. On the other hand, the commission found that Oswald was a Communist sympathizer. He had defected to the Soviet Union, married a Russian woman, and returned to live in the United States. Evidently, he was very pro-Castro."

Gene continued, "The issue of Oswald's motives and politics has become controversial since the commission report and twenty-six volumes of supporting documents came out in 1964. For one thing, before he defected, Oswald was a radio operator stationed at an army base in Japan where the CIA operated U2 spy flights over the Soviet Union. He seems to have returned to the United States from Russia without much scrutiny of his original defection. This seems rather strange since he could have passed sensitive information to the Soviets.

"Also, in this context, the Colonel has been looking into Oswald's friendship with George de Mohrenschildt, a petroleum geologist who was born in czarist Russia and immigrated to the United States in 1938.

"De Mohrenschildt's father was arrested by the Bolsheviks shortly after the Russian Revolution for anti-Communist activities. His older brother Dimitri is a staunch anti-Communist, former member of the OSS, and one of the founders of the CIA's Radio Free Europe.

"In 1952, de Mohrenschildt settled in Dallas and took a job with oilman Clint Murchison as a petroleum geologist. Remember we saw Murchison at the Del Mar racetrack hosting J. Edgar Hoover. De Mohrenschildt was also a member of the right-wing Texas Crusade for Freedom."

"What? Are you sure? You mean this anti-Communist with deep right-wing connections was a good friend of Oswald?"

"We know that in the spring and summer of 1962, just before the assassination, de Mohrenschildt and his wife, Jeanne, befriended Oswald and his wife; they tried to help as best they could and introduced them to the anti-Communist Russian community in Dallas."

I had never known what to make of the assassination conspiracy theories, so this information blew my mind. "Are you implying that Oswald may have been working undercover for some agency of the US government and only pretending to be a Communist sympathizer?"

Gene answered, "Some conspiracy theorists think that de Mohrenschildt was Oswald's CIA handler. But the Colonel has not found hard evidence for that. We can only say for sure that de Mohrenschildt has very high-level CIA contacts. Maybe there is some innocent explanation. Maybe de Mohrenschildt just liked Oswald and thought he could steer him in the right direction."

"Pun intended?" I asked.

Gene ignored my stupid joke. "Here's another little tidbit. The former Deputy CIA Director Charles Cabell's brother, Earle Cabell, was mayor of Dallas when Kennedy was assassinated. He must have had some say in the motorcade route."

Gene continued. "The Colonel has uncovered even more strange CIA connections. When de Mohrenschildt dropped out of the Oswald's lives in April of 1963, Ruth and Michael Paine took his place as the Oswald's benefactors. Marina Oswald moved in with Ruth, who was instrumental in Oswald's employment with the Texas School Book Depository. It's not widely known, but Ruth's older sister Sylvia Hyde Hoke worked for the

CIA at the same time. In addition, Michael's mother Ruth Forbes Paine Young was friend of Mary Bancroft, who was Allen Dulles's mistress during World War II. These coincidences, if that's what they actually are, boggle the mind."

I was stunned. All I could do was to repeat the old adage, "Truth is stranger than fiction."

Gene looked grim. "If the Colonel finds hard evidence that parts of our government were involved in the assassination, he may consider leaking this information to the press in an attempt to force a new investigation. But, there are huge barriers to the success of public disclosure. How do you insure the veracity of the next investigation without the full cooperation of the FBI, CIA, and president? Again you are faced with the problem of these agencies investigating themselves. If the Warren Commission report is actually a cover-up, any subsequent investigation may be no better. In any case, the Colonel views public disclosure to be a close call. I don't know what he plans to do.

"I want you to go back to Zurich within the next week. Make sure your new report is fully up to date. We may not have much more time."

Gene was too tired to continue running, so we turned around and walked the three miles back to my car. He hardly said another word; he seemed lost in some inner world.

Chapter 27

Iflew directly to Zurich from New York. I was able to complete my report on the flight, so I called Marco Oliver as soon as I arrived. No fooling around this time—I was all business. Oliver was even more so and had two surprises for me.

"You are now authorized to remove items from the safe box; so from now on your box transfers will occur in our standard private room." He walked me to a closet-like space in another part of the bank near the main vault. "I do not wish to be informed of future transfers; you are now the only person with authorized access."

I was stunned. "Wait. Are you saying that even Gene Stanford can no longer access the box?"

Oliver held up one palm. "I have no comment on whatever past authorizations were in place. I can only repeat what I just said: you and only you are now in charge of this box. The service has been prepaid for five years, through December of 1978. If you wish to continue after that, a new arrangement will be required."

When I submitted my invoice for seven thousand and change, Oliver sprang the second surprise. "After today, I will no longer accept invoices or make payments. I have been instructed to make this final payment of twenty-five thousand dollars to cover your future expenses."

He opened his magic box and counted out 250 hundred-dollar notes. "This will be our final meeting; I will be taking a new position in the bank. I ask that you attempt no further contact with me. Access to the safe box will be arranged through our regular safe-deposit box system. From now on you will be treated as an ordinary bank customer."

"I guess I don't quite qualify as one of your 'high-net-worth individuals'?"

He raised one eyebrow. "Not even in your wildest dreams."

We shook hands, and I left his office feeling like I had just gone bankrupt, even though I was carrying an extra twenty-five grand in the money belt around my waist.

Again I declared the bucks at the immigration check in New York. I arrived late at night in San Diego and grabbed a taxi to my house in Solana Beach. The taxi driver engaged me in several highly intelligent discussions about current affairs. He was about thirty with a well-trimmed black beard.

"The investor class is really taking a beating; the Dow is down fifteen percent from its peak in January."

I responded, "Yes, I've heard. You seem to be on top of many current issues. Do you mind if I ask what your background is?"

"I have a PhD from UCSD in Marxist philosophy."

I didn't hide my surprise. "I'll be damned; you studied under Marcuse. But why are you driving a taxi?"

He laughed. "Hey, I like the job. It's not very demanding, so I have plenty of free time and energy to read and pursue my hobbies. Besides, can you imagine the reactions of corporate America to my job applications? They don't need me, and I certainly don't need them."

Good thing you're single, I thought. That way you won't end up like the poor schmuck in *Death of a Salesman*. It was an interesting taxi ride; I tipped him 25 percent.

I was quite anxious to question Gene about the new Zurich arrangements with Credit Suisse. When I called his home, Marie answered. "Gene's been quite sick; he's sleeping now. When he feels up to it, I'll have him call you."

Several days went by, and Gene still hadn't called. I decided to get going on a new project. I called deSilva. "I'm planning to have a shower, sunken spa, and patio built in my backyard. Can your guys do that?"

"No, that's above their pay grade. But I can refer you to a contractor who does good work at a reasonable price; his name's Kyle Cook."

Kyle came to my house the next day to give me an estimate. "I'll have to dig a trench for the sewer and waterlines from the house to your shower and spa in the back. You really want me to pour a slab and do all the tiling to create the spa? It might be a lot cheaper just to buy a hot tub."

"No, I don't want a hot tub. I'm not going to keep it full; the spa will double as a bathtub or a spa big enough for four friends. I figure an extra fifty-gallon water heater will take care of a four-by-six-foot spa, eighteen inches deep."

Kyle warmed to the idea. "I get it. I take it you don't plan to dick around with permits, so we'll have to be a little sneaky with our concrete work. Fortunately, your yard is private."

I called Gene's house again, and again Marie put me off with some vague excuse.

Kyle's boys dug the trench on the following Saturday. They didn't work on Sunday, but 007 did. I measured ten feet from the house along the trench and then another eight feet perpendicular to the trench where I had planted a flower bed. I dug a hole four feet deep, lined it with plastic sheeting, and filled the space with a box made from treated lumber.

I filled the box with quick-mix concrete and embedded a new metal safe in the gooey stuff so that only the door was visible. I then placed a cover on the box, added another layer of dirt, and topped it with a fake water shut-off valve with connecting metal plate. Finally, I covered the system with a six-inch layer of bark from the garden. Since the whole thing was located within an active flower bed, the ground disturbances due to my accesses should not attract attention. My new hideout was now ready should I have to close down the Zurich box.

I had been following news of the Watergate affair on public radio over the past year. In March of 1974, a Washington grand jury indicted several former Nixon aides for conspiring to hinder the Watergate investigation. Nixon himself was looking guilty as hell.

I found gold prices in the financial pages of the *LA Times*; they had been running around $100 an ounce, way up from $64 at the end of 1972. But I didn't want to buy gold; I wanted leveraged bets on gold. Gold-mining stocks typically moved twice as fast as gold itself, but I wanted even more leverage than that, so I called the Chicago Options Exchange. Homestake Mining stock was listed at $40 a share. The option with a strike price of $45 and three-month expiration was listed at $200. I called deSilva. "I need a stock broker."

"You need a stock broker like you need a poker up your ass," deSilva yelled. "The market is already down by thirty percent, and it's headed even further south. If you have money to burn, buy more houses."

"Don't worry," I said. "I'm just playing with small potatoes in the market. I'll be buying more houses this month."

He calmed down. "My friend Ian Ski at E. F. Hutton can help you."

I called Ian and placed an order for twenty options on Homestake, to be purchased at the rate of one per week over the next twenty weeks. I was pretty sure gold was going up, but the timing was critical—thus the need to stagger the options buying.

Ian said, "At today's prices this will cost you $4,000 plus commission, but I'll call you every day with an update. If you get real lucky and Homestake goes to $60, you can buy a hundred shares at $45 per share and then resell them at $60 so each of your options at $200 will be magically transformed into $1,500. Of course, you will lose all of your dough if Homestake stays below $45."

Marie called me in the afternoon. "Jack, I need to talk to you. Can I come over right now?"

She arrived twenty minutes later looking flustered and more vulnerable than I had ever seen her. I gave her a quick hug, letting go before Johnson could wake up from his hibernation. "What's wrong?"

She sat down on my couch. "Gene's in the hospital. Officially, it's pneumonia, but in reality, he was committed by Dr. Blackwell; he's in the psychiatric ward under an assumed name."

I opened my mouth, but nothing but a few squawks emerged.

Marie went on. "I know Gene told you about the voices. At first it was sort of a game; he was enjoying it. What would they say? How would they respond to his questions? He said he could detach himself and treat the whole experience as a scientific experiment. But in the last few weeks, things have gotten out of control..."

She paused, and her eyes filled with tears.

I never used Kleenex, so I gave her the first thing I could find, a wet bath towel. I moved next to her and put my arm around her. She said, "Sorry, I'm OK now."

I moved back to my chair, and she continued. "Lately, the voices have become more frequent and more demanding. There are apparently two of them, and they seem to work some sort of 'good cop, bad cop' routine. The bad cop might tell Gene to smash one of our windows. Then the good cop might say, 'That's too much; just throw a wine glass against the wall.'"

"Holy Halloween, they sound like gremlins," I said.

Marie answered, "It gets worse. The voices or gremlins or devils or whatever are trying to get Gene to play mean tricks on people—first on our housekeeper, Martha, and later on me."

I was having a hard time believing our conversation was real; it was like a dream. "Like what?" was all I could say.

"The bad cop told Gene to get a knife from the kitchen and jab Martha in the butt when she had her back turned. Gene refused, but then the good cop told him that if he just used a safety pin, Martha would enjoy the joke."

"Don't tell me..."

"Yes," she said. "Gene jabbed her in the ass with a pin, and she screamed bloody murder. She threatened to quit, but I finally calmed her down.

"For several days after that, Gene seemed to be his old, normal self. He assured me that he could control the voices in spite of evidence to the contrary. Then last night he became very romantic; he came on sexually like the old Gene. We were in bed, and he was kissing me everywhere. At first I was very thankful to have my husband back, but then things really got weird."

Oh hell, this was going from bad to worse—much worse.

Marie then stood up. "I want you to see this so you really understand what I'm up against." She pulled her loose-fitting dress up around her waist. She was wearing skimpy white panties, but I could still make out her full brown bush through the material. Her legs were spread wide.

She waited for me to focus a little lower. On her inner thigh just below her panty line was an ugly wound. Black-and-blue marks surrounded an area of torn flesh and dried blood. "He took a big bite out of me," she sobbed.

I grabbed her in my arms and sat her down on the couch. She cried for several more minutes in my arms before continuing her story.

"Gene chewed slowly on the flesh in his mouth for some time and just sat on the bed with a blank look on his face. I immediately called Dr. Blackwell's emergency number. He arrived at my house with paramedics in thirty minutes. They put Gene in a straitjacket and took him directly to the hospital. He didn't resist and never said a word."

"This all happened last night?" I asked.

"Yes. This morning I went to the hospital; Dr. Blackwell met me there. Gene was heavily sedated. Blackwell claims he can treat Gene's psychosis with a combination of drugs. But I'm not feeling very optimistic after what I've experienced."

Mental illness was way off my radar screen; the whole story just didn't even seem real. But I now understood why Marie had gone to the extreme of lifting her dress to show me the bite wound, which was all too real.

Marie had more to tell me, but we both needed a break. I fixed a simple meal and opened an expensive bottle of chardonnay that I kept for special occasions. Marie drank her first glass in one gulp. Probably she would have done the same with grain alcohol and rainwater. After our meal and more wine, Marie said, "Jack, have you ever wondered why Gene and I never had kids?"

"I suppose it crossed my mind, but I wasn't about to broach the subject. For one thing, you both have rewarding careers."

"Gene has an older sister permanently in a mental hospital; she's severely schizophrenic. I have an aunt who is also hospitalized with schizophrenia. Gene and I did our homework; this disease is linked to genetics. If we were to have children, their risk might be much more than that of the general population. So we decided to take a pass on parenthood."

I thought for a while. "So Gene is also at increased risk because of his sister's illness?"

Marie just barely nodded her head yes. She was way too drunk to drive home. "You can sleep in my guest room," I said. By this time she had passed out on the couch, so I carried her to the spare bed and tucked her under the covers.

I was so overwhelmed by the day's events that it took me several hours to fall asleep. When I awoke in the morning, I found that Marie was still asleep in the guest room. I closed the door quietly so as not to wake her and fixed us coffee and a light breakfast.

After a quick breakfast, she kissed me on the cheek and said good-bye; she was off to the hospital to get the latest word on Gene.

Chapter 28

Gold prices continued to go up while broad stock market indexes went down the drain. My brokerage account, consisting entirely of options, was now worth over $50,000 on paper, a ten-plus bagger based on my original investment of $4,000. Ain't leverage lovely when it works its magic in your favor?

I sold seven of my options for $15,000 and bought five more houses through deSilva. Now that I had real assets, deSilva's banker was actually able to use honest loan applications to maximize my leverage. No more conjuring up fake incomes. I let the remaining $35,000 ride with my E. F. Hutton broker, Ian, aiming to graze in even loftier options pastures in the future.

Gene's intensive drug therapy seemed to be working. After three months he was released from the hospital but remained on an extended leave of absence from IPS and stayed in his home office most of the time. He even made peace with Martha, his cook and housekeeper, whose ample ass had fully recovered.

In July Marie invited me for a visit. Gene was pale and subdued as we sat with Marie in their living room. I avoided any discussion of his illness but provided a running account of my adventures with stock options. "You were right on two counts. First, gold prices really went up after Nixon closed the window. Second, your analysis of option pricing seems right on the money."

At first he didn't seem to remember much of anything about his earlier analysis. "Tell me again how you use the normal distribution?" He struggled with these kinds of basic questions as if I were the expert teaching him. He was not the same Gene; apparently Blackwell's anti-psychotic drugs had dulled his intellect.

In August of 1974, physics professor Frank Halpern and his friend Trudy, along with Bob and Ava, came to my house for dinner and to watch Nixon's resignation speech, delivered from the Oval Office. The Watergate scandal had finally got a hold of Nixon's short and curly hairs. He said he was resigning for the good of the country and asked the nation to support the new president, Gerald Ford. Nixon went on to review the so-called accomplishments of his presidency, especially in foreign policy.

Trudy was particularly scornful. "Yeh, peace with honor in Vietnam—only three million dead, right?"

Frank added, "Well, I guess we should give him some credit for improving relations with China, but I'm damn glad he's gone."

In late October I drove downtown to a movie theater with Jim, my old friend from Astro.

We went to watch a closed-circuit live broadcast of the so-called rumble in the jungle, the fight in Zaire between Muhammad Ali and George Foreman.

Foreman was heavily favored after having demolished Joe Frazier to win the heavyweight title, but Ali won by knockout and regained the title.

It was the fall of 1974; I was thirty-four and Gene was forty. The Dow stock market index hit six hundred, down more than forty percent from its peak in 1972.

I ran into Ruthie by accident at the Mission Valley shopping center. We grabbed some coffee and sat at an outside table. She brought me up to date on Bicycle Bill's players. Fast Eddie had moved on to play elsewhere. More dramatically, Jersey Joe had jumped off some tall building in New York. "We didn't know it, but Joe had over a million in stocks. When the market crashed, he crashed through the roof of a Mercedes—very symbolic."

"Jesus, if he had a million in 1972, he still had six hundred thousand after the crash. For most people that's hog heaven. Why would he kill himself?"

Ruthie displayed wisdom born of long poker experiences. "For a lot of guys, self-worth equals net worth. Joe just couldn't live with his loss of self-esteem."

In November Gene returned to work at IPS. We restarted a limited version of our beach runs, mostly three-mile jaunts at La Jolla Shores. Gene had little to say about the Colonel's investigations or my role as his recording secretary. It was like we now lived in a different universe. After a while I gave up asking.

In December gold closed at $183, three times its value at the end of 1972. My brokerage account grew to $140,000; I withdrew $40,000 and bought ten more investment houses, bringing my cracker-box stash to twenty-five. As promised, deSilva and his boys took care of everything from maintenance to collecting rents and more. All I had to do was write checks every month.

Much of my time was now spent on the study of options pricing. I ran across a reference to an article published in the *Journal of Political Economy*, which I had never heard of. "The Pricing of Options and Corporate Liabilities" was written by two guys named Fischer Black and Myron Scholes. The paper was loaded with mathematics used to estimate the price of an option over time.

I really needed Gene's help to fully understand the analysis, but he was in no condition to offer anything. As far as I could see, however, my graphical approach provided a plausible approximation of the Black-Scholes model. For options trading in the real world, maybe the advanced math was not necessary.

In April of 1975, I was sitting in my living room in front of the TV waiting for the local six o'clock news and working on my second bottle of Negra Modelo, rescued from my freezer just five minutes before ice would have formed. James Bond wannabes like their beer really cold, at least the American versions.

My financial successes over the past year were beyond my wildest dreams. In January I had visited Mom in Cocoa Beach and bought her a new car. My friends were in awe of my beautiful new spa and shower in a nicely decorated outdoor sitting area. My love life was not so good; I really missed Mandy. But in my current mood I felt that the female void would be filled sooner or later. In any case I was enjoying complete freedom from having to worry about money or filling someone else's expectations. Isn't it strange how the impression of a good life can disappear in an instant?

The six o'clock news started with a story about the shooting of someone called Robert Lee Steward at his office in Sorrento Valley, an industrial park seven miles south east of Del Mar. The TV reporter was conducting an interview with his secretary, an attractive blonde named Lisa May. "Please tell us what happened when you came to work this morning."

Lisa wiped away a tear. "I arrived at quarter to eight and knocked on his office door but received no answer. I knew he must be close by because his black Mercedes was in the parking lot. I went in and saw him slumped over, his head on the desk. At first, I thought he was asleep; then I saw all the blood. I tried to find a pulse, but then I noticed the terrible head wound." She started to sob.

The reporter gave her time to compose herself. "Then what did you do?"

"I immediately called emergency and told them that my boss, the Colonel, seemed to be dead."

I jumped out of my chair, knocking over my beer.

The reporter looked confused. "The Colonel?"

Lisa clarified. "Everybody called Colonel Steward simply *the Colonel*. Most of our associates probably didn't even know his real name. Of course, he retired from the military years ago."

The reporter thanked Lisa and went on. "As a young military officer, Robert Lee Steward, also known as the Colonel, worked under General Eisenhower and helped to plan the Normandy Invasion. For the past ten years, he has been president of the think tank called Integrated Parallax Systems, located in Sorrento Valley. Steward was sixty-one years old.

The reporter then interviewed Captain Silas Dixon of the San Diego Police. "I understand you are treating this as a homicide. Some of the people here seem to be from the FBI; what have they got to do with this? What else can you tell us?"

Dixon was a tall heavyset fellow sporting a seemingly permanent scowl. "According to our preliminary findings, the victim died from a small-caliber gunshot to the back of his head. Death was probably instantaneous. The victim was involved in top secret government work, so the FBI is naturally interested in any potential compromise of security."

I wondered why Dixon never used the Colonel's name; he just called him *the victim*. Maybe police who deal with a lot of crime need to detach themselves emotionally.

The reporter pressed, "Are you saying some foreign agent might have murdered Steward to steal government secrets?"

Dixon's scowl grew truly impressive. "No, I never said anything of the kind. We are still in the very early stages of our investigation. I caution you against unwarranted speculation. This interview is now over." He moved out of camera range, thankfully before the reporter could ask more dumb questions.

I called Gene and Marie's home all evening and the following morning but never got an answer. The next day's newspaper accounts added very little to what I already knew.

In the evening I was again plunked down with a cold beer waiting for the news. At six o'clock the TV anchor Tyler Ball came on like gangbusters. "We have breaking news in the murder of Robert Lee Steward, former president of the secret think tank Integrated Parallax Systems. I'm switching you directly to our reporter in the field."

The same reporter from the previous night was standing in a familiar location; I was immediately overcome with a sickening feeling. "I am standing in front of the home of Dr. Gene Stanford, a prominent scientist working for Integrated Parallax Systems. Dr. Stanford has been charged with the murder of his boss, Robert Lee Steward. Stanford is the son of the well-known industrialist George Stanford, who was killed several years ago by a hit-and-run driver."

I was too stunned to talk to my housemates or anyone else; I just opened a bottle of vodka in my bedroom and drank myself to sleep.

I was finally able to contact Marie three days later. She came to my house late in the evening. Her eyes were bloodshot, her hair messy. She looked about as bad as one would expect under the circumstances. "I'm sorry I look like hell," she said. "What have you got to drink?"

I poured us glasses of cheap red wine. I was out of the good stuff, but somehow the cheap crap seemed more appropriate for the crappy circumstances. "Tell me the whole story; all I know is what the damn TV says."

She organized her thoughts. "Last Thursday, Gene called at eight in the evening to say that the Colonel needed him to stay late. He didn't get home until two, but I wasn't too worried since these kinds of late nights were not unusual before Gene's illness. In fact, I thought it was a positive sign of Gene's recovery."

She finished her glass and waited for me to refill it before continuing. "He went right to bed and slept late in the morning. Around noon we got a call from Lisa May telling us that the Colonel was dead—probably murdered. Gene turned white as a sheet but didn't say much. We expected that the police would come, so we just hung around the rest of the day. Other than Gene's father, the Colonel's friends and relatives were unknown to us, so there wasn't much for us to do.

"We hung around all day Friday and went to bed early. At six on Saturday morning, a large contingent of police and FBI came with a search warrant. We were forced to sit in the living room while they tossed the whole house. After several hours they showed us a .38 caliber silver pistol with a black handle. I had never seen it before. They claimed it was in Gene's office."

My mind was racing through all the possibilities. "What did Gene say?"

She took another gulp of wine. "He claimed to have never seen it either. Let me be precise. Actually, he said he didn't *remember* ever seeing it. At that point I called our attorney, Charles Thomas; he insisted that we say nothing more to the police until he arrived, but Gene did not keep quiet."

I fetched more wine. "Who seemed to be in charge—the police or the FBI?"

"They seemed to alternate taking the lead in the questioning. Gene told the FBI that he would fully cooperate with them but all questioning would have to occur in secret with federal government approval. Otherwise he would be breaching his security clearance. When Charles Thomas arrived, all questioning ended; the police and FBI left before noon."

I flashed back to Saturday night's breaking news. "Things must have moved fast after that."

Marie nodded her head. "Yes, they came back at five o'clock with a warrant for Gene's arrest, charging him with the murder of Robert Lee Steward. The press had been alerted, so the whole thing was a circus. Our attorney, Thomas, was outraged; he couldn't believe they had obtained a warrant so fast."

"Have you talked to Gene?" I asked.

"Yes," she said. "And so has Thomas. Gene doesn't remember anything about late Thursday night. He remembers calling me at eight and going to bed after two. He says the six hours in between are a complete blank."

"What about the .38 pistol?" I asked.

Marie looked ashen. "Gene has no memory of the gun, but the police claim to have found the store that sold it and positively identified Gene as the buyer."

"Christ, Marie, I don't know what to say. I just can't believe this is real. I crossed the room to give her my best hug."

Marie got up to accept my hug, but quickly disengaged. "I really have to go now."

A week later, two suits with crew cuts knocked on my door. Unlike my experience of the drug raid, these guys were actually courteous. They sat down in my living room. "Really nice place you have here; did you use a professional decorator?"

"Thanks. No, I have some creative friends; they helped me out."

"You mean like Gene and Marie Stanford?"

"Well, yes, as a matter of fact," I replied. "Hey, guys. I don't mean to be rude, but you are obviously not police. Just who are you?"

The taller one answered. "Let's just say we represent government security. We really just want some general information. No need to deal with formalities. You're not under suspicion for any crime."

I saw no need to play hardball with them. "OK, I'll just pretend you are from the CIB or CIC or whatever. Shoot your questions."

The shorter guy smiled. "We would like to hear how you first met Gene Stanford and the nature of your relationship since."

No problem. Gene had set things up so that interviews like this one would be a piece of cake. I mostly told them the truth—just not the whole truth. "Gene loved sports, and he admired my running career. We ran on the beach all the time; Gene wanted me to push him to faster times. He's a brilliant scientist, but down deep he's also a frustrated jock."

The tall guy asked, "What else did you talk about? What about politics?"

"No, not much. Gene was really interested in my poker-playing career. He also liked to hear about my love life."

Every time they tried to steer me into some sensitive area, I just related another folksy anecdote. "We were basically good running and drinking buddies—nothing deep or serious."

After a while they switched topics and hit me with a first class zinger. "What about Marie Stanford? We hear you're a real lover boy. Did you ever sleep with Marie?"

That stopped me in my tracks, but I recovered quickly. "Absolutely not. Marie and I are friends, but our thing is strictly platonic. Besides, Gene would kick my ass if I ever slept with Marie." Before they could zing me with the question I knew was coming, I volunteered, "A while back Marie was quite upset about Gene's illness. She drank too much to drive home, so she slept in my guest bedroom. Just like a good sister should."

They looked uncertainly at each other and then got up to leave. As they walked out, I followed them to their car. "Hey guys, do you think J. Edgar will be visiting the Del Mar track this year? Tell Hoover I have a few hot tips for him."

The short guy gave me a dirty look as he got behind the wheel.

Well, these guys had provided me with valuable information. Either Marie or I, or maybe both of us, had been under surveillance for some time.

Their strange questions, which had little connection to the murder charge, raised a serious question in my mind about the safety of my reports stored at Credit Suisse. Compared to their rich clients, I was essentially a deadbeat. How would they respond to pressure from the US government? In the end, it felt better to take possession. The next day I bought a round-trip ticket, San Diego to Zurich, and I left about ten days after the full moon.

On my return I sneaked a visit to my backyard garden and safe at four in the morning; there was very little light reflected from the new moon. I deposited all the reports that I had written since Gene had hired me ten years earlier. It wasn't a perfect solution but the best one I could think of at the time.

Chapter 29

Over the next few months, Gene awaited trial in the psychiatric ward of the prison system. His attorney, Charles Thomas, met regularly with Marie, and she often invited me to come with her.

Thomas painted a grim picture. Just after he was arrested, Gene had undergone a discharge residue test, which indicated that he had recently fired a gun. His fingerprints were found on the .38 caliber pistol discovered at Gene's house. The police had a witness who would swear he saw Gene buy the .38.

The question of motive was less clear-cut, but the police had found one IPS associate who claimed to have had overheard several heated arguments between Gene and the Colonel in the weeks before the murder.

Our meetings with Gene were of little help. He had no memory of the critical events. One time he came right out with the big question. "They say I killed the Colonel. Did I?"

Marie and Gene's mother, Julia, brought in some big legal guns to defend Gene at his trial, hiring the famous legal team of Cindy Jackson, Shari Belli, and Michelle Green. The defense had Gene's history of psychiatric care and the powerful testimony of Dr. Avery Blackwell. I took the stand to relate my experience with Gene's complete change of personality.

But in the end, Marie's graphic testimony about the awful leg bite clinched the outcome. After deliberating for only four hours, the jury found Gene not guilty by reason of insanity. He was committed to the Atascadero State Mental Hospital for an indefinite period.

In the following months, Marie drove up the coast to visit Gene at Atascadero every week. Sometimes I went with her. Amazingly, Gene seemed to be in relatively good spirits, although the doctors insisted he was a long way from cured.

In 1975 and 1976, the Church Committee of the US Senate published a series of reports on illegal activities and abuses of power by the CIA, NSA, and FBI. Among the matters investigated were attempts to assassinate foreign leaders, including the use of the Mafia to kill Fidel Castro. Also uncovered was Project MKUltra, the CIA operation aimed at manipulating mental states of targets unaware that they had been drugged.

I was amazed at the deadly accuracy of the Colonel's earlier disclosures, the same information contained in the report buried in my backyard.

At about the same time, the House of Representatives Select Committee on Assassinations was established to investigate the John Kennedy and Martin Luther King assassinations.

In November of 1976, Jimmy Carter defeated Gerald Ford in the presidential election.

A year after Gene was committed to Atascadero, Marie and I took the Amtrak train up the coast from Del Mar to San Luis Obispo, a picturesque little town about halfway between Los Angeles and San Francisco. Marie opened her suitcase. "Look at this." She handed me a thick portfolio containing a collection of scientific papers. "They're all articles on neuropsychopharmacology that Gene asked me to bring."

Marie worked in an area of biochemistry that was out of my league. This hundred-dollar word was unfamiliar to me. "Say it again," I said.

She repeated it slowly. "Neuro psycho pharmacology is the study of how drugs affect human behavior. These papers were written by scientists developing drugs to treat mental illness. Gene has begun his studies in this field in earnest. In a short time, he has become amazingly knowledgeable about the field."

"So is Gene looking to find his own cure?"

"It's more general than that. In the short run, he just wants to understand as much as possible about the effects of drugs on behavior. He enjoys the learning experience."

We arrived at the train station and hired a car for the twenty-minute drive to Atascadero.

After Marie had some time with Gene by herself, he asked to see me alone. We were granted only ten minutes. Gene seemed to have become his old self. "I'm probably going to be here for at least several years, but I hope to get out eventually. You remember the CIA's drug projects? I'm working on the theory that I may be a victim of one of their experiments. I'll tell you more on your next visit, but Marie must not know about this or anything else associated with IPS; such knowledge could put her in danger. In the meantime, I want to ask a favor of you."

I didn't know if this CIA talk was just a paranoid delusion, but the recent reports of the Church Committee made the idea plausible. I didn't know what to add, so I just stuck with his request. "I'll do anything."

"I really appreciate everything you've done; you're a true and trusted friend. But I'm asking one more thing. I want you to stay in close touch with Marie. Jack, will you take care of her for me?"

"Of course," I said.

"You answered too quickly. I'm not sure you fully understand," he replied. "I'm asking you to stay real close—basically to be a substitute husband."

For several seconds I was speechless but finally managed to reply, "Gene, do you know what you're saying? And what would Marie say if she heard you proposition me like this?"

"I've already told her. The two of you can discuss it on the train back to San Diego."

Marie was silent for the first part of our train ride, but she finally acknowledged the proverbial elephant in the train car. "I suppose most women would be insulted or badly hurt if their husbands offered them to another man. But from Gene's perspective of facing long years behind bars, I recognize this is a pure act of love. He really wants me to be happy."

"It sure puts me in an awkward spot," I said.

Marie looked at me closely. "I suggest we just pretend to go along with Gene's request. Keep your zipper zipped up tight."

The following week I was relaxing in my living room with no particular plans for the evening. On a lark, I decided to visit the Body Shop. Mandy was there as I had hoped. When she danced to "City of New Orleans," I sat at the stage and ogled at her naked body along with the sailors, rich lawyers, college professors, and several subspecies of dusty old men. I made sure I left the biggest tip to show the bastards just who was boss. It had been a long time since Mandy and I were together. Who knows? Maybe she would like a little fun tonight for old times' sake.

After her dance she came to my table and served me a drink. "Jack, you should know that John and I are living together. It's not that I'm not glad to see you, but I'm really uncomfortable with you watching me dance. My emotions get confused. I'd appreciate it if you would not come here on my performance nights. We had a great fling, and I'll always love you a little, but now it's over."

She was OK with all these strangers looking at her beautiful body, but somehow I made her feel uncomfortable? It was hard to figure. I felt a profound loss, but all I could say was, "I understand."

I now joined Marie on nearly all her visits to Atascadero. Each time Gene seemed more and more with it. Over the next year, he became a genuine expert on the behavioral effects of drugs. He became known to the hospital's psychiatrists as the Walking Encyclopedia of Atascadero. But they seemed no closer to recommending his release if for no other reason than the potential political fallout; after all, he had apparently shot the Colonel only two years earlier.

Gene seemed especially happy with the close relationship that Marie and I had developed. Occasionally he would slyly ask questions that might potentially lead to an explicit sexual discussion, but Marie always steered the conversation to less sensitive areas. Gene never tried to probe deeply; if he thought we were bed partners, we didn't tell him otherwise.

Marie and Julia hired a new set of attorneys, Nolan Neman and Jordan Jacobs, to look into legal strategies aimed at Gene's eventual release. They found good reason to question the story of the witness who claimed to have observed Gene buying the .38 pistol. Neman and Jacobs planned to eventually ask for a new trial, but they cautioned that this would be a long and expensive ordeal. Fortunately, George had left Julia with more money than Genghis Khan; she vowed to get Gene out no matter what it took.

House prices in San Diego really started to go up in 1976 and 1977. I executed several tax-deferred exchanges, increasing my portfolio to thirty-six houses. I continued trading options on a selective basis following my pricing strategy.

Gene reverted to his old brilliant self; he remembered his earlier option studies and was able to clear up some of my misunderstandings of the new Black-Scholes model.

One night, Marie and I were having dinner at my house. After a few glasses of wine, we started reminiscing about the past. We both laughed as we recalled the day she told me that I would be last on her list of men to have an affair with.

I added, "Yes, and you also said, 'If I even made the list at all.'"

We had met for lunch that day, and she had asked my help in finding out what was wrong with Gene. I vividly recalled my dream that night of Marie dancing nude on a bar table. At that time I wouldn't have told anyone, much less Marie, about the dream. But now I felt fully comfortable with her. I relayed the story in great detail, including the parts where my arms were pinned to my sides, the crowd was cheering, and Gene was hauling her away.

Marie smiled and said, "Pour me some more chardonnay, and let's hear some music. I know; Mandy liked 'City of New Orleans.' Let's do that." When I returned from the storage closet with the cassette, she was standing barefoot next to my large coffee table. "Sit on the couch," she whispered.

The music started, and she stepped up on the table. She danced slowly at first but picked up the pace, twirling and raising her dress. Finally, she pulled her dress over her head, revealing everything that I had remembered: turned-up nose, pink nipples, generous patch of brown fur, and beautiful freckled legs. As she moved closer and closer, I noted that this time my arms were not pinned to my sides. Free at last.

The next time we visited Atascadero, we told the truth, the whole truth, and nothing but the truth, so help me Gene.

Chapter 30

In 1977, Mandy and John were married. Their first child was born a year later. He was not named after me.

In 1977–1979, the ultimate demise of San Diego's unique card room culture was set into motion with the legalization of games based more on chance than on skill. Hundreds of seniors on social security were forced to find substitute activities.

In 1977, a request under the Freedom of Information Act uncovered a cache of twenty thousand documents relating to project MKUltra, providing unequivocal evidence that the CIA had used mind-altering drugs against many unsuspecting targets. The subsequent Senate hearings revealed that CIA director Richard Helms had ordered all MKUltra files destroyed in 1973, but the recovered cache had been stored in the wrong location, accidently surviving the Helms purge.

Public exposure of the CIA's drug programs added substantial credence to Gene's claim that his psychosis had been induced by someone in security agencies monitored by Gene and the Colonel.

By 1978, disclosures resulting from congressional investigations and other parties taking advantage of the Freedom of Information Act had essentially confirmed all the information in the handwritten report hidden in my backyard. As there was no longer any need to keep the report secret, Gene asked me to share the report with his legal team of Newman and Jacobs.

Gene's lawyers considered several possible avenues leading to Gene's release. Maybe he could be judged cured by the psychiatrists. On one hand, this might be the easiest route since Gene had seemed completely sane for several years and had even become an intellectual legend at Atascadero Mental Hospital. On the other hand, the prosecution could always dig up psychiatrists who would testify under oath that Gene was still a danger to himself or others.

In the real world, the political fall-out resulting from releasing someone like Gene, who may have killed his boss, was a substantial concern. Thus, the lawyers decided on a more direct strategy— raising reasonable doubt that Gene had actually killed the Colonel.

Over the next two years, Gene's legal team punched more and more holes in the murder case. The Colonel's secretary, Lisa May, signed an affidavit disputing the earlier claim by the IPS associate that there had been heated arguments between Gene and the Colonel. Actually, Lisa said, this same IPS associate had physically threatened the Colonel, but her earlier testimony had somehow been suppressed by the district attorney's office.

The witness who claimed to have seen Gene buy the .38 caliber pistol turned out to have a criminal record that was not revealed in the first trial. Gene's new defense team deposed him in considerable depth as part of the discovery process. Just what kind of deal had he made with the district attorney's office to reduce jail time in exchange for his testimony? His evasive answers caused his credibility as a witness to go south in record speed.

In 1980 Gene, at age forty-six, was finally granted a new trial. Gene's late father George had powerful friends. The defense team was able to call several well respected public figures as character witnesses to testify as to Gene's high moral character.

Newman and Jacobs also planted a backup scenario in the jurors' minds. The defense claimed that Gene did not kill anyone; someone else had shot the Colonel and framed Gene. But, even in the unlikely event that Gene actually did kill the Colonel, he could only have done so under the influence of some drug given him without his knowledge. Either way, justice would be served only if Gene were freed to lead a normal life.

My hand written report was introduced into evidence. Gene's attorneys put me on the stand and questioned me at length about our secret interactions on beach runs over a ten year period. A forensic document examiner was called to verify that my hand written dates in the report were accurate. The defense team made a plausible case that Gene had been a victim of MKUltra or some similar secret government program.

After the prosecution finished its closing remarks to the jury, Marie, Gene's mother Julia, and I showed Gene spirited thumbs up and bid a hopeful goodbye as the marshals led him out of the back of the courtroom. Gene's legal team of Newman and Jacobs expected the jury to take at least several days, maybe even several weeks, to come to a verdict.

Over the previous two years Marie and I had become frequent companions, as lovers and as friends. Marie often spent three nights per week in my king size bed. While our relationship maintained some lingering aspects of the old brother-sister feelings, amazingly this did not dampen the sexual energy between us. On Thursday through Sunday nights, however, we always slept separately, sort of in recognition of our regular weekend visits to see Gene.

Our arrangement seemed bizarre to some of our friends, and Marie managed to keep it from Julia. But to our minds, Marie, Gene and I seemed to have successfully overcome the jealousy and conflicts normally expected in three-way relationships. Gene and I would not succumb to the classic tragedy of King Arthur and Lancelot. Marie would not duplicate Guinevere's ultimate residence in Camelot's nunnery.

On the third night after the trial ended, Marie and I adjourned to my house in Solana Beach to continue waiting for the jury to decide Gene's fate. As we lay in my bed, Marie said, "Jack, I love you. Maybe you all ready knew, but I want to say it just the same. The amazing thing is that my love for you does nothing to diminish my love for Gene."

She continued to reveal her inner self. "I have often been skeptical of the more flaky aspects of the so-called counterculture— the drugs, the unlimited sexual freedom and so on. On the other hand, over past few years, I have come to see humanistic psychology in a positive light. Innovative thinkers like Carl Rogers, Jack Gibb and Abraham Maslow have much to teach us about human relationships. I seem to have evolved into a more worldly person, open to new experiences that I never would have considered in the past.

"Remember that night at Betsy's party when everyone went into her pool naked? I would never have admitted it at the time, but now I can freely confess that I really wanted you to see and appreciate my body. When I saw how you looked at me as I entered the pool, I got quite excited. That night I was all over Gene like a rash; we made passionate love several times before morning."

I was deeply touched and wiped away a small tear. I hesitated for some time before replying, "I love you too Marie. I also love Gene; he is my best friend and big brother. I'm guessing that your freedom to love both of us is partly because of this. You cannot betray Gene when you know how much he approves of our closeness. Gene and I will never compete for you; our love game is not zero sum. When Gene gets out of the hospital some things will change. But one thing will stay the same; we will still be family."

Early in the morning Marie and I went for walks separately so that one of us was always close to the phone. At 1:30 p.m. we were just finishing our pizza lunch when the phone rang.

We both jumped up and banged heads as we reached to answer. It was Newman. "The jury has apparently reached a verdict. Since it has come sooner than expected, the judge is allowing one hour for all parties to return to the courtroom. Get here fast."

We drove downtown to the courthouse in my Pontiac, parked illegally, and found seats that Julia had saved for us in the packed courtroom.

The jury filed in; I could not predict anything from their formal demeanor.

The judge began, "Good morning ladies and gentlemen of the jury. I am informed by the marshal that you have reached a verdict. Is that true, Mr. Foreman?"

The foreman, a tall distinguished looking man of about 50 with white hair and bushy eyebrows, stood up and replied, "Yes, your honor."

Damn. I was struck by the disturbing observation that the foreman looked a lot like Fast Eddie. But I quickly dismissed the impression; just more weird stuff spilling out of my unconscious.

The judge said, "Would you please hand the verdict to me." He looked at it quickly, like it was no more than a recipe for meatloaf. He then handed it to the marshal. "Marshal will you pass this to the clerk?" He paused to allow the paper transfers and then said, "I direct the clerk to read the verdict."

The clerk, a good looking middle aged woman with red hair, stood in front of the judge's bench and responded in one of the strongest voices I had ever had the pleasure of hearing.

"We the jury find the defendant Gene Stanford not guilty on all counts."

The courtroom burst out in applause; Marie and Julia rushed to Gene for big hugs. I was close behind. The attorneys Nolan Newman and Jordan Jacobs were all smiles; even the prosecutor came over to congratulate us.

Gene and Marie resumed their loving relationship as if the previous five years of Gene's incarceration were just a bad dream. The three of us met on a regular basis, but my sexual relations with Marie ended naturally without much discussion. Gene and I continued our runs on Black's Beach and other locations. Gene took an unpaid adjunct faculty position in the UCSD Medical School and continued his research in neuropsychopharmacology.

Six months after Gene's release, Marie introduced me to one of her fellow scientists, a pretty dark haired young woman named Savannah. We hit it off amazing well from the beginning. She combined the perkiness of Mandy with the intelligence of Marie. Savannah soon moved in with me in my house in Solana Beach. Gene served as best man and Marie as matron of honor when we married in late 1982. My mother Rachel was as happy as the proverbial clam.

Epilogue

In the late 1970s and 1980s, candidate and then President Ronald Reagan asserted a need for a more aggressive foreign policy. He coined the term *Vietnam Syndrome* to describe American anti-war sentiment, implying that US soldiers had been let down by Johnson and Nixon administration officials who had been "afraid to let them win" the war in Vietnam. Reagan sought to overcome doubt and guilt over the morality of America's actions during the war, arguing that America had fought for "a noble cause."

In 1983, Kovac, my old friend from Astro, became CEO of a $500 million defense company in Los Angeles.

Bob and Ava gradually settled into a more conventional relationship; aerobics instructors no longer pranced into their house for quickies.

In 1984, Gene and I started a new hedge fund based solely on options trading. We persuaded Jim to quit Astro and join our firm. DeSilva and Kovac were among our first clients. With Gene's contacts and our advanced option strategies, we signed up all the investors we could handle.

In 1985, I purchased the Redneck Mother Bar and Grill in Cocoa Beach and hired my high school friend Sam as full time manager. Sam didn't require a bouncer to control obnoxious behavior. Surprisingly, my mother Rachel had become a big country music fan late in life. After my purchase she visited the bar nearly every week. Our friendly patrons voted her in as the bar's first official "Redneck Mother of the Year."

In 1995 the US announced formal diplomatic relations with the Socialist Republic of Vietnam. In following years United States relations with Vietnam became progressively deeper. Vietnam later evolved into one of the most pro-American countries in Asia.

In 2004, documents were declassified revealing that in 1974, President Ford had wanted to sign a congressional bill to strengthen the Freedom of Information Act, but his advisors, mainly chief of staff Donald Rumsfeld, deputy Dick Cheney, and attorney Antonin Scalia, convinced Ford to veto the bill. However, Congress voted to override Ford's veto, giving the United States the core Freedom of Information Act still in effect today with judicial review of executive secrecy claims.

In 2007-2008, the world experienced the worst financial crisis since the Great Depression of the 1930s. The associated taxpayer robberies greatly exceeded those of the savings-and-loans crisis of the 1980s, but no bankers, Wall Street hustlers, or government officials went to prison for racketeering or other crimes. As expected from its actions in the 1980s, the government again bailed out well connected companies like Goldman Sacks, providing another victory for crony capitalism.

In 2007, *Rolling Stone* featured the deathbed confession of former CIA agent E. Howard Hunt in which he implicated himself, as well as several other CIA operatives in the assassination of President Kennedy. The article was based mainly on interactions between Hunt and his son St. John beginning in 2003. The response of the mainstream media was mostly to ignore the allegations. Other media sources claimed that Hunt or his son or both must be lying.

As of 2014 about two million Vietnamese immigrants and their offspring have became American citizens. Large groups of students from Vietnam also come to America to study. Vietnam has remained independent of China and has good relations with the United States. Could this same state of affairs have been easily achieved in the 1960s without the loss of fifty-eight thousand American and two to three million Vietnamese lives? What would Lyndon Johnson, Richard Nixon, Ronald Reagan and Ho Chi Minh have said?

Endnotes by Author

This is a work of historical fiction. While the characters are fictional, I have attempted to stick closely to the pivotal global events that took place mostly during 1962–1975. Astro (General) Dynamics, Vandenberg Air Force Base, Bicycle Bill's, Crystal Pier, Sandstone Ranch, Atascadero Hospital, Black's Beach, Lester's karate gym, the Body Shop, and more are (or were) real places. *Casino Gambler's Guide* (book cover image) by Allan Wilson, *How the United States Got Involved in Vietnam* by Robert Scheer, *Elements of Advanced Karate* (book cover image) by Lester Ingber, and *A Bright Shining Lie* by Neil Sheehan are also real.

I hope you enjoyed reading this novel as much as I enjoyed writing it. By the time I finished the first half, my characters, especially Jack, Gene, and Marie, seemed to acquire minds of their own, as if I no longer had full control over their actions. The last part of the novel was perhaps as much a surprise to me as to you.

The CIA programs MKUltra, Midnight Climax, Mongoose, and Phoenix were all disclosed in official congressional investigations. In Operation Mockingbird, leading American journalists were (and perhaps still are) recruited to present the CIA's views in the mainstream media. The illegal FBI actions of COINTELPRO against peaceful war protestors under Hoover are also well documented. We don't know if Hoover's avoidance of actions against organized crime was due to homosexual blackmail or if he was just excessively friendly with wealthy mob-connected figures.

In a ruling on a lawsuit filed against the CIA in 1984, the US Supreme Court provided the following description of MKUltra: "…the research and development of chemical, biological, and radiological materials capable of employment in clandestine operations to control human behavior. The program consisted of some 149 subprojects that the CIA contracted out to various universities, research foundations, and similar institutions. At least 80 institutions and 185 private researchers participated. Because the CIA funded MKUltra indirectly, many of the participating individuals were unaware that they were dealing with the CIA."

My insistence on historical accuracy severely limited any genuine probe into the assassination of President Kennedy, a topic for which I lack any special insight. But, to my mind, the most important single event of this period was the Cuban missile crisis, in which hawkish political pressures in the United States and Soviet Union caused events to spiral out of control. Unlike with the Kennedy assassination, the central facts are now well-known; the world as we know it came very close to ending. The behavior of many of our political and military leaders at that time can be summarized succinctly; in my view, it was mob psychopathology.

The world currently has about 18,000 nuclear weapons stockpiled, most held by the United States and Russia. The destruction of any country probably requires fewer than 100 warheads. So why do we have so many? Think money and power. In any country, the influence of the most hawkish groups can be expected to rise is proportion to external threats. Peace is their enemy.

I submit that the prevention of accidental nuclear war should be enshrined at the top of any discussion of national defense. Closer scrutiny of the politics leading to the Cuban missile crisis and Vietnam War is, to my mind, far more important than the narrower question of just who killed President Kennedy. Of course, these events are related, but we may never know the full details.